Learning to Yawp

To Dr. Burkhardt—

Thank you.

By

Christine Margaret Stearns

Christine Stearns

I sound my barbaric yawp over the roofs of the world...

Learning to Yawp

By

Christine Margaret Stearns

This is a work of fiction. Any references to real people, events, or places are only intended to give the fiction a sense of realism and authenticity. All the other characters and places are the product of the author's imagination.

Dedication

This story, like all the other stories I've ever told, is dedicated to the people who have loved and nurtured me on my journey. To my Mom and Dad—my Mom is the first person that ever told me that I should be a writer. She is the best teacher I ever had. About almost everything. My Dad gave me the gift of his stubborn faith—a faith which sustains me every day. To my husband—without which there is nothing—my number one fan and my best friend. To my beautiful children and grandchildren, who continue to teach me every day about courage, love, laughter, and grace. In a very special way to my beautiful grandson Brett Michael, who died in a tragic accident in 2019. I miss him with every beat of my heart, but I listen for his whispers—he is still teaching me every day. To my niece Sarah and my nephew Seamus—please be there at the finish line to show me the way. To my brothers and sisters, nieces and nephews, friends and colleagues, family, and fellow teachers. The people on whose shoulders I stand every day. The writers who have gone before me—whose words I gobbled up eagerly as I learned the power of storytelling. In a good story, well told, we reach for a glimpse of the truth, the universal, the Good. In a beautiful poem, we hear a faint echo of the music of the spheres. *Learning to Yawp* is all about keeping the faith, finding a way to go on, reaching out, and discovering that in helping someone else learn to carry their losses, we learn to carry our own with surprising strength and grace.

Section 52 of Song of Myself

The spotted hawk swoops by and accuses me, he complains of
my gab and my loitering.
I too am not a bit tamed, I too am untranslatable,
I sound my barbaric yawp over the roofs of the world.
The last scud of day holds back for me,
It flings my likeness after the rest and true as any on the
shadow'd wilds,
It coaxes me to the vapor and the dusk.
I depart as air, I shake my white locks at the runaway sun,
I effuse my flesh in eddies, and drift it in lacy jags.
I bequeath myself to the dirt to grow from the grass I love,
If you want me again look for me under your boot-soles.
You will hardly know who I am or what I mean,
But I shall be good health to you nevertheless,
And filter and fibre your blood.
Failing to fetch me at first keep encouraged,
Missing me one place search another,
I stop somewhere waiting for you.
Walt Whitman, 1855

Chapter 1

Sometimes, a fall from grace is grace disguised. But, it takes a long time until you see it that way. Somebody once said that we are just builders; we are not the architect. Maybe. But anyhow, Linda Miller was about to take a fall, although she didn't know it at the moment.

She shouldered her briefcase, took a long, last look around the classroom, turned off the lights, and locked the door. She had been teaching Advanced Placement English for thirty years, and there were so many good memories that would forever be held by the four walls of her classroom. At least for her. She only had two days left, and then, she would retire. She and her husband Rick were all set to move to Fort Lauderdale, where he had a job selling yachts waiting for him. She told herself over and over that they would be beginning a whole new chapter in their lives together.

He sold boats in Michigan for Maitland Motor Sports for almost thirty years. And the job had been very good to them. Although Michigan's summer is way too short, it is also almost painfully beautiful. And there is water everywhere. Not only the Great Lakes, which are completely different animals, but also thousands of small, inland lakes. He had made a good living for their family, and she had always thought that he loved his job. However, lately he had been making remarks that he was fed up with his bosses at Maitland. Linda knew that he had been passed over for a promotion that he wanted, but maybe the new job in Florida would satisfy him.

Linda went out to the parking lot, smelling spring in the air. The forsythia and crocuses were long since done, and the lilacs had almost spent themselves entirely. Every tree was green, almost to the point of bursting, and the sky was a promising blue. She could smell something wonderful—jasmine, honeysuckle, apple blossoms—like a lovely perfume, or just a memory of a perfume, somewhere in the air. She got in her good old Honda, started it up and pulled out of the school parking lot, rolling the windows down to let the smells of summer in. She had shoulder-length blonde hair, kind of thin and wispy, like a baby's hair. She loved the feeling of the wind in her hair. She had green eyes that flashed with golden flecks. Summer was coming. It was her best time of year, because her skin got a golden glow, and a couple freckles popped out on her cheeks. Summer was her best season, and it was almost here!

A couple of her students waved to her as she pulled out of the school parking lot. Seniors. They would graduate in a couple of days. Then, off to the university. Linda couldn't even imagine being that young again. And yet, on the other hand, she could remember it all so clearly. Like it happened yesterday. But she was 54 now, and so that would make it—just about 36 years ago that she left this little town and headed off to Michigan State University, her dream school. Dear Lord, she thought. Could it really be that long ago?

As she drove the six miles to her house, she turned the car stereo up and let the classic rock and roll fill her car. Bob Seger was singing "Night Moves," talking about how the night rolls away, and the years roll away when you're not looking. Suddenly, Linda found herself singing along with Bob, knowing exactly what he meant, surprising herself that she still knew every word. Ain't it funny how the night moves, with autumn closing in. The poignancy of the moment was not lost on her. She fought back a tear and told herself to stop being silly.

She pulled into the driveway, surprised to see Rick's car there. She thought he was working late tonight. With Memorial Day weekend in two days, people were frantically buying boats, wanting them in the water for the first holiday of the summer. Rick would make a lot of money in May and June. He always did. She had told him that she had a faculty meeting after school today and that she would be late. But the meeting was cancelled, and there were no students asking for extra help today. So, she was home much earlier than she had thought she would be. Maybe, if he were home for the night, they could go out and get dinner. That would be nice. She really didn't feel like cooking. She parked in the driveway and grabbed her briefcase from the back seat. As she walked up the sidewalk to the front door, her eyes fell on the real estate sign on the front lawn, now with the SOLD banner across the top. It was a nice little house—a modest

Cape Cod. It had been good to them. They were going to rent an ocean front condo in Fort Lauderdale for a year, until they understood the lay of the land. Then, maybe they would buy something. Linda really couldn't imagine living in a condo. All she had ever known was a house. And she and Rick had been in this little house for almost twenty years now.

She remembered when there were skateboards and bicycles on the front lawn every time she pulled in the drive, but the kids were grown and gone, and the front lawn was much neater. And yet. She shook herself, telling herself to stop being so melancholy. She forced her thoughts to a new direction—where she might like to go to dinner, why Rick was home so early. Things had not really been good for a long time between them. He just seemed to be distracted—always trying to make the big buck, never quite pulling it off. He might have been a little disappointed in his career choice. Here he was, at 55 years old, still selling boats. Maybe he had hoped for more. Maybe he would find it in Fort Lauderdale. Nonetheless, this should be a night of celebration. Her last day with students. They were on the cusp of a new beginning.

The front door was unlocked, so she walked right in and dropped her keys on the little table in the foyer. Rick's keys were already there. She could hear voices from upstairs, and laughter. He must be watching a movie or something, she thought. On busy days, sometimes he liked to sneak away from the office, have lunch at home, and watch a little mindless television before he had to go back. He worked a lot of nights because he had to be at the marina when people got off of work and headed over to buy a boat or a dock system. You have to make hay while the sun shines, and all that. That's what he always said. As she kicked off her shoes in the front room, she heard a different set of noises coming from upstairs. It sounded like Rick might be watching porn. Linda thought about it and wondered how she should handle it.

She had found out about his secret porn addiction in a very uncomfortable way. It had come up in a list of favorites on the family home computer. She was so disgusted and disappointed. Besides that, she felt betrayed. He had reminded her that their kids were grown, that they were both out of the house, one at college and the other working full time in Chicago. He even encouraged her to consider the idea that watching some salacious videos might spice up their sex life. It was all so uncomfortable for her that she couldn't bear to even think about it. Did he find her so boring sexually that he had to use that kind of artificial stimulation? But she didn't feel like fighting right now. She really felt like celebrating. She had just finished her last day with students. Her last day. Surely that called for a celebration. So, she went into the kitchen, opened the refrigerator, and poured herself a glass of Chardonnay—a nice one—and headed upstairs to the master bedroom. The stairs were deeply carpeted, so she moved about the house very quietly. Not on purpose. Just the way it was.

As she walked down the hall, she felt a momentary frisson of confusion—was that Rick's voice? In the movie? Was that his laugh?

She opened the bedroom door quietly, and dropped her glass of wine on the white plush carpeting. She had been teaching a unit on Hemingway's novel called *The Sun Also Rises*. Several years ago, one of her former students had given her a sash from Pamplona. The ones that the men who are going to run with the bulls tie around their waists before they enter the gauntlet and run for their lives. It was one of her favorite teaching props. She had left the sash on her dressing table, folded up neatly. She had always wondered if she ever got to Spain if she would have the guts to sit through a real bullfight. It's one thing to teach about the bullfights, and it's quite another thing to really watch one. Hemingway called those who were passionate about the bullfights "aficianados." Linda suspected, in her secret hearts of hearts, that when it got right down to it, she wouldn't be able to watch.

Now, her beloved Hemingway red sash was tied around the waist of a twenty-something woman who was running around her bedroom with Rick chasing her. She had gigantic boobs, bobbing up and down, and a ton of blonde hair flying behind her as she ran. Rick held his two index fingers up to his forehead as if he were the bull. And he was snorting and laughing. The girl, whoever she was, ran around the edge of the bed, still not noticing Linda standing, open-mouthed, in the doorway. Her husband, also not noticing, leapt across the top of the bed, naked and semi-erect, trying to catch the young matador. She was laughing and squealing; he was snorting and saying over and over, "I'm gonna get you. I'm gonna get you. I've almost got you."

Linda managed to find her voice, "What the hell is going on?" She tried to never say that word, and with one part of her brain, she was astonished how easily it came to her now.

Startled, Rick tripped over the edge of the bed and sprawled on the floor, his nose ending up almost in the glass of wine Linda had spilled at her feet. The twenty-something squealed and high-tailed it into the bathroom, slamming the door behind her. Rick looked up at Linda, saying stupidly, "What are you doing home? I thought you had a faculty meeting today."

Linda stood there, absolutely stupefied. She literally could not believe her eyes.

"What the hell?" she said. "What the hell is going on?" She stared at him, her mouth hanging open. She felt her knees give out, and she stumbled.

Somehow, Linda sat down on the chair at her vanity, trying to breathe. She couldn't take a deep breath. She sat there gulping air, not able to speak. Rick, looking genuinely concerned, grabbed his boxers from the top of the dresser and stepped into them. He came over to Linda and knelt down in front of her, touching her gently on the back. She bashed his hand away, still gulping, tears in her eyes. "What the hell," she repeated. She felt like she was frozen in place. Incapable of moving. Almost incapable of speaking.

Rick stepped into his pants and pulled on a shirt. "Tiffany," he said. "Come out here. You better leave. Get back to the shop."

"Is it safe?" came the voice from her bathroom. Tiffany opened the door a crack. She had a sundress on and high-heeled

15

sandals. Her hair was still a wild mess from their antics. Linda looked at her in complete astonishment. And disgust. Rick nodded to her that he thought it was safe, and she tip-toed out. She looked scared, her eyes a little wild. But Linda thought she saw the glimmer of a smile playing around her lips. Linda wanted to hit her.

"Go on," Rick said. "I'll talk to you later."

Tiffany finger combed her hair and said, "I'm really sorry," as she walked by Linda. She handed Linda the sash from Pamplona. When Linda did not reach out to take it from her, she set it on the chair beside Linda. Rick looked furiously at her, grabbing the sash and flinging it on the desk.

"Go now," he said. "Just go. All right?" Tiffany stood in the doorway, as if trying to think of something to say. But, no words came, thankfully. She pivoted, brushing her hair over her shoulders, and flounced out of the room.

"Tiffany?" Linda said. "Really? I didn't think anyone named their kid Tiffany anymore. And you! Are you her boss? Gross. Wrong. Embarrassing even. And how old is she anyway?" She was surprised to find herself talking, although she really didn't know what she was saying. Now, she wanted to hit Rick.

"She's hardly a kid," Rick said, pulling on a dress shirt and looking for a tie. He actually sounded kind of pleased with himself. Apparently, he was going back to work. As if nothing had happened. What an asshole. Linda stood there, watching him. Stupefied.

"She's not much more," Linda snapped back at him. "What is she, twenty? I think she's younger than your daughter.

16

Do you have any idea how ridiculous you look? What a cliché you are?" Again, there was some corner of her brain that was absolutely shocked that she was managing to speak. At all. She could feel her heart racing and her blood pressure skyrocketing.

"Look," said Rick. "This is stupid. Do you want to argue about her age? I don't think so. Let's talk about the elephant in the room, shall we?" He sat down on the bed, almost as if he were keeping a safe distance from her. Linda bent over and picked up her fallen wine glass, rubbing her toes in the wine that had soaked into the carpet. She couldn't bring herself to look at him.

"How could you?" she said. "How could you?" She raised her eyes and forced herself to look at him. Tears started streaming down her face. She wiped them away with the back of her hand, angry at herself for crying. "You know, I knew about the online porn thing. And I didn't like it, but I let it go, and now this. This is a whole different level of betrayal." She was trying hard not to let go and cry, not wanting to give him that victory over her.

Rick had the good sense to be quiet for a few minutes. He seemed to be weighing his words, trying to find the right way to say the thing he had to say. And there was no right way.

Instead he asked a question. "Did you really never know?"

Linda looked hard at him, trying to figure out exactly what he meant. "Know what?" she answered, feeling completely empty. Obliterated.

"Know that I was fooling around," he answered.

She shook her head. "No. I really didn't. I feel incredibly stupid to admit it, but I didn't have a clue. The online thing, yes. I knew about that. But nothing else." She wondered what he meant. How many times had he done this? How could she not have known? What was she thinking?

She sat there, absolutely numb. Momentarily speechless. And then a new thought occurred to her. She raised her eyes to look at him. "Is this the first time you've done this? Here in our home?"

He looked right at her and said softly, "Honestly? No. There have been others. I kind of thought you knew and just looked the other way."

She just sat there, not moving. Not knowing what to think or do.

Rick stood up and came over to her. He helped her to stand up and then he made a move to try to take her in his arms. She pushed him away, furiously. She didn't even want him to touch her for a minute. And she could still smell Tiffany's perfume. And her musk. She pushed him hard, and he stumbled a little, back into the room. Then, she sat down in her chair again and sobbed. Angry at him, and angry at herself for crying.

"How could you," she cried. "How could you do this to me? Get out of here! Now! Get the hell out of here!"

He came and knelt in front of her, reaching his arms around her. She kept her arms over her chest, her face buried in her hands. She felt the anger surging through her, like a wave breaking over her head. Still he knelt there, trying to hold her. But not with love or passion. With pity. Suddenly, she was just exhausted. She wanted to resist, she wanted to refuse, she wanted to hit him. But she did none of those things. She let him hold her in his arms. She smelled his after-shave and deodorant.

He spoke softly, into her hair, "Honey, I'm really sorry. I feel lousy. You don't deserve this. I haven't been entirely faithful or entirely honest. And I haven't felt any real passion between us in several years now. Except occasionally. And then it seemed like an accident." He took a deep breath and then he went on. "I have been wanting to ask you for a divorce for a long time now. I just never found the right moment to say the words I'm saying right now. I don't really feel like we've been husband and wife for a long time now. We've raised Andrea and Matt, and we've stayed together for them. It's time to move on. Give ourselves a chance at a second life." She was shocked at how easily he was speaking these words, as if he had rehearsed them for some time.

She pushed him away, using all of her strength. She looked at him, and for a minute, it felt like she didn't even know him. He was some other middle-aged man. Not her Rick. Her Rick? Apparently, he hadn't been that for some time now.

She took a deep breath, trying to calm her heart. "Well, I just feel incredibly stupid, that's all. Shame on me. I thought that when you were married, you stayed married. And not just for the kids. For a deeper promise." She felt like she was saying things he didn't want to hear, and suddenly, she just ran out of words. There were no words.

She pulled herself together with all the courage she could muster. "And I am angry. Really angry. Obviously, promises mean nothing to you. Get your things together, and get out. Don't come home tonight. This is not your home any more. Get enough to get you through the night and then come and get the rest of your stuff when I'm at work. Honestly, I don't know what I'm going to do yet. But, as far as I'm concerned right now—get out of here. Right now, a divorce sounds good. I'm tired of trying to patch this thing up anyhow." She sounded braver than she felt. He looked her in the eyes, said nothing, and nodded.

"All right," he said finally. "All right." He grabbed some things out of his dresser and out of the bathroom, and then left the room. She waited until she heard the front door shut. Then, she lay down on her bed and howled. Her whole world had just shattered—everything she thought she knew—gone.

Chapter 2

Linda sobbed for an hour, gut-wrenching sobs, until she felt completely empty. Then, with her stomach grumbling, she stumbled into the kitchen. She found a different wine glass—the other one was still lying on the carpet upstairs. Maybe. She couldn't really remember. This time she got a big one and poured another glass of Chardonnay. Then she sat down and called her daughter, who ran an upscale bar in Chicago. She had graduated with a degree in hotel and restaurant management and had several job offers immediately. She loved living in Chicago. It was only about three hours away from Linda, but right now, it felt like a million miles away. She pulled herself together before she called her daughter, knowing that she had better not be hysterical when she spoke to her. Andy had little patience for that kind of behavior. She herself was always under control, or so it seemed to Linda. She only saw her about once a month now, but they talked every couple days, and her daughter was her best friend.

She suddenly realized that it was Friday evening, and that was a big drinking night in Andrea's bar. But she had to talk to somebody. Andrea would be busy, she thought. But still.

"Hi, Mom," Andrea answered quickly. "Happy Friday. Your last day with students, right? Congratulations. Pour yourself a big glass of wine and make the old man take you out for dinner to some place nice." She spoke quickly, and Linda could picture her hustling around the bar, mixing drinks and schmoozing with the customers. She could hear laughter and the tinkle of glassware in the background.

"I walked in on your father and a girl named Tiffany running around naked in our bedroom after school today. They were apparently playing bull and matador. She had my Hemingway sash knotted around her ass. I guess I got there during the foreplay session," she spoke flatly, trying to keep the tears out of her voice.

"Shut up! What did you just say? Are you kidding me?" She could hear Andrea almost scream into the phone. "Just a minute, Mom. Let me get somewhere quieter than this, and then tell me all over again what you just said. I must not have heard you right." Linda could hear Andrea issuing orders to the other staff members, telling them to finish the drink order she had been working on. She could tell that Andy was walking fast because she could hear her breathing hard. Then, she must have gone in her office because she heard a door slam. And then there was quiet.

While all of this was going on, Linda walked in to the living room and sat in her favorite chair, looking out the front picture window. The neighborhood had that happy Friday hum. Dads and Moms arriving home from work, kids riding bicycles up and down the street, neighbors calling out to each other. It occurred to her that it was very strange that all these people seemed to be going on about their business, blithely ignorant of the fact that the world had just ended. And then she realized—all at once—that for them, it hadn't. Only for her.

Now Andrea came back on the line. She said, "Now, tell me everything that just happened. Tell it to me slowly. I am hoping that I didn't hear you correctly the first time." Linda could hear the tension in her daughter's voice. Tension—and anger.

Linda told the story from the moment where she was driving home, listening to Bob Seger. Leaving out no details. And when she got to the part about Tiffany running around the bedroom with her boobs flapping up and down as the Hemingway sash fluttered behind her, Andrea started swearing. At least, Linda thought she was swearing. In between swear words was something that sounded like laughter or snorting.

Puzzled, and a little bit angry, Linda said, "Are you laughing?" Here she was, pouring out her story of her betrayal, and her daughter was trying not to laugh?

There was a moment of choked silence in the air, and then Andrea said, "Not really. I actually want to kill him. What a jerk. But the picture of this Tiffany running around the room with her boobs flapping up and down and the sash trailing was just a little bit funny. I didn't mean to laugh. I cannot believe what an asshole Dad is." She paused to take a breath and then went on, "I mean, I actually can believe it. I have been suspecting for some time now that he might have been fooling around."

Linda was flabbergasted. And a little bit angry. "Do you mean to tell me that you knew he was being unfaithful to me? Why didn't you tell me? I feel like such a fool. How could I not know?"

Andrea quickly corrected her. "No. I didn't know. Not for sure. But I just had the feeling that things were not quite right between the two of you. And Dad has that look of wanderlust or something in his eye. Remember, Mom. He's a man in his 50's. I think that's the time when the midlife crisis kicks in these days. At least for some guys."

"You make it sound like that's something acceptable. Even mandatory. Since when did the world change so much? I thought married people were supposed to stay together. 'Til death do we part and all that. We took a vow," Linda blubbered. She didn't mean to, but she started crying again. She tried not to let it sound in her voice. But Andrea knew her way too well for that to work.

"Listen," said Andrea. "I've got to finish my shift at the bar tonight. It's too late to get someone to cover for me. But I'll get up early and drive home to you. I'll be there by lunchtime."

"How can you take the whole Memorial Day weekend off," said Linda, trying not to sound too hopeful. She needed her daughter nearby right now.

"I just can," said Andrea. "I'm the boss, and that has some perks. So, just make it through tonight, and I'll be there by the time you finish your second cup of coffee. Promise."

"I feel stupid asking you to do this," said Linda.

"Don't be ridiculous. Now, pour yourself a glass of wine and turn on something good. Some chick flick. Crying is acceptable if you're crying at a movie. And I'll be there in the morning. I love you, Mom. Hang in there. You'll get through this." There was a long pause, as Andrea seemed to be weighing the idea of saying something else. Then, she apparently decided to plunge ahead. "Do you remember when you taught me what the ancient Greeks said about the Truth?"

"Yes, of course," Linda answered woodenly. "That Truth has a power of its own, and that it will reveal itself in time. That it's better to know the Truth, even if knowing it hurts. That eventually Truth will set you free." Linda felt a little bit like the good student who knows the answers and can recite them by rote, whether or not she understands what she is saying.

Andrea paused, seeming to let Linda's words hang in the air between them. Then she said, "Well, you have answered correctly. Did you listen to what you said?"

"Yes," said Linda.

"And?" Andrea prodded her, looking to push her understanding or acceptance of the new normal along. "And?" she repeated.

"And I think the ancient Greeks were full of shit," Linda said, pouting.

Andrea burst out laughing, and almost in spite of herself, Linda joined in—a little. "Atta girl," said Andrea. "All right. Now, just get through tonight and I'll be there in the morning. I love you so much. Be tough, Mom."

"I'll try. But I've got to tell you. It's not my forte."

"You're tougher than you think," said Andrea. "I'll see you in the morning. Good night, Mom. Love you." Then, she hung up and the silence loomed large. She suddenly knew what she had to do. She had to call her son, Matt, and tell him what had happened. He was a first year law student, down at the University of Miami. And this was finals week. What lousy timing. She thought about not calling him, but if he found out from Andrea instead of her, he would be mad. So, she called up his name on her list of favorites on her phone and called. She was surprised when he answered by the third ring. With him, her calls often went to voicemail, and then he called her back. But here he was. Now that she had to speak, she couldn't really find where to start.

"Hi, darling. Sorry to bother you during finals week. Are you doing all right?" she asked, searching for a door into the terrible words she had to say.

"Hi, Mom. Good to hear your voice. Yeah, I'm doing okay, I guess. I have my Criminal Law final exam tomorrow. And I hear from everybody that it will be tough, so I'm locked up in the library, cramming. But, it's still good to hear you." Now, she understood why he seemed to be whispering.

"Well, maybe I should call back later," she said, tentatively.

"No, here. Let me slip outside. There's a balcony here where I won't be bothering anybody, but I can still see my books and stuff, so no one can mess with it. What's up?" he said.

Linda took a deep breath, wondering how much to tell. What to keep back. She said, as calmly as she could, "I came home early from school today and found your dad with another woman in our bedroom." As she spoke, she could picture the long blonde hair flying, the boobs bouncing, the red sash trailing behind.

Matt gasped, "What do you mean? Do you mean naked? Doing it?"

Linda almost laughed at that expression. Almost. She took a gulp of wine and said, "Well, let's just say they were still engaged in a rather active sort of foreplay." She let that hang in the air for a minute. Then she went on, "However, I don't want you to come home or anything like that. Andrea is coming home tomorrow. And she'll help me get through the weekend. And then, I'll gradually get my head around it. You've got finals, and you need to concentrate on them. I just didn't want you to hear all this from Andrea and be mad at me because I didn't tell you myself."

Matt spoke very slowly. Linda could hear the rage in his voice. "Well, I appreciate that. And you're right. I would have been mad if I didn't hear it from you and heard it from Andrea. I hate being out of the loop. But, Mom," he said, with a catch in his voice, "this sort of changes everything. I mean, you two were going to move to Fort Lauderdale together. Now what? Do you think it is something you can forgive, or do you think it is all over between you?"

"Honey," Linda said. "The truth is that before he left tonight, he asked me for a divorce. He said that it had been over for a long time. That we had stayed together to raise you and your sister, but he now wanted a chance at another life. And I don't really know where I go from here. But, we will figure it out. It's a lot to process all at once. Now, go back to studying. I'm more or less all right. We can talk again tomorrow. I love you."

"Mom," he said. "Do you want me to call him and talk to him?" Linda almost smiled. Her sweet son had a little bit of arrogance in that he always believed that if he could just sit down and talk to someone, they would have to see it his way. Maybe that arrogance would help him be a good attorney one day. Or at least a successful one. Maybe. Anyhow, his "wisdom" obviously wasn't going to help right now.

"Matt, you can call your father if you like. In fact, you probably should. But, don't expect him to change his mind about this. He sounds like he's given it a lot of thought, and frankly, I don't think I can ever get over what I saw today. Ever." She heard a catch in her voice and knew that she had to get off the phone before tears started coming. The last thing Matt needed to hear right now was her crying.

"So," she said. "Get back to studying. "I'm all right. Honestly. I feel myself coming to terms with the new normal. Whatever that will be. And I'm so proud of you and all the things you are doing. So, get back to preparing for those exams. I'll see you when you get through with them. By then, I should have figured some things out. I love you so much." She knew she sounded braver than she felt.

"Are you sure you're all right, Mom? I can come home if you need me," she could hear the hesitation in his voice, almost praying that she would not say yes.

"That is the last thing I would want. Really. What I want is for you to focus on what you have to do for school. I'll see you when exams are done. I love you so much. Now, get back to work. I'm going to call my sister, your crazy Aunt Carly. She'll certainly cheer me up. Or get me drunk, whichever comes first."

She could hear Matt chuckle. "I would tend to bet on the latter, personally. All right, Mom. I'll talk to you in a couple of days. I'll tell you the truth. Dad's been a jerk for a long time now. I mean, I love him. Because he's my dad. But I think he's been stuck in this weird middle age crisis thing for a long time. I think I saw it and I'm pretty sure Andrea did too. Maybe the only one who didn't see it was you. And that might be because you're just too kind to imagine such a thing. Anyhow, if he gets a second chance, don't forget, you do too."

Linda tried to laugh, "You mean what's good for the goose is good for the gander? Or something like that?"

Matt said, "Well, Mom, I don't think I've ever heard that expression before, but I think I get the gist of it. And, yes. That's what I mean. Just hang on for tonight. Andrea will be there in the morning. And I'll be there as soon as my finals are over. If you want me to. Or are you still going to move down here? Well. Too much to think about tonight. So, just remember this. You're a tough cookie, and you can do this. You don't deserve what he's done to you, but you can triumph over this. And, Dad is a complete asshole. He will never find another woman like you. And he doesn't deserve you."

"Thanks, honey," Linda said. "Good luck with your exams. We'll talk soon. I love you. Thanks for being there for me." In her head, she was thinking, well—obviously, he doesn't want another woman like me. She flashed back to Tiffany's boobs flapping up and down, the red sash trailing. She closed her eyes, stomped her foot, and tried to shake the image away.

"Good night, Mom. Love you." Matt sounded worried. Linda knew she should say something more, to quiet his fears, but she was completely at a loss as to what that could be.

Linda hung up and got ready to make one more call—the call to her sister. She was already dreading it, knowing that Carly had said that Rick was no good a long time ago. Now, she was going to get to say 'I told you so.' And Carly would thoroughly enjoy that. On the other hand, Carly only lived twenty miles away, and Linda felt like she needed some company tonight. So, she dialed her sister's number and found that she was holding her breath as she did so. Carly answered, almost immediately.

"What's up?" she said.

"How do you know something's up," Linda answered.

Carly snorted, "Because you're calling me on Friday evening. Which is something you never do. So, something must be up."

Linda tried to sound brave, but even she could hear the undercurrent of a sob in her voice. "Rick's left me. I walked in on him and another woman."

"What the hell! What did you just say?" Carly gasped. "You are absolutely kidding me, aren't you?"

"Nope," Linda said. "I wish I were. I don't think I'll ever be able to unsee what I've seen tonight. It's burned on the back of my eyeballs forever."

"Do not say another word," said Carly. "I'm getting in my car right now. I'll be there in fifteen minutes. Do you have anything to drink?"

"I've got a bottle of good Chardonnay," Linda answered. She had been saving it for their celebration dinner. Her last day of teaching celebration.

"Well," said Carly. "We're going to need more than that. I'll come armed with more booze. I love you. Sit down. Breathe. I'll be right there." She hung up, and Linda could picture her running around, gathering things to bring over for the night.

Linda sat down, as ordered, and looked out the front window, where the life of the neighborhood was settling down into a beautiful early summer evening. And where everything looked the same as it had always been. And where nothing was the same at all.

Chapter 3

About fifteen minutes later, Carly roared up in her bright red Porsche Boxster. The whole neighborhood turned to wave at her. Everybody knew Carly and that car. It was so exotic in this very middle class, domestic-car, Michigan neighborhood. Carly's long blonde hair streamed out from under her baseball cap, and she looked like a college kid. The truth is, Carly was a perfect example of the notion that "arrested development" can sometimes be a good thing. Although she was only eight years younger than Linda, it kind of seemed as if Carly had decided to never grow up. She was a very successful attorney, and very happily *not married*. Carly had had several long-term relationships, but every time she got close to getting serious, she ended it. The result was kind of beneficial for Andrea and Matt, because since Carly had no children of her own, she had spoiled them rotten every chance she got. She was the coolest aunt on the planet, if you asked either one of them. And they were probably right.

Carly parked the Porsche in the driveway and came right in to Linda. She pulled her into a bear-hug and rocked her gently. Then, she grabbed a grocery sack from the car and led Linda inside the house. "First, let's get ourselves a glass of very good wine, something to eat, and then we can sit out here on the porch, watch the evening come down and you can try to convince me not to kill him," she said.

"What purpose would that serve?" said Linda.

Carly looked at her with some surprise. "That was just a figure of speech, my darling. I am not going to kill him. And neither are you. In fact, I'm here to tell you that this might be the best thing that could have happened to you." She poured them both a glass of wine, set out cheese and crackers, and led Linda outside. Linda suddenly realized that she actually might be a little hungry. She had only had an energy bar for lunch because she had hoped they might be going out to dinner. However, as she thought about it, that seemed like an eternity ago. A different era. She thought about what she had said to Matt, about trying to get used to the new normal. She had heard that phrase from someone, and now it seemed to apply. Or truthfully, it seemed like something she *should* say. But the truth is, she did not understand it at all.

Carly settled into her chair, looked at Linda, reached over and gave her hand a squeeze, and said, "Tell me everything. Start from the beginning, and don't leave anything out." Linda realized that she sounded like Andrea. She leaned back in her chair and looked out over the neighborhood. A light breeze was rustling the trees overhead, trees that were showing off their new showy, summer leaves. Trees that just a few weeks ago had been bare, pointing their dark branches into a gray, wintry sky, revealing their bony architecture in the stark reality of winter. But now, like young women who are just starting to blossom and who are completely unaware of their own youthful beauty, they lifted their branches, already heavy with big, green leaves, into the evening sky. The pale blue of the early summer sky was darkening into a lovely twilight. In the distance, Linda could hear birdsong. Surprisingly, it sounded almost cheerful to her. Robins twittering in the twilight. Just as if nothing had happened.

Carly waited, sipping her wine. Then she said, "Tell it, Linda. Tell me what happened."

Linda took a deep breath and described what had happened. A weird kind of objectivity set in. She realized, as she was speaking, that this was already the third time she had narrated the scene, and in some bizarre way, it was getting easier to describe. But also, in some ways, not. In some ways, it was just so humiliating. She had been such a fool. How had she not known? Had she not been paying any attention at all?

As she finished, she turned to Carly, who was listening carefully and silently. Now Linda said, "So, what do I do now? The house is already sold. I have to be out in a week. I already have a moving van set up. I have a big yard sale scheduled for tomorrow. I took out an ad in the paper and everything. And put up signs around the neighborhood. I thought Rick would be here to help me. Now, he won't. And I've paid the first month's rent on the condo in Fort Lauderdale. And I just quit my job. And I can't undo any of that." She felt like she was babbling senselessly. She turned a tear-stained face to Carly, suddenly tired of trying to be brave.

Carly reached over and took her hand. "Nor should you," said Carly, with some strange kind of certainty in her voice. "Nor should you. You don't need to undo any of that. It's still a good plan. I will stay the night and help you with the yard sale. It will be fun. Let's sell all his shit and sell it cheap. One additional thing, however, is that we will sue him for divorce. I will get someone in my firm to represent you. I could do it, but It would be better if I didn't. I have a friend who will do it for free. This is an easy case. And then, you go ahead with your move. And make a new start down there. Matt's already down there at law school. This will all work out." Carly said it all so confidently, as if were going to be easy. Straightforward. Tears slipped down Linda's cheeks. She tried to smile through her tears. The evening had fallen down all around them, and suddenly Linda was aware of crickets chirping. Her stomach grumbled. She almost laughed, wondering how the animal processes of her body could be going on even when it felt like her brain had stopped.

Carly heard the tummy grumble and said, "All right. That's enough of that. I brought chicken soup. From the deli. You remember how that was Mom's cure for everything? Probably, even broken hearts. So, I'm going to heat that up, and we are going to watch some stupid chick flick on TV, and we are going to drink too much wine. Then, we are going to crawl in your big bed and sleep. Then, we are getting up early in the morning to have the best damn yard sale this neighborhood has ever seen." Carly stood up and grabbed Linda's hand, pulling her to her feet.

Linda followed her sister into the house, slumped down in a kitchen chair, and watched numbly as Carly busied herself around the kitchen. She had to admit that chicken soup actually sounded pretty good. She thought of her mom and dad. It had been years since they had passed on, but in times of crisis, she missed them so much. She thanked God for Carly. And for Andrea and Matt. She told Carly that Andrea was coming in the morning.

"That is awesome," Carly said, as she ladled soup into big white bowls. She grabbed saltines and put them on the table. Put a big spoon in Linda's hand and said imperiously, "Eat. No kidding. You have to take care of yourself physically in times like these. That means eat good food. Drink water. And tonight, drink wine too. Your body is a machine and it runs on fuel. If you don't take care of it, then a whole other set of problems will set in. And I'm not going to let that happen. So, eat."

Linda obediently spooned some of the soup into her mouth. The salt of the chicken broth tasted a little bit like her tears. She was about to share that observation with Carly, but decided to just eat her soup instead.

After dinner, they watched *Pretty Woman* and then crawled in bed together. Linda did not think she would sleep, but numbed by too many glasses of wine, she did. Miraculously.

Suddenly, sunlight was streaming mercilessly through the window, and she opened her eyes to the sound of the shower running and the smell of coffee brewing. For a minute, she was confused, wondering if Rick was in the shower. Then, her head cleared, and the whole terrible mess came flooding back over her. She stood up and stretched, rubbed her eyes, and stumbled toward the bathroom.

She popped open the door as the shower stopped. Carly stepped out of the shower and wrapped herself in a big towel.

"Good morning, sleepyhead," she said cheerfully. "I've been texting Andrea and she is about an hour away. It's eight o'clock and I see that your yard sale is supposed to start at noon. I checked the ad you ran in the paper. So, get in the shower and get ready to meet the day. We have a lot of work to do."

Linda looked at her sister with a mixture of astonishment and envy. How could she have this much energy in the morning? Oh, yeah. She's not the one whose whole world just fell apart. She stepped into the shower and let the hot water sluice all over her body. She almost felt bruised from the previous day's events. Which was nonsense, of course. But still, she felt bruised.

Suddenly, an arm reached into the shower, holding a steaming cup of coffee with cream. "Drink," said Carly.

"But I'm in the shower," Linda objected.

"Are you telling me you never drink in the shower?" Carly asked. "Well then, it's high time you discovered one of life's little pleasures. Drink. Now."

Linda took the cup and drank. It seemed like a ridiculous thing to do. But as the hot water beat on her body and the coffee trailed down her throat, she had to admit that she might have been missing out on something.

Meanwhile, Carly was babbling on. She was saying that she had brought up several card tables from the basement and was hauling them out to the front yard. Linda had gathered many of the things she wanted to sell down in the basement, and Carly was already busy setting them out. She had cookies in the oven, and beer in a big cooler. She wanted to have treats for the folks who came to the yard sale. Suddenly, she stuck her head in the shower and said to Linda, "All right. Enough. Get out her and help me."

"I'm drinking my coffee, like you told me to," Linda said, a half-smile playing on her face.   "Well, you've had enough," Carly said, turning off the water. "Now get out here and help me."

Reluctantly, Linda stepped out of the shower and into the towel that her sister held open for her. Carly said, "You've had your coffee. I have fresh croissants in the kitchen. Andrea will be here within the hour. Let's get moving." Linda looked at her like she was crazy. Her brain was moving slowly, fuzzy from too much wine last night and still in partial disbelief that her life had just been turned completely upside down. But it was pretty clear that Carly was not going to allow her to wallow in self-pity, or even to have a minute to take a breath.

"All right," Carly said. "Now, get dressed. Really. We have a million things to do. I'm going downstairs to get started. Hurry up." She whirled out of the room. At the doorway, she stopped and turned around, "I said, hurry up!" She grinned at Linda. "Get a move on, sister."

Linda groaned and got moving. When she got downstairs, Carly had already taken the card tables out to the front lawn. She was setting out things that Linda had marked for sale, almost singing while she worked. Linda halfway wanted to strangle her for being so peppy this early in the morning, and for not seeming to be all that upset that her life had just been blown to smithereens. Or at least, the life she thought she had. Just as Linda was walking out to the front yard, Andrea pulled up, in a rented BMW. She jumped out the car and ran into her mother's arms, enveloping her in a bear hug. Carly came over and joined in, and Linda found herself being utterly smashed between two crazy women. Almost in spite of herself, she started giggling.

"All right, all right, you two," she said. "I can't even breathe." She untangled herself and gave Andrea a kiss on the cheek. "It was so good of you to come home, my darling," she said. "But, maybe you don't need to be here. This crazy person is taking care of me." She jerked her thumb at Carly.

Andrea said, "Well, to tell you the truth, I needed a break from the city, and your disaster provided me with a good excuse to get out of there." She held her mom in her arms, but at arm's length. She stared into her mother's eyes, as if trying to divine some higher truth. "How are you holding up?" she said.

Linda tried a smile. "Better than yesterday. I guess I'm still trying to get my head around it. It's weird. I keep expecting him to come in the house at any moment."

"Well," said Carly. "He may very well do that. I texted him about an hour ago and told him that his golf bag and golf clubs were sitting curbside, the number one attraction for the yard

39

sale. I know they are his pride and joy. I told him if he didn't want them to go to the highest bidder, he had better get his ass over here and buy them himself. So, I think you can expect to see him at any minute."

Linda could not help herself. She giggled. "Oh, Carly. You did not do that!"

"Oh, yes I did," said Carly. "I've already got a price tag on the bag. $200.00!"

Linda laughed, almost sputtering, "Carly! He has well over a thousand dollars' worth of equipment in that bag! Maybe two thousand! Two hundred would be an absolute steal!"

"Well, then," Carly said, turning back to pricing items she was setting out, "he had better hurry before one of the guys in the neighborhood snaps them up."

Linda looked at Andrea, not knowing exactly what to do, and Andrea put her arm around her mother's shoulder and said, "Mom. This should be interesting." They walked inside the house together, leaving Carly to manage the front lawn, and Andrea threw her duffle bag on the floor in the kitchen.

"Sit with me for a minute, Mom," she said. She held her mom's hand in hers and said, "Now really, how are you doing? How did Matt take it? What can I do?"

Linda smiled, a little sadly and said, "All right. All right. And you're already doing everything you could possibly do. In that order." She kept holding her daughter's hand. There was something comfortable about that, in the midst of all this madness.

Andrea smiled. She said, "I think Matt has finals this week. I was a little worried about the timing of this announcement. I was afraid he would be really freaked out."

"So was I," said Linda. "But he seemed to take it in stride. I have this weird feeling that both of my children were actually more perceptive about the state of the union than I was. Maybe I just wasn't paying enough attention." She felt tears appearing in the corners of her eyes. Andrea put her arms around her mom and held her close.

"Mom," she said, "if you weren't paying attention, it's because you were looking out for me or Matt or your students. You are one of the most selfless people I've ever met. So, don't go making his infidelity your fault. I will not let you do that." She looked into her mother's eyes and said, "I will always love Dad, and he will always be my dad, but that doesn't make this right. And you can't blame yourself for his midlife crisis. That's just nonsense. That good old Catholic guilt, or mother guilt, or whatever it is—throw it away. This is not your fault."

"I know you're right," Linda said. "I just can't believe it's over. "Our anniversary is next month. We would have been married for thirty years." A tear trickled down her cheek.

"Are you sure it's over? Can you forgive him?" Andrea said. Linda suspected that the business person in Andrea was playing devil's advocate. Negotiating.

"No," said Linda. "It's over. In fact, he told me that, as far as he was concerned, it had been over for a very long time. He even asked me for a divorce."

Andrea sat there in silence, staring into her mother's eyes. "Well then. It sounds like you think he really meant it. Not like it was something he just said on the spur of the moment."

"No," said Linda. "It had an air of finality about it, if you know what I mean. I think he really meant it. In fact, I think, now that I really think about it, that he was just looking for a way to tell me. And then he had it. A rather spectacular one."

Outside, voices were yelling and swearing. One was Carly's and one seemed to belong to her husband. Linda and Andrea went to the front door. What they saw out there was almost comical. Almost.

Carly and Rick were engaged in a full-on tug of war over the golf clubs. Both of them had a death grip on one side of the bag. They were hurling epithets at each other. Colorful ones. There were about six or seven other patrons of the yard sale milling about, and they were standing there, mouths open, aghast. Although some were laughing pretty hard, enjoying the scene. Carly, slender but tough, was holding her own against Rick. Several of the neighbors were drifting over, interested in the sideshow. Linda felt helpless, embarrassed, and kind of naked. Emotionally.

Two little kids were standing in front of Carly's platter of cookies, touching each cookie and deciding which one had the most chocolate chips. Their mom, embarrassed by their behavior, was making an effort to turn them around, ushering them rather forcefully back to her SUV, parked in the driveway. Neither kid was going to leave without a cookie. Or two.

"Carly," Rick said, trying to keep his voice under control. "You cannot sell my property. Linda doesn't even want you to do this. You are being completely unreasonable and doing nothing more than performing for these good people, who, by the way, are not amused by your antics."

"I'm amused," a rather chunky blonde woman said, raising her hand. "I just stopped because I saw the yard sale signs, but from what I've heard, I think she has a right to sell those clubs. And you probably owe that good woman two hundred dollars." Linda had never seen this woman before. Carly grinned at Rick and tugged again on the bag, enjoying the moment.

"Ma'am," said Rick, putting on his salesman voice, "I will thank you to mind your own business."

"Well, it's a little bit my business too," she said, "because I just gave that woman you're arguing with a deposit on the golf clubs. I bought them for my hubby, and he is on his way over here right now to claim them. They are too heavy for me to drag home. But my Kenneth is coming over with cash, and those clubs are already sold. To me." Linda looked around and saw that several more people had joined the other buyers in the front yard. She could see that the entertainment value of this scene was going up by the moment. She looked at Andrea, not knowing what to do. Andrea grinned at her.

"Hi, dad," she called out. "Good to see you. I'm sorry about your clubs. This is very awkward. But Aunt Carly says that she gave you fair notice. And told you to be here early this morning if you wanted them. It's now noon, so I think Aunt

Carly, and Mom and I thought that maybe they didn't matter to you anymore." She smiled at the chubby lady who was not yielding her position and who was now being joined by a man who had two hundred dollars in his hand and obviously wanted that set of clubs. Must be Kenneth, thought Linda. In some strange way, Linda felt like she was just an observer. She sat down in one of the big Adirondack chairs on the front porch, cradling her now lukewarm cup of coffee, and decided to watch how it all played out. Andrea looked over her and said, "Mom, these other people over here have made their selections and are ready to pay for them. Could you take their money?"

Linda hopped up obediently, walking over to the cashbox and smiling, with what she hoped was a pleasant smile. She saw what they had collected and added up the price tags. "Let's see, that will be fifteen dollars." The woman, who had long brown hair and smiling eyes, handed over a ten and a five.

She grinned at Linda, obviously not knowing who she was and how she fit in, and whispered, "You know, just between me and you, I kind of find myself pulling for the lady here. Obviously, this looks like a messy divorce in the process, and that man seems very arrogant and very sure of himself. Kind of annoys me." Linda looked over at Rick and Carly, still engaged in their warfare, with Kenneth pitching in. She was already emotionally distancing herself from Rick, and it surprised her to feel that going on. She looked at Rick yelling at both Carly and Kenneth and saw him getting redder and redder in the face. She even heard that supercilious tone in his voice that this woman was talking about. She was looking at him with new eyes, and for the first time in her life, she was looking at him as just another man. As she watched for another minute or so, Rick reached in his wallet and took out a $100.00 bill.

He practically threw it at Kenneth and said, "Here. I'll give you a hundred dollars to let go of my golf bag and just go away!" Kenneth threw back his head and laughed.

"Let me get this straight. You're giving me a hundred dollars to *not buy* your golf clubs? Is that right?" He grinned at his wife. "Honey, the way I look at it, this is a win-win. Buddy, you got a deal." He grabbed the hundred-dollar bill out of Rick's hand, spun his wife around to the curb and waved goodbye to the crowd on the lawn. Several of the spectators laughed and clapped. Linda realized that no one standing on her front lawn liked her husband very much. This was all new to her. Rick was fuming.

Dragging his clubs up the sidewalk, Rick approached the front door. "Can we at least be civilized about all of this, Linda? Get your crazy sister to stay away from me, before I say something I will regret." He dragged his clubs in the house and stood them up in the foyer.

Linda said, "I'm sorry about that scene. I didn't really know that Carly had your clubs out there." She looked out at the yard sale which was humming along merrily. The crowd was still buzzing and laughing in the aftermath of the battle for the golf clubs. Andrea and Carly had everything under control, so she followed her husband (ex-husband) into the house. "Are you going to get your other stuff today, too? You know the movers are coming next weekend, so whatever you want, you should

45

probably take today. I'm going to be packing all week, and I move out of here one week from today." She sounded a lot braver and surer of herself than she felt.

"I get it. I know the schedule." He looked a little embarrassed. "Look, Linda," he said. "I never really wanted it to go down like this. I thought of telling you a hundred times, and I never pictured it happening the way it happened. I feel really bad about that."

"A hundred times?' said Linda softly. His words stung her. How casually he had said it. Once again, she found herself wondering how she could have been so oblivious to what was going on.

"Oh, I don't mean that literally," he said, embarrassed. "I just mean that, at least for me, the magic went out a long time ago. I mean, I haven't really felt like the man of your dreams for a while now. In fact, I haven't really felt like there was any fire between us for a long time."

"Do you have that fire with Tiffany? Or whatever her name was?" Linda asked, fighting back tears.

"To tell you the truth, she's just the latest in a long line of distractions, Linda." He couldn't meet her eyes. He sat down on the couch, folded his hands in his lap, and looked down at his feet. Linda realized that he was a little ashamed, but not much. Mostly, he just seemed tired. Resigned. She considered the thought that she had not been paying very much attention—to him or to her marriage.

Rick took a deep breath and then said, "No, I don't feel any real fire with her, not like the kind we used to have. And maybe I'll never find that fire again. But I also haven't felt it with you, and I got tired of waiting for it. At least I'm back in the chase again, and in some weird and probably very juvenile way, it makes me feel more alive." He looked into her eyes. "Does that make any sense?"

"Nothing makes sense to me right now," Linda said, embarrassed as the tears trickled down her cheeks. She was angry at herself for crying, and giving him that victory over her. And then, all of a sudden, a weird thing happened. That fleeting sense of compassion or understanding or whatever it was, left her completely. She just got angry. Not so much sad at this particular moment as just angry. She felt herself starting to tremble, but not with tears. Rather with rage. She realized that she had been holding words in for a very long time, and suddenly, they just came spilling out.

"No," she said angrily. "Nothing makes sense. You are a damned fool. I loved you, and I honored you, and I was a good wife to you. You could always depend on me. You were the one thing I thought I could always depend on too. And I was wrong. Anyhow, I'm sorry if you didn't feel like I loved you. I think I did. I never thought I would love anyone else. But in spite of that, I hear you. It's over. So, I will let you get your things together. And just get out. You will hear from my lawyer." She fought back tears. "You better take your stuff quickly before Carly comes up here and gets them and puts a price tag on them."

"She's a crazy person," Rick said, shaking his head in disgust. "You know that, don't you?"

"Yeah. Well. She seems perfectly sane to me lately," Linda said. "And making a hell of a lot more sense than you make. Like I said before, you are a sad middle-aged fool. Good luck with your return to mid-life crisis." She turned around and left the room. She held her head high, pushed her shoulders back, and took a deep breath. She could do this, she told herself. She went upstairs to the guest room to give him some space while he gathered his things. She didn't want to watch that final gathering. She could do this, she told herself again. But as she sat down on the couch, tears continued to flow.

Chapter 4

Clearly, nothing about any of this was going to be easy. Somehow, Linda got through the last week of school obligations. There was the responsibility of closing up her room, filing all her grades, and packing up her personal possessions. Saying goodbye to everyone. There was a farewell luncheon, and so many of her colleagues reached out to her, telling her how happy they were for her. Retiring. Starting a new life in Fort Lauderdale. Fort Lauderdale. The words still had a kind of magic to them. She remembered the first time she had seen the old beach town, when she was just a kid and her family had gone down there for vacation. That was a long time ago. A lifetime ago.

Linda had decided to keep the whole fiasco with Rick and the failure of her marriage to herself. It just didn't seem like anyone's business but her own. And her immediate family. So, she somehow pasted a fake smile on her face and her heart and got through the week. She was fully aware of the fact that it was the best acting job she had ever done, and she knew that when she looked back on this week, she would see it through a prism of utter gray fog and bewilderment.

Then, on Saturday, the moving van appeared. Four strong young men loaded her whole life into a semi and set off for Fort Lauderdale. Many of the neighbors had come over to say goodbye. Two of the neighborhood women each brought her a cake. After they said their farewells and left, Linda looked down at the cakes, wondering what on earth had made the women think that she might need or want a cake as she drove south. Was she supposed to return the plates?

Anyhow. Carly had spent Friday night with her. On Saturday morning, she got up before the movers arrived so that Linda would be ready to face the morning. The men were so matter-of-fact about the whole thing that it actually kind of helped. They moved families every day. It didn't really matter to them, one way or the other, if the family they were moving had just been shattered or not. They didn't ask any questions, and Linda was grateful for that. All they cared about was that she was moving. And that gave them a job to do. Period.

So, the last of her stuff was loaded up, and they shut the tailgate, telling her that they would see her in Fort Lauderdale in two days.

Linda and Carly stood side by side in her living room, which somehow looked a lot smaller now that it was stripped. Linda moved to pick up some imaginary lint off the floor when Carly stopped her.

"No," Carly said. "This place is spotless. You've done an amazing job. It will probably never be this clean again. These people are lucky that you are so meticulous. But it is not your house anymore, and it is time for us to hit the open road." Linda choked back a sob that somehow had been able to sneak up on her. She turned to her sister with tears in her eyes and Carly said, "No. No tears. We are all done with that for now. At least for a little while. We are on a grand adventure. Let's go." Carly grabbed her hand and headed for the front door.

Linda took one last look around the house. In some weird way, it already looked like it didn't belong to her. She took a deep breath and looked into her sister's eyes. "Okay. I guess I'm ready." Carly gave her a hug and led her down the front porch stairs to her car.

The plan was that they would drive south together in Linda's car, stopping halfway down the continent for the night. Carly had arranged to take a week off work to help Linda get settled. Then, Carly would fly home and Linda would begin the next phase of her "great adventure" alone. The whole plan sounded desperately hopeful and just a little bit ridiculous to Linda. Andrea said that she was standing in the wings, ready to come down at a moment's notice if and when she was needed. Linda knew, in her heart of hearts, that it would be hard for Andrea to get any more time off work, but she appreciated her offer of help.

They drove out of the neighborhood at noon on Saturday. One lady was out in her yard, watering her flowers. She lifted a hand in a casual wave. Linda wondered if the woman knew that she was driving away from a life she had known for thirty years. She suspected not. In fact, Linda was thinking about how, at times of momentous changes in a person's life, it seems so strange that the rest of the world is spinning on, obliviously. She remembered experiencing that bizarre disconnect at the moment of her mom's death, and her dad's. How could the rest of the world not know that her world had just fallen apart? And yet, it really did not. Things went on as before, regardless of your sense of dislocation.

Carly had said that she would take the first shift, and Linda was glad that she had, watching the neighborhood move into her rear window with this weird sense of other-worldliness. She wondered briefly if Rick remembered that this was the day she was leaving town. In the next half thought, she scolded herself for thinking of him. Old habits die hard, she thought.

Carly said, "All right. I put a playlist together for this moment. I have it all cued up and I hooked my phone up to your Bluetooth, so, here we go." She pushed start on her phone and "Hit the road, Jack, and don't you come back no more, no more, no more, no more," blasted out of her sound system. Linda couldn't help but smile at the raucous old song. She let herself just listen for a while, letting those amazing voices speak her thoughts for her. The day was warm, the beginning of summer in the air, and the sunshine felt flirtatious. Light-hearted. They had the windows down, and the warm air rushed over her.

Carly reached over and patted her on the knee, but she didn't say anything. Carly was really very smart, and some part of her knew that this was a moment when no words would suffice. Ray Charles kept singing, and the warm air kept rushing. Goodbye to Michigan summers, thought Linda. Goodbye to my old neighborhood. Goodbye to teaching. She looked down and saw her wedding ring on her finger. Carly had her eyes on the road, thank goodness. And while Carly wasn't looking, Linda slipped her ring off her finger and put it in her purse. She thought about dropping on the roadside, but it was worth a lot of money, and her kids could use the money for sure. So, she slipped it in her purse, determined to give it to Andrea or Matt to sell at her first opportunity to do so. And then, she closed her eyes again, feeling the summer wind in her hair.

Before she knew it, Carly was pulling off the highway, saying she had to go the the bathroom, and it was Linda's turn to drive. Linda roused herself and looked at the clock. Her poor sister had been driving for four hours, and the car was on fumes. Linda said, "Geez, Carly. Why did you let me sleep that long? I don't know what got into me. I'm sorry."

Carly shook her head and said, "No. Don't be sorry. You were obviously exhausted. I really don't know how you are even standing up, given what you've been through. But anyhow, it's your turn to drive." They got out of the car and stretched, and Linda pumped gas while Carly went in to use the restroom and get some drinks. She brought out a Gatorade and an ice-cold water. Linda took the water and gulped some down gratefully. Then, after using the restroom, she got into the driver's seat and pointed the car south. Carly grabbed the phone and got her playlist going again.

"Next stop, Lexington," Carly announced. "I've arranged for us to stay the night at a really nice Marriott, right off the interstate. And, it has an awesome restaurant right across the street. I got one of the best filet mignons there I have ever had last time I passed through town. And, girl, I am buying you a good steak tonight."

Linda laughed. "I don't even know how long it's been since I ordered a steak at a restaurant. I always order fish, trying to keep it on the light side. But, I guess it's time to try new things. Let's live dangerously!" Carly smiled at her.

"You are such an innocent. I love you." Then, she went on. "But you are being really brave, and I'm so proud of you." Linda didn't really feel very brave, but she felt herself getting used to the rhythm of the interstate. She had been staying in the center lane, tucked in between a couple of huge tractor trailer trucks. But now, she put on her blinker and entered the fast lane, where everybody was going at least ten miles over the speed limit. She brought the car up to 80 miles an hour and settled in. Oddly enough, she felt good, having left Michigan behind. Or maybe it was the physical act of moving forward? Hard to know what was the primary motivator, but she felt a kind of lightness in her heart. At least for a moment.

They were almost through the long flat prairie of Ohio, and the mountains would be appearing soon. Carly closed her eyes and pushed her seat back after checking that Linda was doing fine. Linda relaxed into the drive, letting thoughts roll through her mind, letting the miles roll away under her car. Soon, dusk came and Lexington appeared before them. Her navigational system guided her to the Marriott, and she parked the car and got out and stretched.

The city was just lighting up, and the air smelled wonderful. It smelled like freshly cut grass and charred steaks. They checked in, cleaned up, and headed over to the restaurant. It was Saturday night, and a lot of couples seemed to be out for a night on the town. The crowd at the bar was already roaring. A lot of the men were watching a soccer game, a preliminary to the World Cup. They were screaming at the players on the American team, who were down by two goals to Costa Rica. The hostess said that it would be about half an hour until they could be seated, but they could go to the bar and get a drink.

They took two bar stools, right in the middle of the bar and ordered drinks. Linda got a glass of Chardonnay; Carly got a Margarita, rocks, salt. They started to half-heartedly watch the soccer game. Because it was there, right in front of their faces. A handsome young thirty something came over and jostled Carly. "Excuse me, ma'am. Can I buy you a drink?" He had this Southern drawl that sounded kind of fake to Linda, and she frowned at him, telling him with her eyes to go away.

But not Carly. She swiveled around on her bar stool and looked him over, from head to toe. "Well," she said, slowly, "You see. I have just ordered myself a drink. And I will pay for it myself. Why don't you go down there to the end of the bar and give us a little space. We just got off the road, and the highway is still echoing in my ears, if you know what I mean." He looked at her closely, trying to follow where she was going with this. "And so," she continued, "I am going to drink this lovely drink I've ordered, and when it's gone, maybe I will let you buy me another. But until then, I need a little peace and quiet. All right?"

He gulped and said, "Why sure. I'll be right down there at the end of the bar, and I'll watch to see when you're ready for a new one. Then, I'll be back." She smiled at him, nodding him away, and he went, like an obedient little puppy.

"What the heck was that?" Linda said, as soon as he left.

"What do you mean?"

"That Jedi mind trick you just worked on him. You want to buy me a drink, but you must wait until I am ready," Linda recited, using her best Jedi master voice. "It's like he couldn't even think for himself. You pretty much rendered him speechless." She really was in awe of what she had just witnessed.

Carly laughed, easily. "That," she said, "my dear sister is the power of womanhood. Something you have yet to learn to use to your advantage." They received their drinks from the bartender, and Linda took a sip of her wine. It was good. Carly grabbed the bar tab and pulled it toward herself, smiled at the bartender, turned to Linda, and said, "Cheers."

Linda smiled at her sister. Her wonderful younger sister. "How," she said, "did you get to be so cool and confident? I'm the older sister, but I feel like I'm getting lessons in coolness from you. I somehow missed these lessons earlier in life."

Carly smiled. She said, "Don't be too hard on yourself. You got married young and raised a family. And did a really good job with that. And you tried to raise a husband. That's something I've never done. I think I'd like to, and I think I'd like to have kids of my own. But I'm pretty sure that ship has sailed. I'm 46 already. My child bearing years have passed me by. And I have never found a man I like well enough to marry. At least not yet." It occurred to Linda that Carly had her own kinds of sadness. Different from her own, but just as real to her.

"Well," said Linda, taking a big gulp of her wine. "I feel like a fish out of water. I watch you flirt so easily with that guy, who is probably ten years younger than you, and I realize that I don't have a clue how to do that. Not a clue. I feel like an old maid around you."

"You are hardly an old maid," Carly said. As she spoke, she reached over and undid two more buttons on Linda's shirt. Linda gulped, completely unprepared for this assault.

"What are you doing," she sputtered.

"Just getting you a little more comfortable," Carly grinned. Linda reached down to do a button back up and Carly gently pulled her hand away. Then, she reached out and mussed Linda's hair. Linda looked up at her, aghast. Carly smiled and said, "You are really very pretty. Your hair is still blonde, and you've got great skin. And absolutely beautiful eyes. You just need to show your good qualities off a little better. Lesson one complete. Our table buzzer just went off. Let's go get some steaks." As they passed by the guy at the end of the bar, he rose to follow.

Carly put her hand up to stop him. "Sorry, buddy. Been thinking about your offer. You seem like a really nice guy, but we have a lot of stuff to talk about tonight. Sister stuff. Maybe tomorrow. All right?"

"Yeah, sure," he said. "If I'm here tomorrow." He sounded like he was trying to suggest that this was a one-time only offer.

"Well," Carly smiled at him, "if you're not, our loss. Thanks for the offer, anyhow. Have a great night." She patted him on the arm as they walked past his bar stool. Carly's smile seemed to take the sting out of her gentle rejection.

Linda watched, open-mouthed, as her sister negotiated these perilous waters. She managed to turn the guy away without making him feel stripped of his dignity or his manhood. Even though she knew full well that she would not be back here tomorrow, he would be all right. Linda marveled at how much she had to learn.

Chapter 5

Two weeks later, Linda was all moved in. Carly had stayed a week and helped her get settled. But she had to get back to work, so Linda drove her to the airport and put her on a plane back to Michigan. As she hugged her goodbye, she tried to tell her sister how much she appreciated everything she had done.

Carly brushed her words away. "Don't be silly. I loved every minute of it. It was like a vacation for me. Now. It's the middle of June, and you're in South Florida. These first days and nights are going to be a little tough. But it looks like there are a lot of nice people in your building. So, just take it cool. And give it a chance."

Linda tried a smile. "All right. Quit acting like a big sister. I'll be all right."

Carly said, "Yes. You will. And if you feel lonely, just call me. Night or day. I'm right here for you." She reached over and messed Linda's hair up a little again, grinning at her. "You may discover that you are more all right than you ever realized before." Linda hugged her again, and then Carly left to go through security. Linda watched her until she was all the way through. Carly turned around and waved her hand and headed to her gate. Linda went out, got into her car, and tried to navigate the twisting turns that were the exit roads from the airport. She accidentally got in the wrong lane and ended up circling back through the terminal drop off lanes again. Frustrated, she was determined to pay closer attention the second time, and this time, she got it right. While Carly was here, she had made her learn her way to the best grocery store, and now she thought she would go by there and get a few things. She had it programmed into the GPS in her car, and that made everything a little bit easier.

She liked the grocery store. Everybody was busy, and the people who worked there all seemed very cheerful. She picked up a few things and headed home. As she pulled into her condo garage, she slowed way down. She was still not used to parking in a parking structure, but that is how this worked. She had a spot assigned to her and that is the only place she could park. She managed to nudge her Honda into its spot, got the groceries out of the trunk, and headed to her elevator. As she waited for the elevator to come, she could feel the breeze, moving through the open-air parking garage. When she got up to her unit, she put her groceries away and stepped out on the balcony, which was finally deep in shade since it was the afternoon. To the east, she could see Mother Ocean, today a dark blue with white caps. Looking powerful and aloof. But so blue. And to the west, she could see the Intracoastal, the inland waterway that supposedly ran all the way up the coastal landscape, from here to New England.

Today, all kinds of boats were out there, from old pontoon boats to yachts. She went into her kitchen, poured herself a glass of white wine, and grabbed her novel. She was reading a mystery about stolen art. She had a comfortable chaise lounge on her porch, and she sat down and put her feet up. She heard laughter coming up from the pool. Gingerly, she peeked over the edge of the railing. There were about ten young people down at the pool, drinking beer and wine and laughing. They all looked to be in their 20's or 30's. They were fit and tan. Linda suddenly felt very much alone, and in unfamiliar territory. She thought about calling Andrea, but her shift at the bar would just be heating up. She thought about calling Matt, but what could he do? She thought about Carly, but she was somewhere up there in the blue. She thought about Rick for a minute, and she felt herself about to tear up. So, she took a gulp of her wine, opened the mystery book, and following the words of the writer, took herself back into the museum, where the piece had been stolen. She forced herself to read the next scene, and the next.

And soon enough, the words worked their magic and she was back in Paris, for a while. The evening settled down, and the city lit up. The moon rose over the ocean, and a cool breeze came in. Linda told herself that she would be all right. In time.

Chapter 6

The next morning, she decided to go for a walk before breakfast. There was an awesome sidewalk that ran along the ocean, between A1A and the sandy beach. The sidewalk was pretty busy with early morning walkers and joggers, many of them in pairs, but lots with headphones in, doing their own thing. Linda told herself that tomorrow she would remember to wear her headphones and bring her Iphone along. She could listen to the new playlist that her son had made her. But, as for this morning, she would just make do with walking and listening to the ocean. And the wind, and the seagulls.

But that wasn't quite true, was it? Because right next to her were hundreds of cars, zipping along. Everybody had someplace to go. Something to do. And Linda felt conspicuously out of it. She felt herself slipping into a shallow pit of self-pity. Not a good thing. So, she picked up her pace, kept her eyes firmly on the sun-swept horizon, and put in three quick miles. As she finished and was heading back to her condo, she noticed a French bakery, right across the street from the entrance to her condo. Feeling virtuous after three good miles of walking, and feeling further like she needed a treat to go with her morning coffee, she made a quick detour and entered the little café.

There were about eight small tables, and people bustling about everywhere. There was a long counter with all kinds of croissants and baguettes displayed. And a very attractive French woman working the register. She had her hair cut short, like a boy, and a beautiful face. She spoke French with many of the customers, and Linda was so impressed. She began to wish she were not so sweaty. She felt a little out of place with many of the other people in the restaurant dressed as though they were on their way to work. She almost turned around and left, but suddenly, the French woman was speaking right to her.

"Bonjour," she said. "How can I help you?" Linda noticed that she had immediately switched to English, which, although heavily accented, also sounded beautiful.

"Bonjour," Linda answered. "May I please have a croissant?" She stammered out her question, stunned by the woman's lovely eyes and smile.

"But, of course," she smiled. "Which kind? Any special kind?"

"Oh," Linda said, "just a plain one. Although they all look beautiful."

The woman smiled and said, "Any coffee?"

Linda said that all she needed was the croissant. As she was paying, a Frenchman came out of the kitchen and bumped into the lady working the counter. He was even more beautiful than she was. Dark wavy hair, piercing blue eyes, hands covered in flour, and a brilliant smile. Linda wondered if they were married. Probably. Suddenly, he grinned at Linda, wiped his hands on his apron, and said something in rapid French to his wife, who giggled in return. Linda suddenly felt like a fifth wheel, or a sixth or seventh. Or all of the above. She paid for her croissant, mumbled out a "Merci," and made her way to the door. The conversations swirled around her as she opened the door to leave. Suddenly, someone called out, "Au Revoir! Merci." Linda turned around but couldn't see who had spoken. So, she smiled quickly, sort of half-heartedly, and went on her way, clutching her little white bakery bag.

She entered the lobby of the condo building to find the desk man busily talking with a delivery man, so she slipped by him. She was still getting used to the idea of a lobby where you might have to talk to people. Where you would run into other people. She was thinking to herself that houses didn't have lobbies like this. It was just another new thing. As she waited by the elevator, a woman came and stood beside her, also waiting to go up to her unit. Linda had noticed her yesterday, down at the pool.

She was definitely not in her 20's or 30's. Linda looked sideways at her, and judged her to be at least in her 50's. Probably about the same age that Linda was. But she was as different in her bearing from Linda as night from day. She had tight Lululemon leggings on and a jog bra. Linda wondered if that was considered appropriate outerwear down here. This woman was very tan. Maybe almost too tan. Her hair was pulled up in a high pony tail. She wore a heavy gold chain and carried a water bottle. She had obviously been running or walking or something. Linda was clutching her white bakery bag. She realized that she needed to get some better running clothes. She thought about saying something, but before she could speak, the other woman turned to her and smiled.

"Hi," she said. "I'm Eva." She reached out her hand for Linda to shake. "I think you're new here, is that right?"

Linda said, "Yes. Brand new. I'm still trying to find my way around. I just moved down from Michigan."

"Well, good move," said Eva. "The first couple months might be tough, but it gets absolutely beautiful around here just about the third week of October. You just have to hang on for a few more weeks and then we will be having the most beautiful weather in the world. I'm in unit 2001, and I'm the president of the owner's association here, so if there is anything I can do, just let me know."

They got on the elevator together and Linda got off at her floor, thanking Eva for her kindness. She thought to herself, where do I start? I have so many questions that I don't even know where to begin.

She made herself a pot of coffee and went outside on the balcony. She sat down with her croissant. Which was absolutely heavenly. So light it felt like bread flavored air. As she drank her coffee, she read the newspaper. She realized that school had started a couple weeks ago here. It was already September, and schools all across the nation were in session. It was the first September in 30 years that she wasn't in a classroom. She didn't really want to teach full-time anymore. She had done that for a long time now, and she was done with it. But she needed some way to get connected to the community. She couldn't rely on her sister, or her kids.

She realized that she needed to rely on herself. She remembered a time when she had been very confused about something, and she had called her mom, who had told her to keep putting one foot in front of the other. Just keep moving, and pretty soon, you find out where you are supposed to be going. Such a strange notion, but she felt like it might be the best advice at the moment. In fact, maybe the only advice that made any sense, or had any practical application.

She stood on her balcony, looking down at the pool sparkling in the early morning sunshine. A light breeze wafted over her, lifting her hair. As she glanced down at the pool, she saw a very handsome young man sunbathing. He had slathered himself in suntan lotion, and his skin almost sparkled in the sunshine. He saw her staring at him and grinned at her. He waved. Mortified, Linda realized she had been staring, thinking that the height of the balcony made her invisible or something. She blushed right down to her roots, spun around, and went back inside. Had he been genuinely friendly, or was he mocking her? She couldn't be sure. She didn't want to make a fool of herself, and suddenly she felt like she was playing in a game where she did not know the rules.

She took a shower and then sat down at the kitchen table, pulled out her laptop and went over her finances. She wanted to make sure that she could make ends meet on her retirement pension. She would receive her share of the proceeds from the sale of the house. But that was a one-time thing. She had not asked for alimony from Rick because she didn't think she would need it. She had done the math about a hundred times before, and she was pretty sure that it would work. But just barely. There was no room for extra spending. Not much room for any entertainment expenses. In fact, not much wiggle room at all. She thought about the tightness of her financials for a few weeks, on and off, as she started to familiarize herself with the city.

She spent some time every day, just driving around, finding the nearest Target, finding a church she liked, finding a restaurant with good carryout offerings. At first, she relied very heavily on the GPS in her car, but pretty soon, she started to get the lay of the land.

She kept up her morning walks or runs, depending on how she felt that particular day. In fact, she was religious about it. And she got herself down to the pool to swim laps every day, trying to arrive there before it got too crowded with the young people who seemed more intent on sunning themselves than swimming. Soon, it was fall. She felt a slight change in the weather. Ever so slight. The sun's arc in the sky was changing. She watched it every morning as she walked, and she realized that the arc was getting lower. That changed the angle of the light on the water. It was sharper, and the morning light dazzled her, like sunlit diamonds. The clouds striated themselves across the sky, and the wind was freshening. She started to notice that she recognized many of the faces on her morning walk. Not to call them by name, but she felt a kind of unspoken camaraderie among the morning people. Most of them were very quiet about their walking, almost reverent in the early light. Some had earbuds in, but others just seemed to drink in the beauty of the ocean and the sky.

She had realized that her finances were a little bit tighter than she wanted them to be, so she decided that she needed to get a part time job, just to pick up a little bit of spending money. She researched the local high schools, and it seemed like St. Michael's was the best high school in the area. Everything she read online made it sound like a great school. Good, solid academics and a vibrant sports program. A very diverse student body. Lots of National Merit kids. A very strong alumni association. Sounded like it might be a very good place to make connections, if she could.

So, she put on her navy-blue suit and a pink blouse and put the school's address in her GPS. She pulled into the parking lot labelled "Visitors" and walked up to the main entrance of the school. There she was greeted by a Fort Lauderdale policewoman, complete with a Kevlar vest and a gun on her hip. Linda explained that she was a former teacher, that she was coming to present her credentials as a possible tutor.

The officer filled out a visitor's badge after checking Linda's identification and asked a student to escort Linda down to the guidance center, which apparently also doubled as the Human Resources function for the school. As Linda walked through the halls with the student, who introduced herself as Amy, she felt overwhelmed. This was a big school. Very big. Much bigger than her old school. Thousands of teenagers were moving through the halls. All dressed in uniforms. Khaki pants.

Or dark blue and green plaid skirts. Light blue shirts. But, they were loud and busy, and just a little bit terrifying en masse.

Amy got her to the door of the guidance center and explained that she had to go back to her class but asked if Linda could handle it from there on her own. Of course she could, Linda assured her and opened the door. Inside the center, there were four receptionist desks, several offices behind them, and students milling around everywhere. Linda waited in line, and finally, one of the secretaries looked up and acknowledged her.

"Good morning," she said. "Who are you and how can I help you?"

Linda smiled at the somewhat awkward but very effective greeting. She held out the envelope that had her credentials, a copy of her teaching certificate, and letters of recommendation.

"Hi," she said. "My name is Linda Miller. I just retired after teaching for thirty years up in Michigan. My husband and I are no longer together, and I have moved down here alone. Making a fresh start. I reviewed my finances and realized that I need to make a little pocket money. I really don't want to be a substitute teacher. I'm kind of spoiled in that I was a real teacher, and I don't want to take that step backwards. But, I was thinking that maybe you could have your HR person take a look at my credentials, and maybe you could feel comfortable recommending me as a tutor for some of your students." Linda was just a little bit surprised at how easily all of this had poured out of her. Telling the truth was always best.

The secretary, whose placard said that her name was Mrs. Davis, smiled a little sadly and said, "Well, that is a good beginning. You know who you are and what you want. I think we can work with that. You have your references in this envelope?"

Linda nodded and said that she did. The secretary stood up and beckoned Linda to follow. "Come this way. Our Director of Guidance handles these sorts of things. He is just finishing up with a student. I will give him a minute to finish, tell him about you, and get him to have a look at your resume. Are you sure you don't want to be a substitute teacher? We could probably use you." She added this as a kind of afterthought.

"Really, I'm not looking to work full time," Linda answered. "I did it for thirty years. I just want to work about four or five hours a week or so. One on one with students where I can really make a real difference."

"I understand completely. It just so happens that we are looking for a couple professional tutors, for some of our athletes," Mrs. Davis said, and showed Linda to a chair outside the director's office. She handed Linda back her envelope of credentials and said that she would get her in to see Mr. Williams as quickly as she could.

After she stepped away, Linda quietly observed the business of the office. Kids were typing on computers along one wall, chatting with the secretaries, and talking to the guidance counselors in every office. It was a very busy place. Once again, Linda felt weirdly out of it. She had been in it for so long, and now, she realized that it must have seemed overwhelming to all the people who visited the school where she had been teaching. Teenagers in large numbers are really pretty scary. It doesn't feel that way if you are a regularly scheduled teacher, and this is your everyday scene. However, if you are on the outside looking in, it can be pretty intimidating.

Eventually, a good-looking man came out, finishing his conversation with a student. He then turned his full attention on Linda who stammered a hello. He was tall, had dark hair and very blue eyes. He looked to be about forty years old, very fit, maybe a runner. Linda stood up quickly, extending her hand.

"So," he said. "I hear that you are flatly refusing to be a substitute teacher but want me to look at your credentials as a possible tutor. Is that right?"

Linda said, "That's right. Thank you for seeing me on such short notice. It's very kind of you."

"Well," he said. "For some reason, Mrs. Davis found you very interesting. In other words, you kind of charmed her, or else you wouldn't have made it past her desk." He gestured to a chair in front of his desk. "Please sit down."

He opened the envelope that held her credentials. "So, let's see what your story is." He turned his attention to the papers she had brought in with her. Papers that attempted to summarize her professional life and give some indication of her capabilities.

He finished reading and smiled. "We actually do have need for a tutor. For some of our athletes. It looks like you worked a lot with the top tier students at your old school. Some of the kids you might be tutoring for us are not that gifted. How would you feel about that?"

Linda was wondering how much this job paid. She was, however, quick to reassure Mr. Williams that she was used to

71

teaching all kinds of kids. She smiled and said, "I think that lots of kids who are labeled as 'not gifted' just haven't found their voice or their particular gift. I'd like to think that I could help them find those things. Voice. And maybe confidence academically."

"Well," said Mr. Williams, shuffling her papers together. "I like that answer. Can you start tomorrow? You have to be fingerprinted, but the sheriff is here in the faculty lounge, doing fingerprints for staff right now. I can walk you down there to him. You would come here to the study session room on Tuesday and Thursday, working from 3:00 until 5:00. Never any later than that. And, to tell the truth, you may very well not have to stay until 5:00. When the athletes' needs are met for the afternoon, you are free to go. We will pay you a hundred dollars for each session."

Linda thought about it. It wasn't a lot of money, but, then again, it was two hundred dollars a week, with no papers to grade and no lesson plans to submit.

"I accept," Linda said, extending her hand to Mr. Williams. "I can start tomorrow if you want."

"Perfect," he said, shaking her hand. Let's get you fingerprinted, and then you can come back here and fill out the paperwork. But I want to get you down there while the officer is still here. Grab your briefcase and let's run down there." Suddenly, Linda was being ushered down the hall, still full of teenagers milling around. But she didn't feel quite so out of place as she did when she walked in to the school. St. Michael, she thought, pray for me.

Chapter 7

The next morning, Linda got up at seven and went out for her morning walk. As she went through the lobby, she called a hello to Henry and the valet. Out on the sidewalk, the morning walkers and runners were already bustling about. The sun was just coming up over the ocean, splashing its gold on the water. Pelicans soared overhead in a long, deep V, and Linda remembered something her father had said when she was a little girl. Then had been at the ocean together for her first time when she was about sixteen years old, staying at a little cabin somewhere around Daytona Beach. She and Carly had been splashing around in the pool with her mom and dad, and a group of pelicans had flown by, squawking and flapping as they communicated the flight pattern with each other. Her dad had looked up and said, "There goes the Daytona Beach Air Force."

It's funny how memories wash over you, when you least expect it, and with such power and clarity. Proust had said something about that. Something about how the past never really disappears. That it's right under the surface, ready to reassert itself. The past and the present and the future—all intertwined. The words escaped her right now, but she knew that they would come back. When she least expected them.

Anyhow, she put in her earbuds and turned on her new playlist from Matt, and soon the three miles clicked off. By the time she was done, she was good and sweaty. The sun still had a lot of power, even though it was September, and almost the autumnal equinox. But this time, she had remembered a washcloth, so she could wipe herself down before heading into the French bakery, where she intended to buy another one of those amazing croissants, and maybe a baguette to have with dinner.

She entered the café and found the place buzzing again. The pretty French woman was at the counter, helping another customer. The good-looking Frenchman stood right beside her, talking and laughing with the lady they were serving, who seemed to be buying about ten baguettes. Maybe for an office party or something. She had a suit on, and her blouse was very open at the neck, revealing her figure, to say the least. Linda watched as they concluded her sale, waiting for her turn. Feeling like a sweaty little loser compared to the lady at the counter.

She finally left, saying something in French to the owners, and then it was Linda's turn. The French woman whispered something to her husband, smiling, and went in the back room— the kitchen. Linda noticed two young men back there, both with dark hair and big smiles. They must be their sons, she thought. They look just like their father, only about twenty years younger. They both wore big white aprons, and one of them had flour on his face. They smiled at her over the counter and went on speaking in French to each other, laughing as they worked. She wasn't entirely sure, but she thought one of them smiled right at her.

Suddenly, the Frenchman was speaking to her. He had a name tag on, and it said Michel. The French form of Michael, Linda thought. She decided to try a little of her college French. What the heck. Might as well.

"Bonjour," she said. "Je voudrais acheter une croissant. Chocolat. Et une baguette. Si vous plais," she spoke slowly, but she was pretty sure she had said it correctly. Although she wasn't sure if it should be une or un. Couldn't remember.

"Ah," he smiled. "Vous parlez Francais?"

"Un peu," Linda said. But the truth was, she was now at the end of her repertoire. Unless she hit the books and really worked to get it back. He fired off something in French, and her eyes must have reflected her confusion, because he laughed. Charmingly. And said he would go more "lentement." She knew that was slowly. He gave her the last baguette, and a croissant. He warned her that it was "tres chaud." Then, he took her money and said, "S'il te plait, reviens!" And Linda knew what he said. He said, please come again. She smiled at him, racking her brain for the right words, and suddenly had them!

"Je vais le faire," she said—lentenment! He smiled and nodded at her, indicating that she had said it correctly, and then—he winked at her! He winked at her? With his wife right in the back room? Right there? In the kitchen with their sons? Linda gulped and felt herself blush. It was kind of a forgotten feeling. How long had it been since she had blushed? Had felt that weird little fluttering?

She picked up her white bakery bag and left the café. She couldn't even imagine what her face looked like at that moment. She walked across the street to the entrance to her condominium and realized that she was navigating in unfamiliar waters, in every way. She called out a 'good morning' to the desk attendant, who was this elderly black man named Henry. Henry had a sweet tooth. He reminded her of Winnie the Pooh, in all the best ways. He saw her coming in with a white bakery bag and immediately was interested in what she had.

Linda wished that she had thought to buy him a croissant, but instead she came over to him and said, "Would you like a piece of this lovely baguette? It is still warm from the oven."

He absolutely twinkled and said, "Well, that would be just lovely."

Linda wasn't really sure how to handle this, so she just ripped off a hunk and handed it to him. Apparently, that was all right with him. He grinned at her and thanked her. "Now," he said, "we break bread together. We are family."

Linda smiled and said, "Wow. That is just exactly what my mom used to say. Those very same words. So, I guess we are." She smiled at him and said, "Have a great day. Oh. I forgot to tell you. I got a job tutoring at the local high school. After the school day. Two afternoons a week." She was secretly pleased with herself as she announced this, although she wasn't really sure exactly why she felt that way. It was nothing much, really.

Henry said, "Well, they are very lucky children. Have a great day, Mrs. Miller."

She said to him, "You can call me Linda, if you like."

He smiled back and said. "No, if you don't mind, I will call you Mrs. Miller. My mama always taught me to err on the side of being a little more formal. The habit is deeply ingrained, if you know what I mean."

"I do indeed. Well, have a good morning," Linda said, and she headed for the elevator.

"If there is anything you need to know about the area, please let me know, and I will try to help," Henry called after her.

"Thank you," Linda said. "Thank you very much. I will definitely take you up on that."

She headed up to her apartment, brewed herself a cup of coffee, and took her croissant out on the balcony porch, where she could look east and see the ocean, glimmering in the morning light, and west to see the Intracoastal, where pleasure boats were already starting to move around. Everything from yachts to good old-fashioned pontoon boats. She could even see a couple people working their way up the waterway on those stand-up paddle boards. The morning was already heating up, but there was a little bit of shade on her porch and she pulled her chair and little table into it.

She took a long sip of her coffee, closing her eyes and saying a good morning in her heart to her mom and dad, both of who had passed on years ago. But, she kind of honored them every morning with her first sip of coffee, in remembrance of all the cups that they had shared together over the years. It was her little morning ritual, silly though it might seem to others. She opened the white bakery bag and took out the croissant. Once again, it seemed to actually melt in her mouth. She savored the first bite, grabbed her cell phone, and called Carly.

Carly answered right away, with a note of panic in her voice. "Are you all right?" she asked quickly.

"Yes, yes," Linda said. "I'm fine. Actually, I'm really fine. I'm sitting out on the balcony, having a cup of coffee and eating a croissant from a French bakery across the street. I was in there this morning, right after my morning walk. And there is this husband and wife that run the place. And the husband waited on me this morning, and I spoke a little bit of French to him, and he winked at me when I left. He winked at me. And his wife was right behind him in the kitchen. With their sons. I don't know what to think." Then she added, "But I kind of liked it!"

Carly just roared laughing. "Well, you little hussy. Flirting with a married Frenchman? I cannot believe I am talking to my sister. Well, I say, good for you. You certainly need a little practice with your flirting, and who better to practice on than a French baker."

"You're right, of course. I do need practice," Linda said. "But isn't that completely inappropriate?"

"Don't take everything so seriously," Carly said. "It's just a little game. The French are notorious flirts. It's just the way they interact with attractive women. Nothing will come of it. Except you might get a chance to improve your French."

Linda then told her about the tutoring job she had accepted at the high school. "It is a very big, very well-respected

Catholic high school. They have a very prestigious athletic department, and lots of their athletes go to college on athletic scholarships. So, twice a week, I am going over there to tutor some of the athletes that need a little extra help. Just two hours an afternoon. I don't have any papers to grade, and I don't think it will be all that hard."

Carly said, "Well, I hope it works out for you. I'll tell you the truth—it sounds absolutely terrifying to me. To go in there, and not really know ahead of time what you will have to be teaching? Yikes. But you're very smart, and you'll be great at this." She was quiet for a minute, and then she added, "I don't want to overstep or anything here, but if you need money, I will be glad to give you some." She spoke carefully, and Linda could tell that she was worried about hurting her feelings.

"Not at all," Linda said. "I think my finances are fine. I just want to pick up a little spending money, and I honestly think it will be a nice way to meet some people in the community. Maybe. Anyhow, when can you come for a visit?"

Carly said that she was in the middle of a big trial, but she might be able to come not this weekend but the next. She added that she was very interested in meeting this handsome Frenchman anyhow.

Linda laughed and said, "He's married, Carly. Married to a very attractive French woman."

"So you said," Carly laughed. "Anyhow, I'll see you in about ten days. I'll send you my flight info as soon as I arrange the flight. Good luck with your first tutoring session today. I'll talk to you soon. Love you."

Linda hung up and looked out at the morning. The day was certainly advancing. It was already almost 11:00, and she had to report for work in a few hours. She took a deep breath and smelled the morning air. The warmth. She realized that she was feeling pretty good. It was almost a surprise. She thought to herself—I'm going to be all right. Then, she went into her bedroom, and got in the shower, remembering to bring her cup of coffee. Indulging in that newly discovered pleasure.

Chapter 8

She reported to the high school, checking in with the policeman who guarded the front door. He was expecting her and pointed her in the direction of the coaching offices. She had arrived a little early, and classes were still in session. It was about five minutes to the dismissal bell, and there was an actual hum about the building. Linda thought to herself that it must be the pent-up energy of 2,000 students about to make a break for it.

Sure enough, as she made her way down the main corridor, the dismissal bell rang, and the doors exploded—spilling thousands of teenagers, or every color and size out into the hallways. Linda started dodging kids, some of them coming right at her, their eyes already lowered and connected to their phones, where they were frantically texting somebody. But there were some whose eyes were up, and they looked at her with frank interest, wondering who she was. New teacher? Substitute? Others had a very different look in their eyes. Disdain. That's what it felt like. Like they wanted her to know that, whoever she was, she did not matter to them. Just an obstacle to get past in the hallway as they made their way to their cars. Linda fought back the impulse to return to her car.

Linda kept her eyes peeled, and she finally found the door that said "Head Football Coach. Max Pearson." She noticed that the door right next to the coach's office said "Boys Locker Room." She knocked on the door, uncertain if she was supposed to wait to be admitted or not. But she need not have worried, because two seconds later, the door burst open and a physically imposing young black man burst out. Maybe a junior or a senior. Certainly not a freshman. He looked too mature for that. He was obviously annoyed about something.

Linda stepped out of his way, not wanting to be knocked down, and entered the office. She smiled warily and stuck out her hand, "Coach Pearson? I'm Linda Miller. I'm the tutor that was hired to help some of your kids. Twice a week after school?" She smiled uncertainly. "Am I in the right place?"

Pearson looked at her as if he were trying to place her and figure out what she was talking about. He was a physically impressive black man, about 40 years old. He was in very good shape, although he wasn't very tall. Only about five feet ten. Linda found herself wondering in passing how he was a football coach. He didn't look big enough to have actually played the game, and yet she had heard that he had played at Vanderbilt. He had very dark hair, cut short. And dark brown eyes. He wore a St. Michael long sleeve T shirt, and it showed that he was very well built. The logo on the shirt showed St. Michael slaying a dragon. She caught herself looking at the artwork, just a minute too long, and realized that he was staring at her just as hard as she was staring at him.

She was suddenly overwhelmed by the awkwardness of the moment. In fact, she wasn't at all sure that he was expecting her. He continued to stare at her, as if sizing her up. But suddenly, he cleared his thoughts, almost with a visible shake of his head, and then looked at her and smiled.

"Yes," he said. "Yes. Of course. We are expecting you. That young man that almost knocked you down is your first challenge. Come in and sit down. Please." He moved a chair into position for her, and then he went behind his desk and sat down in his chair. Linda had thought that a big-time coach like Pearson would have a secretary or two, but it seemed to be a one man show. For the most part.

As they were speaking, several other men came in, nodded or smiled, and went to the rear of the office. There were bins with equipment back there, and they grabbed stuff and left, talking to each other all the way. Linda also noticed a big cardboard box full of snack bars, granola bars, and protein bars. Several players popped in, grabbed one, mumbled "hey coach" or something like that, and went back out.

Coach Pearson continued to look long and hard at her. "I hope you're not easily intimidated or discouraged. What I need you to do it is prepare a couple of my men to take the ACT or the SAT with more success than they have experienced so far. That young man you just saw, Kelly Dunn, has offers from five Division I programs, but he has not yet been able to get his score on the SAT up to their minimum requirement. I am going to have him work with you for an hour before practice. First Kelly, and then another young man named John White. I will tell you the truth—neither of them is very excited about the tutoring program. But they need to get those SAT scores up. Besides that, they may need help preparing their homework for their English classes. No. Not may. They will. I hope you can help them."

Linda said, "I hope so too. Do you have their previous test scores, so I can get an idea about where they need help. I mean, what I should work on. And is Kelly missing practice time to work with me? He seemed angry or irritated as he left there. I'm getting the feeling that maybe he does not want to be tutored. Am I right?"

Coach Pearson looked her in the eyes and answered honestly, "Well, he has to miss practice time to work with you, so, no. I don't think he's very excited about it. But he has a real chance to do something special with his life, if he can clear this hurdle. That's where you come in." He shuffled papers on his desk, and Linda had the feeling that he was ready to move on to something else. He stood up, ready to dismiss her.

"All right," she said. "I'm ready to go. Where do we work?" Then she gathered her courage and said, "Also. I strongly suggest that I meet one hour with Kelly and then one hour with John. If I can get them to give me one good hour, then I can send them back to you and they can blow off some steam on the field."

Coach Pearson looked at her and nodded slowly. "Okay. I think you're right. You work with Kelly from 3:00 to 4:00, and I'll send you John White for the second hour. Basically, they need the same kind of help. In fact, they are both in regular

American Lit. They even have the same teacher for the class." He led her out of the office, opening the door to a small room next to his office. "This is the room that we coaches use to look at film. You can use it as a study room. Kelly will be right in." He looked at his watch. "Two minutes."

Linda grabbed her briefcase, and went into the study room to get ready for Kelly. Luckily, she had brought and ACT and a SAT practice book, pens and paper, and highlighters. She tried to gather her thoughts, when suddenly, the door burst open, and Kelly came in.

He was the same young man that had almost knocked her over as she was coming into Coach Pearson's office. Unfortunately, he still looked angry as he slumped into the chair, kind of glaring at her. He was a huge presence in the room. So young and strong. Muscles everywhere. It felt like he could explode right out of his chair and run through the wall.

Linda put her hand out and said, "Hi. I'm Mrs. Miller. I know your name is Kelly, and I've heard so many good things about you. Coach has hired me to be your personal trainer for English skills, to try to get your SAT and ACT scores up. As well as your English grade. I'm honored to have the chance to work with you."

It was just an ordinary speech. An ordinary introduction. But, it had a surprising effect on Kelly. His eyes sort of softened, and he said, "I dunno if you can really help. No one else can. Seems like." But underneath the disappointment, Linda heard a kind of hope. He sat in the chair, raising his eyes to look at her, as if appraising her potential.

"Well," she said. "Maybe you never really had anyone work one on one with you. That might make all the difference." She took a deep breath. "Let's start with what's going on in your English class. Do you have an assignment there for tonight?"

He said, "Yeah. I do. And I don't understand it at all. Grammar shi..." He caught himself just in time. "Sorry," he said. Then, he pulled a chrome book out of his book bag and looked at his schedule for homework.

Linda pulled her chair up close to his. "May I watch you? I've come from Michigan and we don't use the same programs you do. I need to familiarize myself with how your school does things." He moved over a little so she could see better.

"Sure," he said. "Michigan, huh? Some good football teams up there. Or, at least they used to be good. Not so much recently. No offense." He searched his chrome book for the homework assignment. He pointed his finger at the screen and said, "We got this assignment in grammar tonight. I hate grammar. Active voice or something. I could use some help with that."

Linda said, "Okay. Pull up the pages on your grammar book. I'm betting that you don't have a paper copy of the grammar textbook. It's all online. Is that correct?"

"Yup," Kelly said, as he worked his way around to the right page. "Here's the questions. But I don't understand any of it. So, don't expect me to get them right."

Linda reached for a sheet of paper and a pen. "Let's start here. On paper. Okay?" Kelly said nothing.

Linda looked at him. "What position do you play on your football team?" The question caught Kelly off guard, and he sort of smiled at her. Then, in a minute, he almost lit up.

"I'm a wide receiver. I catch the ball. Anything they throw anywhere near me, I catch it. And then I run for the end zone. I run like the wind," he grinned at her, excited to be talking about the thing he loved.

"I bet you do," Linda smiled. "Okay. Now. Here are two sentences," she wrote them on the paper as she spoke. "1. The football was caught by Kelly who then ran like the wind. 2. Kelly caught the football and then ran like the wind." She glanced up at him. "Which one do you like better? And why? Read them to me and listen to yourself."

He read them out loud to her, thinking about it. Then he looked at her, puzzled. "Actually, they're just about the same."

Linda smiled, "Yes. And then again no. They convey the same information, but they do it differently. Which one do you like better? And why?"

Kelly thought about it for a minute and said, "I like the second one. Because it puts the focus on me."

Linda nodded, "That's exactly right. That sentence is written in the active voice. Because the subject, in this case Kelly, is doing the acting. And it seems to make the sentence more powerful. More active. The other one puts the thing that received the action up front, and that makes it more passive. Let's try another one."

On a whim, she made up the new sentence, with Kelly as the star of the action, once again. And then she diagrammed the sentence, just like she had been taught to do a long time ago. With arrows and things. Kind of like a football diagram, she thought. Very quickly, he got it, and then they attacked the grammar assignment. Before she knew it, the hour was over. Even Kelly seemed unaware that the hour was over.

He stood up and shook her hand. "Thanks, coach," he said, grinning at her. "It's not exactly x's and o's. But I get it. Now, I am going to go out there on that field and catch the ball. And then run like the wind," he said, purposefully echoing the grammar exercises she started the hour with. He grinned at her. "See you next time," he said.

He gathered his book bag, computer, and varsity jacket and left. In came John White. He, too, was a junior. In the same classes as Kelly. Linda smiled at him, got him comfortable, and did essentially the same lesson. With the same results. Soon it was 5:00, and she was done for the day. She gathered up her briefcase and papers and let herself out of the office. Honestly, the two hours had flown by, but she also felt exhausted. The one on one thing is entirely different than teaching a class. In some ways, it was even more intense.

As she walked down the hall, she noticed that it was essentially empty at this moment. As she passed the locker room, she was hit by a really bad smell. Sweat. And dirt. A manly stink. Not one man's stink. Rather more powerful than that. A hundred men. But the hall was very quiet. Everyone must be out on the field. She detoured to take a look at the football field. What she saw almost took her breath away.

This was a big-time program. The high school where she had taught in Michigan had been a distinct "also-ran"—that is, they hardly even had a winning season. But this—this was different. A whole different level. There were about 100 young men out on the field, running through drills. It looked like there were about twenty coaches. It all looked very organized, in a chaotic sort of way.

Coach Pearson was in the middle of the field with a clipboard, almost like a ringmaster at a three-ring circus. She looked to see if she could spot Kelly or John, but to no avail. Everyone had a helmet on, and that kind of rendered them anonymous. She would have to ask them what their numbers were. That would help. Maybe she would come to the game on Friday. Maybe.

She felt hungry, but also too tired to fix anything for dinner. She thought she might swing by the French café and see if they were still open. A croissant would be perfect. She had some cheese and jam at home. That, and a cup of tea would be perfect. It had absolutely nothing to do with the handsome Frenchman who ran the café. Absolutely nothing. Besides, he was married.

As she parked her car at the French café, she could see Michel outside, pulling in the little café tables they had on the sidewalk. Clearly, he was getting ready to close up. Dinner time. But he stopped what he was doing when he saw Linda.

"Bon soir, madame," he said. "Ca va?"

Linda's heart jumped a little, or seemed to flutter. Ridiculous, she thought. He's a married man. His wife is probably in there right now, cleaning up and getting ready to go home to their beautiful French-styled home.

"Je voudrais un croissant," Linda stammered. "If it's not too late?" She searched for the French words, but they failed her. Plus tard? Plus lentement? Oh, well.

Michel seemed to notice her fluster, but said nothing. Except, "Mais, non. C'est partait. Come in, come in. I will give you one to take home. On the house, as you say." He held the door for her and ushered her into the café, where his beautiful wife and two of their sons were, in fact, cleaning up. Getting ready to go home.

Michel went behind the counter, picked out two croissants and put them in a white paper bag. He handed the bag to her and smiled, "Au revoir. Bon soir. Merci."

Linda said, "Please let me pay you for these." But he smiled and say no, no. They are a gift. Come again and we will take your money next time. She smiled and said good night, and walked back to her car, in a kind of tired daze.

She drove the rest of the way home feeling absolutely worn out, but strangely, something else too. She wondered if she dared to admit it to herself. She felt a tiny little bit happy. The evening was still hot, even though the sun was setting over the Intracoastal. She drove her car over the bridge and into the parking garage. She grabbed her briefcase and got into the elevator. Which she took up to her little condo on the water. Not too shabby, she told herself. She put her croissant on a plate, poured a glass of wine, cut a nice piece of cheese and went out to the balcony. As she sat down on her chaise, a light breeze whispered by. She closed her eyes and sighed. She might be all right.

And then again, she might not. After dinner, she went down to get the mail. There was a big envelope there, from the law firm of Spencer and Trenton. Up in Michigan. When she opened it, she found the papers requesting a divorce and a settlement of the assets. Her fragile good feeling shattered, like glass that is too thin to survive ordinary life.

Chapter 9

She read through the papers, felt overwhelmed by all the legalese, fought back tears, sat down out on the balcony again, and called Carly. She answered right away, fear in her voice, "Hey, Linda. Are you all right?"

"Errr. Yes and no," Linda said. She fought hard to keep the sound of crying out of her voice. "I just got home from my tutoring job at the school, and it really went pretty well, all things considered." She took a deep breath and tried to calm her voice. She could hear the quaver. That meant that Carly could hear it too. "And I went by the bakery and got some dinner. I didn't feel like cooking anything. And when I got home, I received the divorce papers in the mail. All nice and neat and formal, and it really screwed me up." Now, she lost her battle against the tears, and they just came.

Carly said quickly, "Hey, hey, hey. Linda. Listen to me. You knew they were coming. This is not a surprise. It's just a formal declaration of what you already knew to be true. It's actually a good thing if you think about it. You've got to move through this thing. You've got to walk through the fire. And I am going to be right by your side. This is really a good thing. You've got to make a clean break of it. You have the right to happiness, and you have the right to live with someone who loves you and knows what a wonderful person you are. And that ain't Rick. That asshole never deserved you." Linda could hear the pitch of Carly's voice rising—ready to launch into an anti-Rick tirade. She quickly cut her off.

"No," said Linda. "I don't hate him. I mean—we had some good years together, and we had Andrea and Matt. Whom I love more than life. And they're half Rick, you know. And I know you love them too. So, we have to remember that." She was a little bit surprised to feel herself defending Rick. But everything she was saying was actually true. "Anyhow, I'm feeling a little better just talking to you. Will your partner handle the legal aspects of this? Do you think he has a copy of the filing?" She could feel herself trying to come to grips with things.

"I will make sure that he does. His name is Tyler, and he is a very good lawyer. Very handsome too, by the way. I will see him at the office tomorrow and make sure that everything is under control." Carly took a deep breath. Linda could feel her pulling herself together, dialing back her anger. "So, you just sign those papers on the dotted line and put them back in the mail. Right away. No kidding. Now, tell me where you are and what you are doing. Exactly and precisely. At this very moment."

Linda looked around, sized up her surroundings, and said, "I'm sitting out on the balcony. I have fresh croissant and a piece of cheese in front of me. And a nice glass of Chardonnay. And I am sitting on the chaise lounge, looking out at the ocean and talking to you. It's a warm evening, but there is a breeze. The sun is setting over the Intracoastal, painting the sky pink and orange, in layers. The color of a Creamsicle. Do you remember those, or are you too young?"

"No," said Carly. "I remember them well. I think they were always your favorite. I'm a fudgsicle girl myself. All right. That sounds good, although you eat like a mouse. You need some protein in there, but that's a discussion for another time." She started her summation, and Linda could hear the lawyer in her. "Now, you just remember that this is all good. That it is necessary, and that you are going to be much better off when we finish this thing. So, pull yourself together and finish the wine. Take a picture of that sunset and send it to me. I wish I was sitting there beside you. It's chilly and rainy up here in Michigan tonight."

"Well, come on down," said Linda. "I've got the guest room all fixed up. You could probably use a couple days of sunshine anyhow."

"Be careful what you wish for," Carly said. "Now, call Matt and Andrea and tell them what has happened, just to keep them in the loop. That will be important to them. Then, like I said, finish your wine, read a good book, and go to bed. This is all good. It hurts a little, but it's all right. I love you. Call the kids."

After Carly hung up, Linda called both Matt and Andrea. She actually handled all of it much better with them. Maybe, she realized, she had been practicing during her call to Carly. And now she sounded in control of herself. Even if she didn't feel that way. She finished her wine, watched the sun dip down below the horizon, watched the city light up all around her, heard the voices of the people walking down the street below her, smelled the charcoal broiled hamburgers from the restaurant up the street, and closed her eyes. She would be all right. At least she felt safe, like a princess up in the tower. Waiting to be rescued? Or maybe figuring out a way to rescue herself.

Chapter 10

Before she knew it, it was time to report to St. Michael's again for her next tutoring session. She got there on time, learning how to navigate the traffic. And—most importantly, learning to get there before school got out, when thousands of kids poured into the halls. She parked in the faculty lot, which made things easier, showed her identification lanyard to the policeman at the front gate, and made her way back to the coach's office. This time, she felt like she actually belonged, or a little bit closer to belonging, somehow. Coach Pearson said hi and pointed her to the film office, where Kelly was already waiting for her. She wasn't late, so he must have been early. He was seated at their study table, his gym bag on the floor beside him, and he was already in his workout clothes for football practice. Linda wondered how he had been able to get ready so quickly. He was texting someone. Using that two-thumb method that absolutely flabbergasted Linda. The kids were so quick with that. She still used the old pointer finger, one digit at a time method. Laughable to these kids. Anyhow.

"Hi, Kelly," she said, sitting down beside him. "Better put your phone away and let's get working. We only have an hour."

"Oh, geez, only an hour," he grinned at her. "Hey, Ms. Miller," he added, remembering something. "I got a 90 on that quiz about active or passive voice. I never got a 90 on anything in English before. I just kept remembering that Kelly caught the ball. I translated every sentence that they gave me into that basic pattern, and I got it." He was a little bashful about the whole thing, but Linda could tell that he was really pleased with himself.

So was she. "I am so proud of you, Kelly. That is a concept that gives a lot of people a lot of trouble. So cool that you figured it out."

"With your help I did. I told Coach, too. He was very happy," Kelly added. "But you got your work cut out for you today, as Coach would say. I gotta figure out a poem and write a paragraph about it."

"Oh, man," Linda said, forgetting her sort of formal manner. "I love poetry. It's my forte. My strong point. What poem is it?"

"I dunno. Something weird. By some Emily chick," Kelly said. "About the brain. I don't get it at all."

"Oh, wow," said Linda. "The brain is wider than the sky! I bet it's that one."

"Yup. That's the one. You know it?" Kelly asked.

"I do," said Linda. "And I really like it. It makes you think," she added. "Let's have a look at it." She checked the page in his assignment and found the poem.

"I hate poetry," said Kelly.

"Ha!" said Linda. "You remind me of my son." She was searching for the poem in his lit book.

"Your son black like me?" asked Kelly. He wasn't looking at her. He seemed to be studying the poem they were about to read. His question caught Linda off guard.

"No," Linda said. "He's white like me. But he says he hates poetry, just like you do. So, that's what I meant when I said that you remind me of my son. That was always his first response to any poetry assignment. Let's see if you hate poetry as much as my son Matt does. I didn't mean to presume anything at all."

"Hmph," said Kelly. "Well, I bet I hate poetry just as much as he does. What's your son do?"

"He's still a student. In law school now. But he played football in high school, up in Michigan. Not very well, mind you. But he loved the game." She found the poem and pointed to it in the lit book. "Okay. Now, you just sort of let it roll over you at first. I'll read this little monster of a poem to you. You see that it's very short. And it doesn't look too intimidating. But many people can't make heads or tails of it. Listen...

> The Brain—is wider than the Sky—
> For—put them side by side—
> The one the other will contain
> With ease—and You—beside—
>
> The Brain is deeper than the sea—
> For—hold them—Blue to Blue—

The one the other will absorb—
As Sponges—Buckets—do—

The Brain is just the weight of God—
For—Heft them—Pound for Pound—
And they will differ—if they do—
As syllable from Sound—

Linda finished the reading and looked at Kelly. He was staring at the page, frowning. Suddenly, he laughed out loud, with a laugh that sounded like something between a bark and a cough. "I hate poetry even more than I thought I did. I say this lady's crazy, and I don't know what the hell she's talking about. Oops. Sorry about the hell. It just slipped out." He glanced at Linda to see if she was angry. Instead, she laughed with him.

"Okay," she said. "That's an honest first reaction. And, I'll tell you the truth. It's the exact same thing my son said when I tried to teach this poem to him. So, I was right. You do remind me of him. A lot."

"But, what does it mean? I gotta write a paragraph about it, and I really don't get it. And I gotta say—there's one thing I noticed. This lady does not know how to use capital letters. She musta skipped that chapter in grammar. And what's with all them dashes? Crazy stuff."

"All right," said Linda. "We don't have much time because you have got to get out on the practice field. So, let's start with the first stanza. You read it out loud, and tell me what you think it might mean." Kelly looked at her with a look of utter bewilderment in his eyes, but he gamely dove in and reread the first stanza. Then he sat back in his chair and thought about it.

He looked at her and spoke slowly, "Maybe our brain is wider than the sky because we can think about the sky and other things at the same time?" There was a question in his voice, as if he was almost afraid to say what he was thinking.

Linda smiled at him. "That's absolutely brilliant. Now, how is the brain deeper than the sea? That's what the second stanza says, right?"

He studied the second stanza, reading it out loud under his breath and looking at Linda when he was done. "Well, I think it's basically the same thing, but I don't get the part about buckets. I don't get that at all."

"What if the poet purposely is trying to play games with you? What if she left out a couple words that might make that line clearer? What if that line said, 'The one the other will absorb as sponges buckets of water do?' What if she is running a deception or a decoy or a feint on you by leaving those two words out, making you figure out the puzzle?"

"Hmph," Kelly said. "She's running a trick play? A hidden receiver? Well, I don't know how ordinary people are supposed to figure that out without your help, but if that's the way the line should read, then I get it. And like I said, it works like the first part. Our brain is deeper than the sea because we can imagine the sea and other stuff at the same time."

"Perfect," said Linda. "And the sea seems kind of bottomless to us. Infinite. And yet we can imagine it and other stuff at the same time, right?"

"Right," he said. "But what about that last part. I don't get that at all."

"Well," Linda said. "You're absolutely right. That's the really hard part. First off, what in the world does she mean by 'the brain is just the weight of God?' Is she being disrespectful of her heavenly Father? Just so you know—she was a Christian, but she battled with many doubts about her faith."

"That's like me," Kelly said. "I believe and I don't. Makes my mama mad when I say that. My Dad died of cancer four years ago. He was my first coach and my best friend. That's when I stopped believing in God. If there is a loving God, why did my Dad have to die." Linda saw that his voice had dropped very low, very quiet, that he was fighting back anger or tears, or both.

"I understand exactly what you mean, and I've been there myself." She waited for a couple minutes. "So, what do you think it means," she said, very quietly. "Is she being disrespectful? You could read it that way. You certainly could. Or, could it mean something else? Could it mean that, at least in some ways, we are a little bit like God?" She kept her voice very quiet, and with a question in it, to let him know that she was thinking right along with him.

"What does the word heft mean," Kelly said.

"It means to hold something in your hand and estimate the weight of it, get the feel of it," Linda said. She got up and grabbed a weight from a nearby station, a five-pound weight. She put it in Kelly's hand. "Do you feel that? You are hefting it, getting the feel of it, getting a sense of it." Kelly nodded, and put the weight down, looking hard at her.

"How does a syllable differ from sound?' he asked, obviously moving his analysis forward, waiting until he figured it out before he gave his answer.

"Good question," said Linda. "A syllable is a part of a word. A spoken part. It has a vowel. It causes you to open your mouth. The word butterfly has three syllables. And sound—well, sound can be used in many different ways. A syllable is a sound, that's true. But a sound could be much bigger than a syllable. Not a word at all. Like the sound of a crowd cheering at a football game." She looked at Kelly, watched him weighing everything. His dark brown eyes intense.

"Is there only one right answer to this?" he said. Linda thought to herself that this was a very perceptive question. There was a very good mind at work here.

"No," she said quickly. "That's kind of the beauty of poetry. And it's also what makes it so frustrating to some people. There may be many interpretations that are valid. It all depends on how you defend your viewpoint. If you are staying true to the text, and not forcing your interpretation on the lines. What do you think it might mean?" He sat quietly. Staring at the words. Then, he spoke very tentatively. Linda was impressed with his patience, the way he thought carefully before giving an answer.

"I think it might mean that we are a little bit like God, but he is way bigger than us. And we can't even begin to imagine that. Even though we try." He spoke slowly, feeling his way.

Linda was absolutely overcome. She just sat there for a minute, and then, without thinking, she gave him a big hug. "That is absolutely brilliant." She was laughing, and so was Kelly.

"Do you think you can write a paragraph about that, now that you figured it out?"

"I really think I can," Kelly said. He glanced up at the clock on the wall and said, "I gotta go. My hour's up." He gathered his things and John White came in. He added, as he went out the door, "I think I still hate poetry, but maybe not as much as I used to." He was gone, and Linda turned her attention to John White. Suddenly, Kelly stuck his head back in.

"Hey," he said. "I just thought of something, Ms. Miller. You should come to the game tomorrow night. See what I can do. I wear number 80. Just like Jerry Rice, the greatest wide receiver to ever play the game. He my hero." Linda noticed that Kelly let his grammar slip a little. She knew he was doing it on purpose. She smiled.

"I just might do that," she said. "Thanks for the invite. Number 80. I'll remember."

Kelly said, "I'll tell Coach you need a ticket." And then he was gone. She turned her attention to John, who quickly informed her that he wore number 3, and that she should watch for him too. She said she would. Then, she started on the Emily Dickinson poem again.

As she was leaving that evening, after her session with John, she walked by the football field. Once again, she was startled by the scene. Over a hundred young men, all doing something different under the watchful eyes of many coaches. Organized chaos. Somehow, Coach Pearson saw her leaving and waved her over to the fence.

"Hey," he said. "Both Kelly and John really like you and like what you're doing for them. I appreciate it. Here's a season pass to our regular season games. The best seats are actually assigned seats, right around the 50-yard line. I got you one on the 50. Row L. My treat. The boys would really like it if you could come and watch them play. Should be a decent game tomorrow. We're playing Fort Lauderdale High, and they are supposed to have a pretty good team this year." He handed her a plastic pass that looked like a credit card.

Linda was startled, and more than a little bit pleased. These little things were adding up to make her feel like she fit into her new community just a little bit better all the time. She said, "Thanks, Coach. I'll be there. Right on the 50. I had a good session with both of the boys today. They're good kids."

He smiled and nodded. "They are. Well, once again. Thanks. See you tomorrow."

Then, he turned and ran easily back out to the field. Linda stayed for a little while, watching the practice. The sun was setting, all golden and orange behind the field. The autumn was deepening, even here is south Florida. The evening air was starting to cool off. A flock of seagulls swooped low over the football field, yawping and crying in the sky. Linda took a deep breath, and a moment to appreciate the beauty of the scene. Then, she picked up her briefcase and headed out to her car.

Chapter 11

Friday night rolled around, and Linda headed over to the school. The game was scheduled to start at 7:00, and she pulled into the faculty parking lot about ten minutes before the start of the game. The custodian who was manning the front gate recognized her and waved her in. It was a privilege to park in the faculty lot, and it saved her a lot of time because hundreds of cars were trying to pull into a parking garage behind the school. When she walked out to the field, after showing her season pass, she was absolutely flabbergasted. This was not high school football the way she knew it from up north. This was completely different.

The stands were already full of thousands of people, both on the home side and the visitor side. The smell of hot dogs and popcorn was in the air. The marching band was settled into their reserved seats in the end zone, and they were roaring their way through the school fight song. Linda stopped at the concession stand and bought a dark green St. Michael's T-shirt to pull on over her tank top. Everybody was wearing a St. Michael's shirt or sweathshirt, and she felt out of place until she pulled her new T-shirt on. Then, she felt like she kind of blended in.

She climbed the stairs to the bleachers and inched her way down to the 50-yard line, and then she climbed up to row L—her row. When she climbed over everyone that was already seated—the seats all had numbers—she realized that she had just about the best seat in the house. Right in the middle of the field. Linda had always liked football, and she knew what she was watching when she watched a game. She scanned the sidelines and spotted Kelly and John, numbers 80 and 3, and smiled. She thought she saw Kelly glance up to where her seat was to see if she was there, but she couldn't be sure.

Then some senior said a short prayer over the public-address system—that was different, she thought. Next, everyone rose for the National Anthem, which was sung beautifully by some girl with long dark hair. Finally, it was time for the game to begin. The other team won the coin flip and elected to defer to the second half, so the St. Michael Warriors went on offense first. Both Kelly and John were starters, and Linda kept her eyes firmly on them. The quarterback was a kid named Dan something—very young, just a sophomore, but he played with an astonishing confidence. And then suddenly, Kelly went long, leapt into the air, snagged a floating long pass right out of the atmosphere, and then ran for the end zone. Touchdown Warriors! And the crowd went crazy. Linda was on her feet with everyone else, high-fiving complete strangers and screaming her head off. It was such a different feeling to see football being played at this level of excellence, and to actually know the people who were out there making the plays. Kelly and his teammates celebrated in the end zone and then trotted over to the sidelines. When Kelly got to the bench, he actually turned around and gave a thumbs-up to Linda. She waved frantically at him, grinning from ear to ear.

The man next to her smiled at her and said, "Is that your son?"

"Oh, no," said Linda. "Nothing like that. I'm his English tutor. I work at the school a couple days a week, tutoring some of the athletes. That's Kelly. I've just started working with him, but I really like him. Last week, one of the practice sentences we were working with was 'Kelly caught the ball and then ran like the wind,' and I think he was showing me that he could actually do just that. He's a great kid."

"My name is Steve Mercado," the man said. "Well, that young man, the kid you're tutoring—he has a very promising future. He has another year here at St. Michael's and he will continue to grow and fill out. Kelly will probably play Division I football somewhere. I think he already has several offers. What did you say your name was?"

"I'm Linda Miller. Pleased to meet you," she answered, shaking his hand. She turned her attention back to the game and watched with great interest. Steve told her that his son played on the offensive line. He pointed him out to Linda, and she kept an eye on him too. He was a big kid, wearing number 75, and he made his presence felt on that line.

At halftime, the marching band took the field, and they did some decent formations. Nothing fancy. But Linda had always liked marching bands. Back when she did her undergraduate studies at Michigan State, her dorm had been right across the practice field for the marching band. Now, that was a band.

Then the second half began. Fort Lauderdale had a good team, and it was a hard-fought game. Both Kelly and John were playing well. Linda sat there in the bleachers, feeling alone and not alone—both at the same time. She didn't really know anybody yet, but she sort of felt a connection because of the boys she was tutoring. She closed her eyes and listened to the sounds of the crowd, the men shouting out instructions to the players, the band's drum line keeping a constant beat, the cheerleaders working their way through their chants. She smelled the grass and the night, the hot dogs and the popcorn. In some strange way, she felt tired and happy. And not entirely alone. Part of the Warrior home crowd.

Steve kept up an idle chatter with her throughout the game, and she enjoyed hearing his insights about some of the other players. He expected that his son would go Division I too. He already had offers from several schools. This was his senior year. Linda listened to his patter, smiling and nodding. You didn't really have to contribute to the conversation with Steve, she noticed. He was glad to do a one-man show, and that was all right with her.

Soon, the game was over, with St. Michael winning 35-14. She headed back home, filing out of the parking lot with thousands of other fans. It had been a really good night, a night that had revealed to her just how big this program was. She drove home through the city streets, all lit up like a holiday. Fort Lauderdale was a tourist destination, and the restaurants and bars were hopping as she drove down Las Olas. Part of her wished that she were one of the women sitting at a table, laughing over a glass of wine. Alas. That was not in the cards right now. Maybe never again for her. Still, it was such a lovely scene. She could smell the steaks cooking and hear laughter and the tinkling of clever conversations. She kept her eyes on the road, drove east to the ocean, pulled into her parking garage, went up to her condo, got undressed and took a long, hot shower. Then, she crawled gratefully into her bed.

Chapter 12

Saturday morning. Linda woke up about eight, surprised that she had actually slept, and slept so late. The sun was already high in the sky, even though the autumnal equinox was approaching. She pulled on her running gear, grabbed her apartment key and a bottle of water, and headed out for a morning run. She called a hello to Henry, who was at the front desk, as she left the building. She walked a bit, letting her leg muscles warm up, and then after a while, broke into a run. A slow run, but a run. She had her earbuds in and listened to a playlist that her son Matt had put together for her. All the songs and artists were new to her; she did not even recognize the names of the groups. But he had chosen well, and she liked almost everything she heard. She was good and sweaty by the time she got back to her condo building. Luckily, she had brought a washcloth with her, and she quickly toweled off before going in the front door of the building. Henry was at his post, the faithful sentinel, guarding the building. She smiled and waved.

"Good morning, Ms. Miller," he said, in his soft Bahamian drawl. "I believe you have some visitors to see you." Linda cocked her head, puzzled, and Henry stood up and made a sweeping gesture with his arm, indicating the couches along the wall. There sat Matt and Andrea, watching the whole scene and giggling with delight at her surprise. It was only ten o'clock in the morning. Linda wondered how in the world they had pulled this off. She was flabbergasted, but she had never seen anything more beautiful in her life. Suddenly, they were both in her arms, talking at once. Henry sat at his high desk, watching the reunion, smiling as if he had planned the whole thing.

"How in the world," Linda sputtered. "How are you here? So early? You both look great."

Matt said, "I just drove up this morning. Easy for me, and Andrea took the red-eye out of Chicago. We are going to spend the weekend with you." Matt looked kind of all-grown up, in a very handsome way. He was very tanned, and his blond hair had sun streaks in it. His jeans hung a little loose on his hips, and Linda found herself worrying if he was eating enough. Andrea had her long blond hair pulled back in a ponytail, high on the back of her head. She had jeans and a cute little T-shirt on, and Linda realized how beautiful they were, all over again. Their eyes twinkled merrily. Clearly, they were very pleased with themselves.

"Well, let's get upstairs and let me get cleaned up. Then, I will take you to breakfast," Linda said.

Andrea laughed and said, holding her mom in her arms a second longer, "I think a quick shower might be in order, Mom."

Linda laughed and said, "Yes, I'm afraid I'm rather sweaty. Sorry. It got hot out there."

They headed for the elevator and Henry said, "I've got the elevator all set up for you, Ms. Miller." She called a thank you to him and they got in and rode up to her floor.

Her elevator opened right into her front door. It was one of the really cool features of her building. No interior hallways. And when she opened her front door and showed the kids in, they both exclaimed with pleasure. For, right there, right outside her front windows, was deep, blue Mother Ocean. The sight always took her breath away, and the kids were wowed. Luckily, she had bought a two-bedroom unit, so she showed Matt into the guest room. Andrea would bunk with her. The kids made a pot of coffee and went out to sit on the balcony while Linda cleaned herself up. Linda thought, not for the first time, that they were very capable.

She showered quickly and pulled on a sundress, black with red and coral flowers. She grabbed a coral sweater in case it was cool in the restaurant, for she had learned to dress in layers here in Florida. As you move in and out of air conditioning, the temperature changes can be pretty surprising. Her hair still wet from the shower, so, she fluffed it up with her fingers. A hairdresser suggested that she should wear it shorter, and had cut about four inches off. Linda was still getting used to it, but it was better in the Florida heat. In fact, the humidity made her hair a little curly, and she kind of liked it. She came out on the balcony to see Matt and Andrea sitting on the two chaise lounges, sunglasses on, staring out at the ocean. Laughing and talking. When she stepped out on the patio, they both exclaimed.

"Looking good, Mom," Matt said, grinning.

"Mom," Andrea pitched in. "I agree. In some crazy way, you look younger. I thought I was going to find you wasting away down here, huddled in a corner and crying. But that is not what I am seeing at all. I can't even begin to tell you how proud I am of you. You are handling this like a champ."

Linda laughed. Sort of. "Well, there's not really any other option, is there?" Even as she said it, she realized that it sounded a little too existential or philosophical for this early in the morning. So, she quickly changed directions. "Where do you want to go for breakfast?"

Andrea laughed. "Oh, I think you know the answer to that. The French bakery, where the handsome French baker awaits." She rolled her eyes knowingly.

Matt sputtered indignantly. "What? What the heck? What are you two talking about? What don't I know?" Linda felt herself blushing like a kid.

"Mom's been making eyes at some handsome French baker who has a shop around the corner. She thinks he might be married to the woman who works there with him." She added the last part with a mischievous grin.

They had stood up and were walking toward the door. Matt grabbed his mother's arm, gently stopped her, and said, "Mom. Explain."

Linda gave him a hug, seeing the worry in his eyes. "It's nothing like Andrea says. There is just this very nice man who owns a French bakery, and he has been kind to me. That's all." Andrea tugged them toward the door.

113

"We shall see for ourselves," she said, pushing the elevator call button.

They walked out of the building and down the street, talking about nothing. When they entered the French café, the place was bustling. The lovely woman who must be Michel's wife met them at the door, smiled warmly, and guided them to the one open table, near the back of the restaurant.

"Are these your children?" she asked, smiling. Linda noticed that she had a name tag on today, and that her name was Maria. Like Michel, she had absolutely beautiful green eyes. Or were they blue? They seemed to change a little in the light. She seemed to be quite taken with Matt.

Linda nodded and introduced Matt and Andrea quickly. Maria smiled and said, "I think you are about the same age as my oldest son. Michel." Aha. Linda thought. Michel Junior, she might as well have said. Well, that just about removes any doubt about that.

Andrea smiled charmingly and ordered coffee for all of them and orange juice for Matt. Then they perused the menus. Andrea glanced over her shoulder. "So, where is the charming Michel the baker?" Linda quickly shushed her, not wanting her to draw attention to them.

But all of a sudden, there he was, at their table, a white apron tied around his waist.

"Bon jour," he said, smiling at all of them, but particularly at Linda. "It is so good to see you. Are these your children?"

"Yes," said Linda. "Yes. This is my daughter, Andrea, and my son, Matt. They are here visiting for the weekend."

"So nice to meet you both," Michel said. "Your mama loves our croissants. And we are always happy to see her. Now, what can I get you for breakfast." He scribbled down their orders, smiled, and bowed away.

And with that, both Matt and Andrea started talking at once. Mom, I think he's married. But he's a hunk, that's for sure. He seems nice. Really nice. His wife is beautiful. Oh, I think I see the sons working in the back, smiling out at us. They were both talking at once, their words swirling around Linda's head. She sipped her coffee and said nothing. Smiling, and just enjoying the sound of their voices. Soon, the conversation switched directions, as she knew it would. They never stayed on any one topic for very long.

Matt said, "I sometimes wonder if I'm making a mistake going to law school. I've survived my first year all right, and am well into the next term, but I feel a kind of boredom setting in. Like I wonder if I'm investing all this time and all this money, and when it's all said and done, and I'm a lawyer, I'm going to hate it." He ate his eggs while he spoke, not wanting to meet Linda's eyes. Not wanting to worry her.

"Unfortunately," Andrea said. "I think I know exactly what you mean. I'm doing really well at the bar, but I'm 30 years old. I have a boyfriend. But I don't think I want to marry him. I'm not sure he's the marrying type. I think I want to have a baby, sooner or later. I'm making good money, and yet I don't really see a career path upward from where I am. Sometimes, I think I want to quit everything and go back to school and get an

English major and teach. Like you did, Mom. I never met anyone who loved their job as much as you did."

Linda was absolutely flabbergasted. She thought that both of her children were pretty settled in their direction and professions. And now she realized that this was not true at all. She sipped her coffee, closed her eyes, and thought. "I really don't know what to tell you. Either of you. I think you're both really good at what you're doing right now, but I know you can do anything you want to do." She decided to tackle Matt first. "If you didn't go to law school, what would you do instead?"

"I really don't know," he answered. "I feel kind of like I'm drifting."

"I understand completely," Andrea nodded. "I kind of feel like I'm going through the same thing. But, Mom, you loved being a teacher. Didn't you?"

Linda smiled at Andrea. "Yes, there were some days that I loved it and some days that I hated it. More love than hate. But it's a lot of hard work. And most days I was exhausted, both physically and emotionally by the end of the day. Still, I really think it's a calling. I don't think you can go into teaching half-heartedly. If you do, kids will smell a phony. And they can make your life miserable." She had never really thought about the whole thing before, but now that she listened to herself describing her profession, she thought she was telling the truth—as best she could.

They shared their doubts and their questions as they ate their breakfasts, and Linda realized that they really didn't want her to solve their problems for them. Not like she could, anyhow.

She let them talk and let the music of their voices and their youth surround her. As she listened, she felt that they were so young. Everything was still in front of them. Who knew what the future would hold? She didn't feel that way about herself. She felt like things were pretty settled for her. There would only be minor changes now. No great shifts in direction or possibility. Just small adjustments.

When they ran out of steam with their arguments and questions, Linda said, "I won't presume to advise you. You are both so smart. I will just tell you one thing my Dad said. He said that when you are in the middle of something, just finish it. And when you are trying to make a difficult decision, make a chart. Put a heading on each column and draw a line down the middle. Put the pros on one side and the cons on the other. Then, put the list away for at least 24 hours. Like my mom used to say—sleep on it. Then, in the light of the new day, see if anything looks clearer to you. That's all I've got."

They both looked at her for a long minute, saying nothing. Then Andrea said, "Well, that's something to think about. That actually sounds like pretty practical advice." They finished eating, picked up their things, and headed out. When they got to the door, they thanked Maria, who was standing at the hostess stand, greeting new guests. "So nice to meet you," she said to Matt and Andrea. And to Linda, "See you again soon. Au revoir."

"Au revoir," Linda answered, smiling. The rest of the weekend passed so quickly. They went down to the ocean and swam. Or rather, bounced around in the surf. They went out to dinner and sat on the balcony, drinking wine until late at night. Watching the city light up.

And before she knew it, it was time to kiss them goodbye and send them back to their own worlds. Their own battlegrounds. Her words made her think of her Hemingway lessons she used to teach her AP classes. Hemingway had a central metaphor that underscored all of his work—life is a battleground, and everyone is eventually wounded. When you receive a serious wound—a sacred hurt—it changes everything. A whole lot of things that were once possible, no longer are. Your future looks completely different—diminished somehow. And there is no changing what has happened. You can't run from it. You can't drink or drug yourself away from it. The escape that offers is only temporary, and when you finally emerge from your three-day bender, you find yourself in even worse shape. In fact, you have probably only added to your problems. Changing where you live doesn't help at all, because you always bring yourself with you. And most of all—you can't lie to yourself about it. Because even as you lie to yourself, you know you're lying, and that makes it worse.

There's only one thing you can do. Face it. Dive down deep into the sacred hurt, and allow yourself to grieve the loss of your innocence, your love, your hope for a happy future. Dive down deep and feel it. Acknowledge the hurt. Grieve. The truth is that things will never be the same. Dive down.

And then, after a while—however long it takes—swim back to the surface. Knowing full well that you will never be the same, find a way to live with joy. Maybe not with happiness. But with joy—something deeper. Learn to appreciate the good things that happen—good food, good drink, the company of genuinely good people, good literature, good music. Whatever it is that moves you—learn to really appreciate it. Learn to live in the moment, and to appreciate the good moments when they come. And they will—if you are open to them. Value experiences—not things. Look forward, not backward. There is no escaping what has happened to you, but learn to carry the loss with dignity. And appreciate the gifts that an ordinary day can bring.

Linda had suffered a sacred hurt. Rick had betrayed her trust, had broken faith with her. Had left her for—who knows what. But wallowing in self-pity wasn't going to get her anywhere. She had to face the loss and learn to live with it. Carry it, but also find her joy. In explaining a poem to a young man who hates poetry. In a warm croissant. In a sunrise over the ocean. In birdsong and breezes. In the hugs and laughter of her children—who were growing up, but who were still keeping her in their lives. They would face their own sacred hurts. There was absolutely nothing she could do to prevent that. All she could do was be there to walk beside them and believe in them. Carry the loss with them. When they talked about their misgivings tonight, she had wanted to offer advice. But she realized, in the nick of time, that they didn't really want advice. They just wanted someone to listen, and someone to love them, no matter what. *That* she could do.

Chapter 13

Before she knew it, it was Tuesday afternoon and time for her tutoring sessions with Kelly and John. She reported to school right as the dismissal bell rang, and students poured out into the halls—seemingly by the thousands. She ducked into the coach's office to say hi and check in with Coach Pearson before her sessions began.

There were several men standing around his desk. Some were coaches, and some were scouts from universities and colleges. They had come to check out some of the players. Linda stood quietly in the corner, not wanting to interrupt their discussion, which was actively ongoing. But Coach Pearson put up his hand, sort of waved everyone to quiet and spoke directly to her.

"Ms. Miller," he said. "Hello. Just wanted to let you know that both Kelly and John speak very highly of you. I've been tracking their grades in their English classes, and both of them are seeing significant improvements since you've been working with them. And I wanted to thank you for that." Linda was happy to hear this.

"Thank you, Coach," Linda responded. "To tell you the truth, I am really enjoying working with them. They both seem pretty eager to learn. We have not been doing any SAT work to speak of. Both times, they have had homework for their English classes, and it seems like—at least in their minds—that comes first. I just wanted to be up front with you about that."

Coach Pearson nodded. "That does come first. They are right. But, if and when you have a few extra minutes, please spend some time on SAT prep. I would appreciate that."

"I will," said Linda. "And I don't want to speak out of turn here. But—I've found that kids that learn to read and think better, by reading and thinking with a good guide, start doing better on the SAT test. Just as a kind of auxiliary benefit. So, the work we are doing for their class is actually teaching them to read and think analytically. And their scores may go up just as a byproduct of that." She knew that a lot of people were skeptical about this theory of hers, but she truly believed it to be true, and for that reason, it was easy for her to talk about it. She had done so many times before.

"Hmmmmm. Interesting," Coach Pearson said. "Well, I guess we will see. Both of your students are registered to take the November SAT. It would be nice if we could see some payback for what you are doing with them." He seemed to consider what he had just said, and he realized that it might seem that there was an ultimatum implied. He backed away from that quickly. "However, aside from that, both of the boys seem to be doing a lot better in their English classes. And they seem to honestly enjoy their time with you. At least, they don't hate it," he added with a smile.

Linda laughed. "Thanks a lot," she said. "Or maybe I should say, thanks a little. Anyhow, I've got to go. Kelly will be waiting." She said a quick goodbye and headed into the film room, where Kelly was waiting, his computer opened up to his assignment page, his head bent over his phone, on which he was frantically texting with two thumbs. No matter how many times Linda had seen kids do this, she still marveled at the sheer dexterity of it.

"Hi, Kelly," she said, coming up behind him. "What do you have for me today?"

"Hey, Ms. Miller. More of your favorite stuff, I'm afraid. Poetry," he added gloomily.

"More poetry," Linda answered. "Awesome. Who do we have?" She kept her voice light, on purpose, hoping her pleasure might be contagious.

"Paul somebody," Kelly answered. "I never heard of him." He opened his book to the right poem, and showed her the assignment on the computer posting. Read the poem and answer the questions that follow it in the lit book.

"Okay," said Linda. "Let's see what we have here." She opened the book to the correct page. She had been lucky enough to find a paper version of the textbook they were using for American Lit. Although the kids mostly worked off of the digital book, Linda was old school. She liked paper. She found the assigned poem. "Sympathy," by Paul Dunbar.

Linda looked it over, remembering it like an old friend. She smiled. "I am going to read this to you, without telling you anything about the poet. I'd like to hear your thoughts before I give you any background information. Then, I will tell you a little bit about his life. Fair enough?"

Kelly nodded. "Fair enough."

Linda read the poem out loud, slowly. Tasting every word:

Sympathy

I know what the caged bird feels, alas!
When the sun is bright on the upland slopes;
When the wind stirs soft through the springing grass,
And the river flows like a stream of glass;
When the first bird sings and the first bud opens,
And the faint perfume from its chalice steals—
I know what the caged bird feels!
I know why the caged bird beats his wing
Till its blood is red on the cruel bars;
For he must fly back to his perch and cling
When he fain would be on the bough a-swing;
And a pail still throbs in the old, old scars
And they pulse again with a keener sting—
I know why he beats his wing!

I know why the caged bird sings, ah me,
When his wing is bruised and his bosom sore,
When he beats his bars and he would be free;
It is not a carol of joy or glee,

123

But a prayer that he sends from his heart's deep core,

But a plea, that upward to Heaven he flings—

I know why the caged bird sings!

Linda and Kelly sat silently together. He just sat there, all young and strong, with his eyes on the page and his hands folded in his lap. He seemed to radiate a kind of kinetic energy, only barely held in check. Linda was determined to let him speak first, so she sat quietly. The silence between them lengthened, but oddly enough, it was not uncomfortable.

Kelly said, "Can I ask a question before I tell you what I think it's about?"

"Absolutely," Linda said.

"Is he black?" Kelly asked, bringing his eyes up to meet Linda's.

"Yes," she answered evenly. Giving nothing away. Waiting. Kelly sat very quietly for another couple minutes.

"He feels like he's in a cage. His life, I mean. And he could be angry. Deep down he might be angry. But he has decided to sing in spite of that," Kelly spoke slowly, figuring it out even as he was speaking. "He doesn't want to be in that cage, but he is. So, he's gonna sing. Even if the song is a song about how bad it hurts. Even if it's full of pain."

Linda sat quietly. She felt her heart swell up with pride, but she didn't want to overstep. "That's exactly right," she said quietly. "In fact, that's a brilliant analysis." She saw Kelly take a deep breath, pleased with himself.

He looked at her and said slowly, "It's like Juice WRLD. His songs are full of pain and hurt. Be he kept on singing. It's like he had to. So he didn't lose his mind. Except then, he lost his life."

Linda quietly thanked her son Matt in her heart for his tireless playlists. Because of him, she knew who Juice WRLD was, and even knew a little bit about his story. She agreed with Kelly, saying, "You're right."

He smiled, kind of sadly. "I thought so. I could feel it."

"Now," Linda said. "Let me tell you just a little bit about Mr. Dunbar. He was born in 1872 and died in 1906. He only lived to be 33. He worked as an 'elevator boy,' that was his term—not mine—in New York City. But he wanted to be a poet. He sold copies of his poetry to people who rode his elevator, hoping to be 'discovered.'"

Kelly thought about that. "So, his cage was real. An elevator."

Linda said, "You're right, Kelly. It was. But it was metaphorical too. He felt caged, limited. But he had to sing. And his song was his poetry."

"Did he ever get out of the cage?" Kelly asked.

"He did," said Linda. "He actually was discovered. And his publisher took him on a book tour, where he toured many cities in Europe. But his publisher kept introducing him to the audiences as a 'rising young American Black poet,' and he hated that. He just wanted to be introduced as an American poet. It bugged him, and it made it hard for him to enjoy his success."

Kelly thought about that. "But he was successful?" he asked.

"Yes," Linda answered. "He ended up publishing several books of poetry. But he battled alcohol, and he lost that battle and died young. Still," she added, "his poetry is beautiful, and he opened the door for a whole lot of young American poets who followed him. His poetry is taught in every major university today."

"So," said Kelly. "You could say that he is still singing."

Linda was quiet, but deep inside, she was so pleased with his insight. She got a glimpse of the young man's depth and his soul. And his eloquence.

"Yes, you could," said Linda. "Now, I know you have to write a paragraph explaining this poem, and your assignment says that you have to quote at least three separate images, or lines, and explain them. Which three lines strike you as important enough to quote? Let's underline them together, so you remember which ones you want to talk about in your paragraph."

Kelly studied the poem. He pointed to the ninth line. "He beats his wings on the bars of his cage so hard that he bleeds. I would want to talk about that." He studied the next line and added, "I don't know what fain means."

Linda smiled, "No wonder. Nobody uses that word anymore. But it means rather. So that line reads that he would rather be swinging on a bough of a tree. In other words—free. Out in the wild." Then she added, "The line you picked is a very good line to talk about. Why do you think he beats his wings until he hurts himself?"

Kelly said, "He knows it's pointless. He can't break that bar. But he can't accept it either. Because if he quits fighting, he hates himself."

"Wow," said Linda. "That's brilliant. Really. What other line do you want to talk about?"

"I think I want to talk about the old scars. But I'm not sure what he means?"

Linda said, "Neither am I. But let's guess. What do you think? This poem was written in 1893. What could be the old, old scars that he still feels?"

Kelly thought about it. "Slavery? That was just over. I mean, the Civil War was over, but I don't think it was easy to be a black man who was free in 1893. It ain't even all that easy today."

Linda nodded. "I think that's a good guess. Any other ideas?"

"Maybe the old scars are from where he has been beating on the bars before?'

"Maybe," said Linda.

"So, what's the right answer?" Kelly said, looking at Linda hopefully.

"Both," she answered, grinning.

"What do you mean?" Kelly said, puzzled.

"I mean, that's the way it works in poetry," Linda said. "You supported both of your answers with the text. Both are possible interpretations. You could go with one or the other, or you could go with both. It's kind of like football at any given moment." She added that, having just realized it herself.

"How's that?" Kelly said.

"Well, like at any given moment, from the line of scrimmage, there are several possible things you could do that might result in a touchdown. You have to look at the defense, and what the other team is giving you, and using that, support your decision and take a stand."

"Huh," Kelly said. "I get that."

"Now," said Linda. "Our hour's almost up. You chose two passages that you want to focus on, and you chose well. We have them both underlined, so you can find them tonight. But you have to choose three. What's your final choice?"

Kelly studied the poem again. "I think I would want to talk about the last two lines. That his song is not a happy song, no matter what anyone thinks. It's a prayer that he is throwing up to heaven, hoping that someone hears it."

Linda smiled. "Good choice," she said. "Really good. Now that you've got all that in your head—do you think you can write your paragraph analysis tonight?"

"Yup," he said, gathering up his stuff. He was already almost out the door. Everything about his demeanor had switched gears somehow, and he was on to the next phase. Football practice. He started to leave and then turned around and said, "See you Thursday, right?"

"Right," she said.

"You coming to the game on Friday?" he asked.

"Yup," she grinned. He grinned back and left. John White came in quickly, and she began the lesson again.

By the time 5:00 rolled around, she was beat. She had only taught for two hours, but it was emotionally exhausting. And intense. Both Kelly and John had decided long ago that they hated poetry, but both of them had very good minds, and were finding themselves intrigued by the poetry they were studying— almost in spite of themselves.

As she gathered up her books and put them in her briefcase, she allowed herself a moment of realization that she was doing okay. She went by the football field, once again overwhelmed by the huge number of young men scrambling around out there. There were about fifteen coaches milling around, and there were people in the stands—just a few, but still. There to watch football practice? This was another level from anything she had ever seen before at the high school level.

She walked by the field. A couple of the coaches waved to her. Seagulls circled lazily overhead, riding the thermals. The sun was dipping lower in the sky, coming closer to the tree line in the distance. Linda felt good. She got in her car, turned the air conditioning up high, turned Matt's music up loud, and headed home.

Chapter 14

She went to the game on Friday night. St. Michael's was playing another local team, and this time, the game wasn't close at all. St. Michael's won, running away. In fact, the score was 42-0 by halftime. Linda realized that the other team would never be able to come back from that, so she slipped out of the stands at halftime and headed home. She waved goodnight to the custodian who was guarding the faculty cars, and drove quickly through the warm Fort Lauderdale night. The whole city was lit up once again. Bars and restaurants had big crowds. Music poured out into the street. Linda drove with her windows down, drinking in the night. And even though she was definitely not a part of the night scene, it still felt a little joyful to even live in such a place. The night air was warm, and it carried the sound of laughter. She pulled into her parking garage and parked her car, headed up to her apartment, and slipped inside. After a hot shower, she read for a little while. Then, feeling pleasantly worn out, she climbed into bed, turned on her white noise machine, and expected to fall promptly asleep. But that's not what happened.

Instead, her mind started jumping around. Thinking about the kids. The way they both felt so unsettled. Thinking about herself. And how she still felt hurt and betrayed by Rick. Wondering what he was doing tonight. Wondering how he had fallen so hard out of love with her. What she had done to bring it on? Then, her mind skipped to her tutoring session. It had gone well. She had to be careful with Kelly and John. They were both fiercely proud. She wanted to know where the line was—what she should talk about with them, and what she should not. She was pleased that Coach Pearson seemed to be satisfied with what she was doing. His season was over half way through, but she knew that there was really a second season—the playoffs. And that started around the first weekend of December and went right up until Christmas. If the team made it to the finals, they would play in the championship game on the field of a major university. She wasn't sure which one it would be. What a thrill that would be for them. But a lot of things had to go right before that could happen.

And then she thought about Rick again. He used to love football. He would have loved to see this team play. The team from St. Michael's. And then she told herself to stop thinking about him. He was gone. Moved on. Done. Divorced.

Divorced. Ugh. It was a word that she never thought she would have to use for herself. It felt a little bit like a failure. No. It felt a lot like a failure. But that wasn't fair either. She had tried to make it work. But you can't make somebody love you. Not when they don't love you anymore. And clearly, Rick didn't love her anymore. She felt her head spinning around and around.

And the more she tried to tell herself not to think of something, the more she thought of it.

She closed her eyes, said her prayers for the kids, and thought about Paul Dunbar. I know why the caged bird sings. We are all in cages, she thought. One way or another. And yet, the caged bird sings. She thought about that, and decided to keep singing. Even if it hurt. Like Juice WRLD. She smiled to herself, thinking that Kelly would enjoy that conclusion. She hoped he had a good game. Soon, she slipped into a restless sleep, filled with dreams she could not even quite remember, let alone interpret.

But the morning came. She went for her walk early, and she noticed, once again, that the sun's arc in the sky was getting lower and lower. It was mid-October already, and the absolutely beautiful weather was moving in. The morning temperatures were more comfortable than she had ever experienced so far down here, and her step was lighter. She listened to one of Matt's playlists, paying special attention when a Juice WRLD song came on. She stopped in at the French bakery, and Michel was there, behind the counter, as busy as ever. He smiled at her, but there was just a little bit of sadness in his smile, or so it seemed to Linda. His sons were in the kitchen, working cheerfully. One of them waved to her as she bought her croissant. Linda wondered if there was a coolness in their reception of her, and if so, what she had done to bring that on. She smiled at them, hopefully, and checked out with the lovely Maria.

When she got home, the mail had just been delivered. She picked it up and found a big envelope from the law firm up north. The one that was handling the divorce. She said a good morning to Henry, the ever-faithful sentinel at the front desk, and went up to her apartment.

She got herself a bottle of water, sat down at the kitchen table, slipped her glasses on, took a deep breath, and opened the envelope. In it was a very formal letter, stating that the divorce was final, the house had been sold, the division of assets had been done, and she should be expecting a certified check in the mail. She sat there, feeling absolutely drained, and suddenly Henry called from the front desk.

"Sorry, Miss Linda. You went by me so fast, I forgot to tell you that I have a certified letter for you down here at my desk. I signed for it, showing that you had received it, as you have given me permission to do. Shall I have the valet bring it up to you?" He obviously had no idea what he was holding in his hand, but Linda suddenly felt like she was unable to walk another step.

"That would be lovely, Henry, if it's not too much trouble," she said quietly.

"No trouble at all, Miss Linda. I will send Diego up with it immediately. Have a good day now," he added.

Two minutes later, there was a knock at the front door of her apartment, and there stood Diego, holding a piece of certified mail. She gave him $5.00, thanked him, and sat back down at the table. Inside the envelope was a certified check for $45, 688.00. The accompanying letter detailed how they had arrived at that amount—the sale of the house, the attorney's fees, the court costs. And that was her half.

Linda sat there, staring at the check, and suddenly, tears were slipping down her cheeks. She felt so alone, so unprotected. It seemed crazy that thirty some years of marriage and building a life together came to such a paltry amount. How can a person's life be reduced to dollars and cents. Actually, no cents. No sense either.

She felt herself spiraling down into a depression, so she called Carly. Carly answered right away, and Linda told her what had happened. She kept her voice as calm as she could, but even she could hear the choked sound of her words. Carly probably could too.

Carly listened quietly and then said, "I'll be there this afternoon."

"No," said Linda. "You don't have to do that. I'm fine. I just needed someone to talk to, that's all."

"No, I get it. You're fine. I know you are. But I need some sunshine and a margarita on the rocks, and some French bread. I need it bad. I have got absolutely nothing to do this weekend, so I am hanging up now, and I am going to book a flight. I'll call you back." She hung up before Linda could even object to her ridiculous, but very kind, and somewhat manic plan.

She set the check on the table and got in the shower, letting the hot water smash on the top of her head. Washing the sweat and the tears off. She stayed in that hot river of grace for a good long time, and then dried off, got in her robe, and went and sat out on the balcony. The sun was rising up over the ocean. It was already pretty high in the sky, but the angle was so much sharper these days since the arc of the sun was lower in the sky.

There was a gentle breeze, and a flock of seagulls flew by, yawping overhead and startling her. She sat down on her chaise lounge and looked out at the water, sparkling with diamonds. She thought about Rick, remembering better times. When he had loved her. When he had taken her to Hilton Head with the kids one summer. They had rented a condo right on the ocean, and she had loved every minute of it. The kids were so little. They had played on the beach and dug holes in the sand. Rick and she had gone for long walks on the beach, holding hands. Sometimes Rick had carried Matt on his shoulders—he was just a baby.

Memory is a strange playmate, sometimes. Here she was, mad at Rick, hurt by his desertion and betrayal, bewildered by her new situation, not sure who she even was anymore, and she was remembering a really good time they had had together. What sense did that make?

The phone rang and Carly said, "Pick me up at Fort Lauderdale airport. I'm coming in on Delta. My flight lands at 3:05. So, take a shower, pull yourself together, and get ready to buy me a margarita." Linda started to object, to say it wasn't necessary, but there was absolutely no point in that. Carly was like a force of nature when she got rolling. So, she agreed to everything, told her how much she appreciated her coming, and said she would be there at three.

Then, she closed her eyes and thought about calling Matt and Andrea, just to keep them in the loop. She had to present this whole thing the right way, or they might feel like they had to come and stay with her, and she wasn't sure that that would be very helpful right now. She didn't even think it was all that good that Carly was coming, but that was happening, like it or not. She lay there on the chaise lounge, listening to the traffic go by. Feeling the warm slant of the sun on her skin, smelling the hamburgers from the restaurant down the street. It wasn't even noon yet, but that place always smelled like grilled hamburgers.

She kept her eyes closed and tried to empty her mind of thoughts and memories of Rick. They weren't going to do her any good at all. She had to let him go. He had obviously moved on with his life, so she too had to close the door on that part of her past. They had had some good times, they had raised two beautiful children together, children who were doing well—facing their own battles. She was living in Fort Lauderdale, the city of her teenage dreams, and she was doing okay. She was doing okay.

She went in and got dressed, checked the refrigerator, realized that she had better run to the grocery store and get supplies in before Carly got here, and got moving. She thought to herself—one step at a time. One step at a time.

Chapter 15

The weekend passed in a blur. Carly kept Linda so busy that she almost didn't have time to think. They went down to the beach, had dinner at an outdoor café, drank margaritas until her head was swimming, sat up and watched an old movie, talked until way past midnight, and dropped by the French bakery for breakfast on Sunday. Both Marie and Michel seemed friendly, but a little bit aloof somehow. Once again, Linda wondered if she had somehow offended them. She noted the coolness and decided to see if she could figure it out, someday.

Then it was time to take Carly to the airport and return her to her own life and her own responsibilities. Linda parked the car in the short-term lot and walked Carly in, as far as she could. She hugged her good-bye, with grateful tears in her eyes. "Thank you, from the bottom of my heart," she said. "I was really blue, and then you roared in here, not leaving me enough time to wallow in self-pity. I know it cost you a lot of money, and I can never really repay you for what you've done."

"Don't be silly," Carly said, hugging her hard. "I needed some sunshine and to just kick up my heels. This was as much for me as it was for you." She giggled. "I gave that cute guy at the restaurant my number. I don't know if he will call, and I don't know what I will say if he does. But he sure was good-looking." Carly was just about ten years younger than Linda, and sometimes Linda felt every single one of those years. This was one of those moments.

She smiled. "I'm pretty sure he'll call. He was really taken with you. I felt like a fifth wheel that night—I kind of just wanted to disappear so you two could take off and enjoy the evening. And getting to know each other better. If that's what you wanted—"

"Well, that is not what I wanted, or I would have done it." Carly smiled at her sister. Then she rapidly changed the subject. "Now, promise me that if you get in a funk you will call. No matter what and no matter when. I'll be here for you." In spite of the fact that she was the younger sister, she definitely seemed to be looking out for Linda, worried about her.

Linda hugged her hard. "You know," she said, "I think I'm going to be all right. I'm sort of feeling my way here, and sometimes I have some pretty dark hours. But not all the time. Sometimes, I think I'm going to be just fine. Eventually." She kissed Carly on the cheek and said, "Now go. You need to get through security and all that. And Carly, thank you so much for being here."

"Like I said, anytime. It was good for me too," Carly kissed Linda on the cheek and grabbed her bag. Then, she turned and walked away, up to where the gates were. Linda stood and watched her until she was out of sight. Then, she went back to her car, got in it and drove home. It was Sunday afternoon, in late October, and the beach was busy. As she drove down A1A, heading toward her condo, she saw that all the restaurants were humming, people were sprinkled all down the beach, huddling under brightly colored beach umbrellas, and out there splashing in the water. Out on the horizon, she could see a cruise ship pulling out. She put the windows down and let the sounds and smells on the beach drift over her. It was hard to stay sad in the midst of this scene. The colors filled her eyes—the blue of the water, the white of the sand, the beach-ball colors on the beach umbrellas, the scarlet of the oleanders. She saw all the families and felt a little sorry for herself that she wasn't out there on the beach with hers. But, in a moment of clarity, she realized that she had done these very same things, when her children were younger. Maybe everybody gets that moment of family beach time, and hers had passed.

This realization almost made her cycle down to tears, but then she had another thought. Maybe, new moments would come. She remembered that the truth is that taking the kids to the beach was always almost overwhelming. All the stuff she had to lug down there. The sand in their diapers. Trying to keep them amused. Matt was always a little bit afraid of the ocean. Andrea was not. She would plunge right in, get knocked down, come up shaking her head and grinning. Matt would be sitting on the beach, right at the surf line, afraid to go in. Linda would be pulled in two different directions at the same time. And now. Now, they were both grown up. Matt at law school in Miami. Andrea running a bar in Chicago. And Rick? Who knew. But anyhow. She had had her moments of family beach time. And they were wonderful, but maybe new pleasures would come. In time. Different kinds of pleasures. She told herself to keep an open heart and wait and see.

When she got home, she turned on the television and saw that there was an NFL football game on—the Miami Dolphins vs. the New England Patriots. They were playing up in New England, and it looked cold. All the people in the stands had coats on, and the wind looked blustery and cold. Everybody down here hated the Patriots and their dynasty of excellence. But Linda harbored a secret affection for them, based on her admiration for Tom Brady. Not only was he very handsome, but he was fighting hard to still keep playing the game he loved, even though he was probably too old, by most people's standards. And there were all these new "wunderkinds" popping up around the league, ready and able to knock the crown off the king. She kicked off her flip-flops, settled down into her couch, and watched the game. Soon, the rhythm of the announcers' patter and last night's margaritas got the upper hand, and she drifted off to sleep.

She awoke to her phone ringing and Carly calling to say that she had landed safely in Detroit. She was absolutely startled that she had accidentally slept for over three hours, and saw that a whole new game was on the television. Again, she thanked Carly for coming down for the weekend, got up and took a hot shower, and dried off, slipping into warm pajamas. Then, she made a cup of chicken noodle soup, and read her novel for a while. Finally, Sunday night was upon her, and she had survived the weekend of her divorce settlement being final.

On a whim, she went over to her jewelry box, opened it up, took off her wedding rings, and placed them in the lower tray, far back. A passing thought came over her—she could go out on the balcony and throw them as far as she could, maybe into the Intracoastal. But then she thought, they are probably worth a couple thousand dollars, anyhow. She could sell them and give the kids the money. The only thing she was sure of was that she didn't want to wear them anymore. So, she tucked them away, to be dealt with at a later time. Then, she crawled in bed, trying to think about Tom Brady. He was much better looking than Rick ever was.

Chapter 16

Tuesday, she went to work and checked in with Coach Pearson before she met with Kelly. As usual, his office had several other coaches in it, talking to each other about players and plays. She always felt like she was interrupting something important, but Coach Pearson always stopped what he was doing and smiled to greet her. Trying to make her feel important, maybe. Part of the team. Linda appreciated the kindness.

"How are you doing? Are you starting to settle in?" he asked.

Wow. She thought. He actually seems genuinely interested. "Yes, Coach. I'm getting a little more used to things every day," she answered. "Thanks for asking." Then, she wondered about how his week was going, if there was something on his mind.

"How does your week look? I know it's about mid-season for you," she said.

"Well, it's actually a very big week for us. We had a hole in our schedule this week, so I invited a big team from California to come out here and play us." He looked down at a bunch of papers on his desk. "Some of my staff wish we were not going to play them. Too dangerous. Too much of a challenge, when we are still finding our rhythm as a team. But I've always believed that if you want people to take you seriously, you've got to play the big teams." He sounded just a little bit skeptical about his own plan. Understandably.

Linda sat down in the chair across from the coach and said, "Do you need me to do anything different with Kelly and John because of this game?"

"Oh, no," he said. "Just keep doing what you're doing. Both of them are really enjoying you. Their grades in English have improved dramatically." Suddenly, he stood up and Linda realized that she had been dismissed. She looked at her watch and saw that it was almost 3:00. So, she excused herself and went into the film room to begin her lesson with Kelly.

He was already seated at the table when she got in the room. But he seemed to give off a negative energy today. He was scowling at his phone. She said hi and he sort of mumbled a greeting. "What are we working on today?" she asked.

"Grammar," he answered. "I hate it, and I don't get it, and I don't know why I have to study it." He was clearly in a very foul mood.

Linda said, "Well, let's take a look at the assignment, and see if I can help. I don't blame you for hating grammar. I hate it myself. And I am not at all sure that it's necessary or helpful to learn it."

"What I said," said Kelly. His mood was not lightened.

When Linda looked at the assignment, she knew that she was not going to be able to work much magic with it. It was on the difference between complex and compound sentences. Identifying relative clauses, and deciding if they were adjectival or adverbial. Enough to put anyone in a foul mood. She struggled through the lesson with Kelly, and then repeated the lesson with John. Neither one of them enjoyed it, and by the time the two hours were over, Linda was exhausted from trying to make the material interesting. Both the boys practically ran out of the room as soon as their hour was over.

Linda shouldered her briefcase and headed out to her car, walking by the football field as she always did. As she passed by, Coach Pearson called to her and waved her over. She walked to the edge of the field, leaned on the fence and waited for him. Instead, he waved her on to the field. She headed out there carefully, not expecting to walk on this hallowed ground.

As she approached, he asked, "How did the lessons go today?

"Not very well," she admitted. "Not the boys' fault. The material we had to cover today was not much fun. Complex sentences and relative clauses. Hard to make that interesting."

Coach Pearson grinned. "Man," he said. "Just hearing those words makes me sleepy. Anyhow, I forgot to tell you—even though you're part-time, you're still considered a part of the faculty, and you have to attend the faculty meeting tomorrow. We have them once a month, in the cafeteria. Right after school gets out. Starts at 2:45. See you then."

He turned and walked back out to the center of the field, calling something out to the players. Linda stood there in the late afternoon sun, sweating a little in her navy-blue blazer. She picked up her briefcase and headed out to her car. She put the windows down to let the breeze in. Although it was warm, there was a tiny edge of coolness in the air. The sunlight sparkled on the water as she drove over the 17th Street Causeway, and she took a deep breath. Well, she had to attend a faculty meeting tomorrow. Had not expected that. He said she was considered part of the faculty, and that was that. Well, all right. She thought to herself—we will see what happens.

On Wednesday afternoon, she got to school right as the kids were getting out. That meant that thousands of hormonal teenagers were milling around and shouting. She waved hi to the policeman at the entrance and ducked right into the cafeteria. There were about a hundred chairs set up. She took one of them, near the back. All around the room, teachers were gathering in their little friend-groups, gossiping and complaining about the day and the meeting. Pretty soon, more and more teachers drifted in, and Linda suddenly suspected that she had seated herself in the men's corner of the room, quite by accident. Big guys were taking chairs all around her, but leaving one empty one, making her feel pretty conspicuous. Suddenly, an attractive blonde woman came over to her and smiled.

"Hi," she said. "I'm Diane Davidson. The English department chairperson. You must be Linda Miller, the new tutor who is working with Kelly and John. I've heard so much about you. You're doing a great job with them. Come sit with me over here so I can get to know you better."

Gratefully, Linda followed her. One of the men from the corner said something like "Hey, Diane. Leave her alone. We don't bite." Or something to that effect.

Diane smiled over her shoulder and shouted back, "I'm not going to take that chance. You've been known to do that on other occasions, and I happen to like this lady a lot."

Linda was impressed with her easy manner. It was obvious that the guys liked her, but there was also a feeling that they respected her. She ushered Linda to another spot, half way down the rows. Then, she turned to her and said, in a very comfortable way, "Those guys are really great. But, you don't want to meet them all at once when they're in their pack mentality. Now, real quick, before the meeting gets going—how are you doing? Do you have everything you need? I have Kelly and John in my American Lit classes, and they really like you. Thought you should know." They sat down together, and Linda realized that she was sitting with several other members of the English department.

Linda said, "Thanks for the encouragement. To tell you the truth, we've had some good lessons and we've had some real duds. Today was a dud. Compound and complex sentences and relative clauses. Not too inspiring."

Diane laughed, an easy and comfortable laugh. "Yes. Sorry about that. That's not much fun, but we build in good old grammar review, hoping that it helps their performance on the SAT and ACT. All the kids hate it." She smiled at Linda, and

Linda felt a genuine warmth and interest from her. It was very compelling. "Now, tell me about you. Who you are and where you come from, and how you came to us."

Linda smiled and said, "I was a high school English teacher in Michigan, mostly American and British Literature. I taught there for thirty years. I recently retired, you know, thirty and out, and on one of my last days of work I came home early to find my husband in bed with his secretary, a girl twenty years younger than he is. Tiffany." She kind of swallowed, took a deep breath, and plunged on. She could feel herself blushing, but there was something about Diane's comfortable manner that invited confidences. "We had already sold our house and bought the condo where I'm living now. So, it was all over but the shouting. I finished out my obligation to my district and came down here and moved into the condo. I decided I needed to make a little extra money, so I applied to be a tutor here, and that's how I came to you." She was actually a little bit surprised at her own candor. It was getting somewhat easier to tell this horrible story. She didn't feel quite so ashamed anymore, for some reason. She was starting to realize that it wasn't her fault. At all.

Diane had never taken her eyes from Linda's face. She shook her head and smiled, sadly. "Wow," she said. "I am stupefied. Speechless." She laughed lightly. "And, believe me, I am never speechless." She looked hard at Linda and asked, "Are you at all interested in working full time again? I might be able to smooth that out if you are."

Linda shook her head. "No," she said. "Thank you very much. But I kind of think that thirty years of full-time teaching is enough. I'm actually really enjoying my work with the boys, two days a week, two hours a day. I get up in the morning, go for a walk on the beach, read the paper and drink my coffee. Lots of things I never had time to do. And, I sure don't miss grading papers for hours every other night."

Diane laughed. "Tell me about it. Well, it looks like Father Thompson is about to begin the meeting. But, after that, why don't you come back to my house for a glass of wine. I'd like to hear more about your story."

Linda smiled. "I'm afraid you've already heard all the interesting parts, but it's kind of you to ask. Anyhow, I'd love to come." She settled in to watch the staff meeting, quietly and anonymously.

"Great," said Diane. "I'll have you follow me home."

Then, she turned her attention to the front of the room where the principal, Father Thompson, was calling the meeting to order with a quick prayer. A prayer he was obviously improvising, because it seemed to meander all over. Rather formlessly, and quite charmingly. Then, he worked his way through several ideas. Lunch duty. The school requirement that at least one grade be given every week, and that the grades would be posted on Blackboard in a timely manner. It was all pretty familiar to Linda. Not unlike what she had known up in Michigan. Except for beginning the meeting with a prayer. She had taught in the public schools up there, and such a thing would have never happened in that setting. Linda thought it was actually kind of refreshing. If ever a profession humbled you, it was certainly teaching. Probably saying a prayer was a really good idea.

Soon enough, the meeting was over, and Diane said goodbye to several of her colleagues, after introducing them to Linda. Then she pulled Linda aside and whispered, "Let's get out of here before one of them asks me to do something or think about something else. I'm feeling really done for the day." Linda actually felt a little overwhelmed, looking at the whole staff buzzing and talking. Everybody knew everyone else, and she felt pretty disconnected. Diane seemed to be aware of that, tugged on her elbow, and headed her out to the parking lot. Linda pointed out her old Honda, and Diane said, "I'm in that little black Mercedes, one row over from you. I will pull out, and turn left. I'll pull over and watch until I know you're behind me. Then, just follow me." Linda nodded and got in her car. Teachers were still calling out their last bits of wisdom to each other as cars started to stream out of the parking lot.

Linda saw Diane's car turn left and pull over, up the street. She pulled into the line of exiting cars, came up behind Diane, who pulled out and led her through town. She turned left on US1 and led Linda down Middle River Drive. It was a quiet neighborhood, that looked like it had been there for a long time. The houses were larger, but they still had that old Florida feeling—like they had been built maybe forty or fifty years ago. The streets were lined with grand old trees, huge spreading mangroves and wild oaks, so the sidewalks were heavily shaded. They pulled into a gated driveway, and Diane pressed a button that opened the gate. The driveway was just big enough for two cars, and Linda parked beside Diane and got out. She threw her blazer in the back seat and grabbed her purse.

Diane led her up the steps, opened the door, entered the security code and welcomed Linda into her home. It may have been an older house, but it was absolutely grand. The interior was done mostly in white and black, and the rear of the house was all window-walls, opening onto a screened in lanai with a big pool and a hot tub. There were deeply padded lounge chairs all around, and the hot tub made a fountain that tumbled warm water into the pool. It was absolutely lovely. Beyond the lanai was a shaded yard, looking out onto a river. There were a couple kids on stand-up paddle boards on the river, laughing and talking.

"Oh, Diane," Linda said. "It's just beautiful. So inviting. Thank you for having me over. This is very kind of you."

"Oh, nothing. Nothing at all." Diane kicked her shoes off and bustled into the kitchen. "Let me pour us a glass of wine and we can go sit in the shade and you can tell me the rest of your story. Or not. Whatever you like. Please make yourself comfortable." Linda kicked off her shoes too, and wandered out to the window-wall, looking out at the river.

"Is that the Intracoastal?" she asked.

"No," said Diane. "Actually, that's the Middle River. But it flows into the Intracoastal, so they're all connected." She handed Diane a glass of wine and led her out through the pool area to the lawn beyond, which was in deep shade this late in the afternoon. They sat down in some wonderfully comfortable chaise lounges, and Linda felt the day's struggles sort of slip away. Diane made her feel very welcome, and her laughter was easy and genuine. "You're doing a great job with John and Kelly. You obviously know your stuff. And the boys really like you." She took a sip of wine. "So, tell me your story."

Linda set her wine glass down, looked at Diane, and let her have it—long story short: "I taught for 30 years up in Michigan, raised two wonderful kids—Andrea, age 30, runs a bar in Chicago, and Matt, age 24, in law school at Miami, then I retired in June, came home early one day to find my husband in flagrante delecto with a twenty-something named Tiffany, (apparently they were playing bull and matador—naked in my bedroom—she had my Hemingway sash tied around her waist— the slut) got divorced, moved into a condo down by the beach, needed a little extra pocket money, got hired at St. Michael's to tutor these kids a couple times a week. And here I am." It sounded wild—almost ridiculous, even to her.

Diane looked at her for a long moment, almost without breathing, and then burst out laughing. Linda didn't know what to make of that. It really wasn't a laughing matter at all—the absolute crumbling of all her plans. But then, for some reason, she burst out laughing too. They laughed so hard that Linda almost started crying. Diane could hardly catch her breath. "Oh, my dear heavenly God," she gulped. "That is the most bizarre thing I have ever heard. She had your Hemingway sash tied around her waist! The illiterate hussy!" She was still laughing.

She got up from her chair and came over to Linda. Without asking permission, she just knelt down and hugged her, kind of laughing and crying at the same time. Linda hugged her back, and she felt a shimmering of lightness all around her. A release of some kind. Maybe it was the wine (which was very good.) Maybe it was the beautiful slant of the light on the water. Maybe it was the gift of laughter. She didn't know what it was all about, but it felt good.

Eventually, Diane stood up and got back to her chair. Then, she suddenly jumped up, grabbed a coconut from under a tree (there were a pile of them there) and shouted, "Damn it!" Suddenly, Linda looked to see what was the object of her fury. Crawling toward them, red tongue out, licking the air, was a dinosaur! Or what looked like one. Four feet long, a spiky crown on its head, a lime green body. Hissing. Linda screamed and jumped up on her chair, barely managing to hang on to her glass of wine. Suddenly, Diane heaved the coconut at the creature, missing him, but coming pretty close. She grabbed another coconut, screaming at the thing and heaved that one too. The iguana turned around, still hissing at her, and high-tailed it back to the break-wall, then fell into the river with a plop.

"What the hell was that," said Linda. "That is the ugliest creature I have ever seen. Are they in the river!"

"I guess," said Diane. "I don't think they live in the water. I've been out on the water on my paddleboard many times, and I've never seen one out there. But you can see that undeveloped lot a couple doors down. I think they live there, in the swampy land. And they're very bold. You are allowed to shoot them, but you're not allowed to throw coconuts at them." She took a big gulp of her wine. "Technically, what I just did is illegal." She smiled a mischievous smile at Linda. "Don't tell anybody," she added.

"Wait a minute," Linda said. "You can shoot them, but you can't throw coconuts at them? What sense does that make? You mean it's legal to discharge a firearm here in the city, with all these houses around? What kind of a crazy law is that?"

"Welcome to Florida," Diane laughed. "This is one beautiful state, but there are a lot of crazy things here too. There's even a website called Florida Man. You can look up any date—like you could look up your birthday—and there will be a story about something ridiculous that took place on your birthday. It's kind of a Florida thing." She pulled her phone from her pocket. "Okay. I can see you don't believe me. What's your birthday?"

"July 26," Linda answered.

"Okay," said Diane. "Here's your birthday story. Florida man loses testicle, toes, and finger to an alligator while bathing in a pond!" She burst out laughing again and handed the phone to Linda, who refused to believe. When she looked down at the phone, she saw the story.

"Oh, my gosh, I never would have believed that!" Linda found herself laughing again. Diane had brought the bottle of wine out with them, and she poured Linda a little more. "Not much," Linda said. "It's the middle of the week."

"Yes, it is," said Diane. "But I've got a new friend and so do you. We should celebrate a little."

"All right," Linda said. "What's your birthday?"

"January 23."

Linda scrolled down her own phone and found Diane's birthday. She guffawed. "Oh, man. Here's yours. Florida man loads car with frozen iguanas. They warm up, come back to life and cause a car accident. What!!" She looked at Diane, completely bewildered. Diane was roaring laughing.

"Oh, perfect," she said. "I love it!"

"But, what on earth can that possibly mean," gasped Linda. "How do they freeze and then come back to life? Is that even true?"

"I don't know how it happens, honestly. But I think at some level it's true. My husband and I were sitting out here last winter. It was chilly. About the coldest it ever gets here is mid-30's. Anyhow, we were sitting out here, looking at the river, wrapped in blankets, having a glass of wine, and an iguana must have been in the tree, sleeping or frozen. And all of a sudden, it fell out of the tree and landed right at our feet. About twelve inches the other way and it would have landed on our heads! I swear—it really happened. Just like that."

Linda laughed helplessly, trying to picture the iguana falling out of the tree. "Was it dazed, or conscious, or what," she asked.

"Well, it kind of shook itself a little, and then waddled away and plopped into the water, or over the break-wall anyhow. I was screaming at Mike to do something, but he was just as scared as I was. We were both running the other way. Anyhow, that really happened. So, the Florida man thing you read for me is absolutely perfect."

Suddenly, she gasped. She stood up and pointed to the break wall. There, tongue out and hissing, was the iguana, rising from the depths. Coming back for another round, apparently. His big green head inched up over the break-wall, a spiny claw clinging to the top, and he started to pull his chunky body up onto the patio, head glistening, waving slowly back and forth. A miniature dinosaur, coming back for revenge.

"Holy shit!" exclaimed Diane. "I guess this guy wants to go a couple more rounds. I'm out of here!" She turned and started running for the house. Linda grabbed her shoes and her wine glass and followed her, laughing so hard she almost couldn't breathe. She just could not believe the whole scene. And she also couldn't believe how much fun she was having. She suddenly realized that it had been a long time since she had laughed that hard. And it was getting late. It was almost 7:00. She thanked Diane for the most wonderful evening she had had in a long time. Diane pulled her in and gave her a big hug.

"I'm so glad you came over. I am very happy to get to know you and welcome you on board. As I said earlier, you are doing a great job for the kids. And if you ever change your mind and want to teach full time again, just let me know, and I will see what I can do to make that happen." She walked Linda out to her car, adding, "I'm in room 201. Stop by any time and see me, if you get there a few minutes early. I had a blast this afternoon." Linda hugged her one more time and drove home, still laughing to herself about Florida man and frozen iguanas falling out of tree. The sun was low in the sky, just the last bit of it still visible above the horizon. The clouds were layered horizontally, streaking orange and vermillion, with shades of purple and pink thrown in. It made Linda think of this wonderful poem by Percy Shelley, where he compared the clouds in the autumnal sky to the long hair of a beautiful woman, stretched out against the sunset: "Like the bright hair uplifted from the head of some fierce Maenad, even from the dim verge of the horizon to the zenith's height, the locks of the approaching storm." Something like that. It conjured up images of a beautiful young woman, dancing wildly to celebrate the harvest. The crops safely in the barn. The last warm rays of the dying summer sun. Knowing the winter is coming, but there is food enough to last until spring. She dances. Her hair whirling in the sunset light, filtering the last bit of gold. And her lover sits at her feet, hypnotized with desire. Firelight flickering on his cheeks, his strong arms.

Linda giggled. Found herself writing a romance novel of some sort as she drove home. She pulled into her parking spot. Took a hot shower to wash the day off, made a cup of soup and got a glass of water. Time to detox. But what a fun night. Iguanas falling out of the sky. What a funny idea. What a funny state. Florida man, indeed!

Chapter 17

She got to school on Thursday for her tutoring session with Kelly and John, and both sessions could be described in one word—uninspiring. Not her fault, entirely. Maybe not her fault at all, Linda thought. Grammar lessons again. Compound-complex sentences, relative clauses, independent clauses. She tried hard to find a cool connection to their football lessons, but nothing seemed to work. Both boys were so jittery about the upcoming game with Madonna della Strada, the powerhouse team from Irvine, California coming to town for Friday's game. The California team actually arrived in town on Thursday, right after her tutoring sessions. Both of the boys had already left to get ready for practice, and Linda decided to swing by the football field on her way out to her car.

There, ranged along the fence, were about a hundred members of the football team from California. They looked every bit as big and mean and ready as the St. Michael's team. Some of the St. Michael's warriors became aware of the team from California, watching their practice, and they didn't like it. There were low cat-calls from both sides until the coaches broke it off.

The California team walked away, many of the members looking over their shoulders, sort of smirking. Saying things softly, so the coaches wouldn't hear. Linda could tell that there would be no love lost here, on either side.

She got home and threw a salad together, eating it quickly and then going out on the balcony for her glass of wine. Suddenly, the sky darkened, and gray clouds rolled in. There was a feeling of electricity in the air. Almost a crackling that you could feel and smell, and it smelled like rain. Then, the wind picked up and the temperature plummeted, falling almost ten degrees in less than a minute. A group of pelicans flew overhead, holding their formation tightly, flying straight into the wind, looking like fighter jets, yawping in the approaching darkness. And then the skies opened up. Linda dashed inside, walking over to the window to watch as lightning ripped the sky apart, thunder crashing and rolling overhead. The storms down here were nothing short of spectacular. Up in Michigan, Linda used to hate the rain, because when it moved in, it sometimes felt like it would never go away. But she kind of liked the rain down here because she never felt like it would last forever. She found that she even kind of liked the feeling of shelter when the world was silvery gray and wet out there.

Linda sat down on her couch, grabbed her book, and turned on the lamp. She pulled a warm little blanket that her mom had made her over her legs and read for a while until the night settled her down. But the rain did not let up. She went to bed around ten and the thunder was still rolling across the sky.

She peeked outside to see the streets, rain-soaked and sparkling in the streetlights. And the rain kept on. All night.

She got up in the morning and the whole world had that freshly scrubbed feeling, but the sky was still dark and threatening. Still, even the brick pavers along A1A looked cleaner. She found herself enjoying her morning walk, even though the rain had not really cooled it off. A huge flock of seagulls flew by, yawping in the stormy sunlight, white wings fluttering against the dark blue. It was steamy, and the ocean was still rolling in with long, even waves. The kind that show up after a storm. The water looked almost brown today—kind of ominous, but the surfers were out there, enjoying the swells.

Puddles still lined A1A. Cars had to wade through some deep water. As she was walking, she found herself looking forward to the game tonight, wondering how the team would do. She had felt a strain or a tightness in both Kelly and John, and she had seen that same strain on Coach Pearson's face. Not exactly strain—there was also a kind of excitement, barely held in check. But there was certainly some tension—in the coaches and the players. This team from California looked big and well-trained. It was a meeting of heavyweights. Beyond all this, the game was going to be broadcast on national television. College coaches from all across the nation would be looking at the Warriors from St. Michael and the Raiders from Madonna della Strada.

Matt called at lunchtime to check in with her. "How are you doing, Mom? Happy Friday, by the way."

"Hello my darling," she said. "So good of you to call and check on me. Happy Friday yourself. Are you done with classes for the week?"

"Um, yes. All done."

She heard some note of tension in his voice, something unsaid, something he was holding in check. "Everything all right?" she asked.

"Oh, yeah. I'm doing fine," he answered. "My classes are actually going pretty well. Funny thing—I'm really enjoying Constitutional Law. And that's a little bit strange because it is the one class I was dreading. I didn't think I would find it interesting at all. And—the truth is—it's my favorite class this term."

Linda breathed a sigh of relief. "Well, that's wonderful, honey. Everything else all right?" She still heard something he was not saying yet, something he still had to say. There was a long pause, and she heard him take a deep breath. She held her own, waiting.

"Um," he said, struggling, "did you know that Dad is in town?"

Linda felt gut punched. She couldn't find words for a minute. A silence hung in the air. Finally, she spoke. "No, I didn't." She swallowed hard and made herself go on, trying to sound normal. "Did he come and see you?"

"Errr, yes," said Matt. "He and Tiffany—I think that's her name—met me for lunch today. Or brunch, or whatever. I met them at the restaurant in the hotel they're staying at. I thought you should know." Linda could hear Matt being careful with his words.

But she had pulled herself together by now. With an effort, but still. "Well, I'm glad you told me, and I don't want you to feel awkward about any of it. He is still your father, and he will always be your father, and he has every right to see you, and to enjoy your company. So, that's fine, honey." She felt good about how she was handling it. The truth is—she was faking it right now. She hadn't really had time to sort out her feelings, but she knew that she had to say the right things for Matt.

"Well, Mom, you're being really cool about this. I know it's awkward, but I didn't want to not tell you. That seemed wrong."

"How does your dad seem to you?" Linda asked.

"I'm not entirely sure how to answer that question," Matt said. "He seemed somewhat like himself, but somewhat not. Like he was a little embarrassed about everything, even though he didn't want to take any of it back. He was dressing a little differently. A little more hip or something. I can't really describe it." Matt faltered, searching for words.

"Did he seem happy?" Linda kept her voice neutral.

"He didn't seem unhappy. He seemed busy. A little distracted. Wanted me to know that he had sold a really big yacht and had come down to see the launch for his client. He was excited about that and invited me to come if I wanted to. He apparently sold it to some rich guy who lives in Michigan in the summer and down here in the winter. Some big-time millionaire. A care dealer, I think. I didn't recognize the guy's name, and I can't remember it either."

"Are you going to go?" Linda asked.

"Nah. I really have so much work to do that I have to ration my downtime very carefully, and going to some boat launch where I don't know anybody doesn't seem like all that much fun to me. Besides, to tell you the truth—I don't really think Dad wanted me to come, but sort of felt like he had to offer. So, anyway—the free food and booze would be nice, but it's not enough of a draw for me at this moment in my life." He paused, gathering his thoughts. "But it was good to see him, and to know that he's all right." He stopped talking, listening for Linda, who said nothing. So he added, "Are you all right?"

Linda smiled to herself, hearing the concern in his voice. "Oddly enough, I think I am," she said. "I'm starting to feel like I'm beginning to move on. He obviously doesn't love me anymore, so that would not be a good relationship for me. No one-sided love ever works out. And I'm keeping busy. The tutoring job has been really good for me. I've met some nice people, and I really like the two boys I'm working with. They have a big game tonight, and I think I'm going to go. If you'd ever like to come up here for a game one Friday night, let me know. I'll get you a ticket. I think you would really enjoy the football. They are playing at a very high level. Much higher than any high school I've ever seen."

"I might do that. Anyhow, Mom. I better get back to studying. I'll talk to you soon. I love you so much. Keep taking good care of yourself." Linda felt like he was trying to take care of her, watching out for her, and she was struck with the idea that there is a strange kind of role reversal that goes on in life. As you get older, the child feels an obligation to act like a parent.

162

Sometimes. It endeared Matt to her, even though she didn't like the idea of him feeling obligated to watch out for her. Complicated.

"I will, my darling. And thank you for calling." She hung up and looked at the clock. Only a couple hours until game time. The sky looked mean, but the rain had stopped. She thought about Rick, dragging around Miami with the luscious Tiffany. He probably looked just a little bit ridiculous since she was obviously so much younger than he. She tried to sort through her feelings, and she realized that they were hard to catalogue.

Many different thoughts were crashing around in her head. But one thing she did *not* seem to feel was any desire to be with him, down in Miami, going to his boat launch. In fact, she was actually looking forward to the football game.

Chapter 18

It continues to rain softly, sort of drizzle, as the evening came on. Linda started thinking that if it didn't let up, she might not go to the game. She didn't want to sit in the bleachers for two or three hours in the rain, even though she realized that this could be their toughest game of the year. At least until the playoffs. But, as game time approached, the rain finally stopped, and she talked herself into going over to the high school. There was some part of her that felt like she owed it to Kelly and John, so she firmly put Rick and Tiffany out of her thoughts. Shoved them in a box, put the box on the back shelf in the closet, and then slammed the doors shut. It was an imaging practice she had read about, and was determined to try. Couldn't hurt. She put on her green and white St. Michael's shirt and got in her car to drive over to the school.

As she got near the school, there were cars everywhere, with long lines waiting to get into the parking garage. Luckily, she was able to weave her way over to the faculty lot, where one of the custodians recognized her and waved her in.

"Wow," she said. "What a crowd! I never expected anything like this." The custodian, whose name was Gus, was about 70 years old. He looked tired and sweaty.

"Do you have to stand out here all evening?" Linda asked.

"No. Not stand. I've got my trusty golf cart over there. Don't worry about me—you have a good time. Enjoy the game," he added. "I'll see you on your way out."

"That team from California must have brought a lot of fans with them," Linda said.

"It sure seems that way," Gus agreed, nodding to the lines of cars trying to find a place to park.

Linda grabbed her sweatshirt and headed into the stadium, where the lights were blazing and the smell of hotdogs filled the air. The stars were out, but they had surrendered to the football lights, at least temporarily. Linda made her way up to her assigned seat on the 50-yard line, grateful for Coach Pearson's thoughtfulness. She sat down and looked out at the field, which looked mucky. The rain had stopped, although it still felt like there was a mist in the air, but the field was basically soft, squishy mud, particularly around the middle of the field. The two teams were out there warming up, and you could see the boys' feet sinking in the muddy grass. Going to be a mud bowl, Linda thought.

Then the teams lined up, the prayer was said, and the national anthem was sung. And everyone stood respectfully for all of this. The coin toss took place at the center of the field, with four players from each side representing their teams. The team from St. Michael's was wearing dark green uniforms, and the team from Madonna della Strada was wearing red. The overall effect was strangely kind of Christmas-like in appearance. St. Michael's won the toss and deferred until the second half. That meant that they would start the first half on defense.

Linda had learned that Kelly was number 80, and John was number 87. Kelly was a wide receiver and John was a tight end. The quarterback was also a junior—a boy named Dan Riley. He wore number 12. Linda had seen him several times around the coaching office, but she had never worked with him. He was apparently a very good student and did not need any tutoring in English. She had the impression that he was very well liked and well respected by his fellow teammates. A good leader, both on and off the field. Supposedly, he too had offers from several Division I teams already.

The whistle sounded and the game began, and it was very clear, right away that this was going to be a completely different game from the earlier games she had attended. In those games, the St. Michael's Warriors had easily had the upper hand. They had led from start to finish, and their victory had never been in doubt. It was going to be a very different story tonight.

The Raiders went on offense first, and they steadily drove down the field, mixing up passing and running plays with ease. The final play of the drive was a quarterback sneak, and their front line crushed forward, opening a relatively easy route to the end zone for their quarterback captain.

St. Michael's then went on offense, and they were able to answer the touchdown, but one of their star running backs got hurt. Neither team scored on their second or third possessions.

Eventually, the Raiders got a field goal. The first half ended with St. Michael's missing a 48-yard field goal attempt, so the Warriors went into their locker room, down 10-7 at the half. As the teams slogged off the field, Linda noticed that their uniforms were covered in mud. Some of the boys had so much mud on them that their numbers were partially obscured. One boy had collapsed on the sidelines and was being administered to by the team doctor and the trainers. Running in mud had exhausted all of the athletes, and they dragged into their respective locker rooms. Most of the boys had their heads down, struggling along. Linda looked for Kelly and John but couldn't really pick them out of the crowd. She had thought that she might go home at halftime, but that was out the window now.

Linda watched the halftime show, amazed that the stands on the visiting team's side were so full. She had not believed that many people would make the trip from California, but it was clear that this was a big-time program. Furthermore, this game had even a larger significance since both teams were ranked in the top ten nationally. That would not be true at the end of the night, because the loser would most certainly drop out of that hallowed status. All around Linda, fans were busy talking about the game. Many of the men in the bleachers were offering their insights as to what Coach Pearson should do to win. Run more. Throw the ball more. Bring in so and so. The conversations swirled around her, and Linda found herself wondering what Coach Pearson and his fellow coaches were saying to the team.

The teams came back out on the field, and a light rain started to fall. People shrugged into ponchos and rain jackets and hunkered down. A few people tried to put up umbrellas, but were asked by others to put them down. No one wanted to miss a moment of the action, and no one was leaving the stadium.

The rain continued and the condition of the field deteriorated even more. Now, patches of grass had been completely torn up by the boys' cleats, and several parts of the field were pure mud. The teams traded touchdowns, with very few mistakes made by either squad. One time, St. Michael's fumbled, and one time Madonna's quarterback threw an interception. Nonetheless, the game came down to the last minute and a half with the score at 17-14, in favor of Madonna. But St. Michael's had the ball on Madonna's 43-yard line and a chance for a big last drive. Their fate was in their own hands. First, they tried a run up the middle. Nothing there. Absolutely nothing. In fact, they lost a yard, and precious seconds ticked off the game clock.

On second down, Dan dropped back into the pocket and launched a ball down the left sideline as Kelly broke free and ran hard down the field. The ball seemed to float in the air, wobbling ever so slightly in the evening breeze. The fans on the St. Michael's side seemed to hold their collective breath as Kelly ran under the ball, his arms outstretched, in perfect position to make the catch, the ball coming over his right shoulder.

And just as it touched his outstretched fingers, the defender for Madonna hit him hard. The ball fell to the ground, incomplete, and Kelly rolled out of bounds, with the defender on top of him. Kelly got up slowly, trudging back to the line of scrimmage. Linda thought she saw him shaking his head slightly, as if trying to clear his vision.

Third down. Still 44 yards to go and the clock showed 24 seconds remaining. One timeout left. Two enemies now— Madonna della Strada and the clock. The center snapped the ball and Dan dropped back to pass, looking for a receiver down the sidelines. But no. Suddenly, he pulled the ball down and started to run up the middle. A quarterback draw! A crazy call with so little time remaining. But he broke free, the Madonna team completely fooled, as he started running for the end zone. All of the fans on the St. Michael's side of the field were on their feet, cheering and screaming, urging him on. Just as it appeared that he might make it, the strong safety appeared out of nowhere, and flew at Dan, flattening him near the end zone. As the players untangled themselves from the pile, two things became clear. The ball was short of the end zone, and Dan was not moving. Players jumped up and immediately started frantically waving to the sidelines for help. Coach Pearson ran out on the field, his clipboard under his arm, followed closely by three assistant coaches. Timeout was called, and once again, everyone in the stadium held their breath. Linda looked around and could see some of the people in the crowd crying, some praying.

His teammates gathered around him, and the coaches used their arms to hold them back. Even the Madonna coaching staff was out on the field. No one was cheering. It was eerily silent in the stadium. And still Dan did not move.

During the game, Linda had noticed an ambulance parked on the field, deep beyond the end zone. She had wondered if that were necessary. Now, she was glad they were there. Quickly, the ambulance crew came trotting out on the field, bearing a stretcher. Four EMT's carefully loaded Dan onto the stretcher, and he still had not moved. A hush fell even deeper over the stadium, everyone straining their eyes to see some movement from the young quarterback. Linda saw Kelly standing close to him. It looked like he was talking to Dan, saying something over and over. The ambulance crew carefully strapped Dan in and removed his helmet. Linda saw Coach Pearson bend close to his young quarterback. It looked like he kissed him on the forehead. Maybe. Maybe not. She couldn't be sure. Then, suddenly, Dan lifted his thumb, giving the universal "thumbs up" sign to the crowd. The fans exploded, cheering, calling out his name, so relieved and so scared—all at once. The ambulance crew loaded him into the back of the truck and drove away into the night, the red lights flashing and the siren wailing.

Suddenly, Linda realized that the game still had not been decided. All the fans on both sides turned their attention back to the field. St. Michael's had the ball. First down. Eight seconds to go. Down by three points. No timeouts. Probably only time for one more play. Their star quarterback out of the game, on the way to the hospital. What to do? On the sidelines, Linda could see the backup quarterback warming up. The coaches stood nearby, their heads together, trying to decide what to do. Kick a short field goal for the tie, or go for the win.

The coaches made their decision. They put in the backup quarterback, deciding to go for the win, against the powerful California team rather than take the unsatisfying tie. During the regular season, if a game ended in a tie—it stayed a tie. No overtimes were allowed. Linda guessed that the coaches had decided that the boys had come too far, put forth too much effort to settle for a no-decision. So, the teams came to the line of scrimmage on the two-yard line. The whistle blew, the quarterback took the snap, turned, and handed the ball off to his star tailback, a senior named Maurice who was a Michigan commit. He headed to his right on a power sweep, feeling for a soft spot in the line as the seconds ticked off. Linda knew that they would get to finish the play, irrespective of the zeroes on the clock. Maurice saw a hole, turned for the end zone, charging forward, his legs churning underneath him. Madonna's defense closed the hole, crushing Maurice, short of the end zone. Victory to Madonna della Strada.

The fans on the St. Michael side of the field were absolutely quiet. A hush fell over the stadium—at least on the St. Michael side. It was as if no one could believe what they had just seen. Victory had been so close—right within their grasp. And the team had played so hard. It felt like no one was even breathing. Then, all of a sudden, several people stood up and started clapping and cheering. Soon, everyone was standing, cheering, whistling, calling out encouragement, honoring the effort given by the team, even in defeat. The team walked off the field to cheers and tears. The fans on the Madonna side were already on their feet, so the whole stadium was cheering, although with wildly different emotions on the two sides of the field. The players for both teams gathered together on their sidelines, and then, with the coaches leading, they walked out to the center of the field to congratulate the other team on a game well played. Every single young man out there was covered in mud. They looked like warriors leaving the field of battle. In a sense, they were. The St. Michael's team then went to the center of the field and knelt to say a prayer, with Coach Pearson leading them. Linda was sure that the prayer included thoughts about their young quarterback who was now at the hospital.

Suddenly, it was over and the stands started to empty. Linda walked out to her car in the faculty lot. Gus was still standing guard. She called a good-night to him and headed home. Traffic was terrible, so it took her longer than she had expected. Hundreds of cars leaving the football stadium and the regular Friday night busy feeling of Fort Lauderdale at the beginning of the tourist season. When she got home, she took a hot shower and went to stand out on her balcony to dry her hair before going to bed. There was a beautiful breeze, so her hair would air-dry quickly, and a full moon had hung itself low over the ocean.

It wasn't its usual distant, cool white. Rather, it was almost gold in color, and it looked huge—like it was somehow closer to the earth tonight. There were whitecaps on the ocean and the moonlight silvered the tops of the waves as they rushed to the shore. Down on the street below, couples walked in the moonlight, holding hands and laughing. Linda wondered if she would ever do that again—walk with a lover in the moonlight after having been out to dinner and having a glass of wine. Sadly, it seemed to her that this experience had somehow slipped away. Moved into the rear-view mirror—at least for her. Apparently not for everyone her age. She had a mental picture of Rick with the buxom young Tiffany, and for just a second, she almost missed him. Then, she shook that feeling off, realizing that she really didn't miss him exactly; she just missed being with a man. Going out to dinner, laughing and talking. Anyhow. Her hair was dry, so she went in, crawled in bed, read her book for a bit and fell asleep.

That weekend, she checked on the kids, having long phone conversations with both of them. Matt was starting to worry about finals—they weren't that far away. Andrea was still considering a radical change of direction in her life, but the bar was busy and she was sort of enjoying the holiday feeling up in Chicago. She said that even though it wasn't actually Thanksgiving yet, the city had decorated the downtown area for the holidays, stringing millions of twinkle lights in the bare branches of the trees down every street in mid-town. They had already had a light snow or two, and it definitely felt like Christmas was coming. At least in Chicago. As they spoke, Linda looked out her windows to see palm trees dancing in the breeze. No snow anywhere in sight. She was still adjusting to the eternal summer of south Florida.

Matt said that he would be coming over for Thanksgiving dinner to her place, but Andrea said that there was no way she could get away. The Wednesday before Thanksgiving was just about the biggest bar drinking night in the whole year, and "Black Friday" was a close second. Her bar was even going to be open on Thanksgiving Day for the people who really didn't have anywhere else to go. Linda reassured her that she understood completely. She was secretly very glad that Matt would be coming over—because she would be one of those people who really didn't have anywhere else to go if he did not.

However, she did not want either of her kids to feel responsible for amusing her or keeping her company. She was a big girl now, and she knew how to take care of herself. Still. If she were going to be entirely honest, the holidays loomed large this year. They were going to be very different. She felt herself starting to dwell on that, and quickly shut it down.

Chapter 19

Next Tuesday rolled around quickly, and she reported to St. Michael's for her tutoring sessions. She got there a few minutes early, and Coach Pearson waved her into his office. He greeted her and asked her to sit down, saying that Mrs. Davidson would be joining them. They needed to talk about Kelly.

Linda said, "Is something wrong?"

He nodded. Clearly, he was really upset. He even seemed to be having trouble speaking. Suddenly, Diane Davidson was there. She walked in the room, walking straight over to Coach Pearson. She pulled him into her arms and gave him a huge hug, saying absolutely nothing. Linda was completely bewildered. She noticed that Coach Pearson had tears in his eyes. Diane backed away from him and came over to Linda. She hugged her too, saying, "You don't know yet, do you?" Linda's heart was racing.

"No. I don't know anything. Will you please tell me what has happened?"

Coach Pearson wiped his eyes, cleared his throat and said, "Kelly has experienced a terrible tragedy this weekend. In fact, we all have." He pulled himself together with an effort. "Kelly has, I mean had, an older brother. Three years older. Played football here too. Name is James. He was Kelly's hero. He had been playing football up at the University of Florida, on a football scholarship." He was overcome with tears again and just sat silently for a minute. Linda knew enough not to say anything, not to try to fill the silence. Diane sat quietly too.

"James got himself kicked off the team last week. He sold his University of Florida jersey and some other equipment. The coach kicked him off. Understandable. James got home last Friday. Came to watch Kelly play against Madonna. Then, things went south in a hurry."

"How?" Linda asked. "What do you mean by went south?"

"Apparently, James got some bad or dirty H. He was down in Miami. Got into one of the clubs. No one here really knows the details, but he overdosed. The paramedics found him outside the club, laying in the street. He was too far gone. They got him to the hospital alive, but he died there. Kelly is missing in action. His poor mom is beside herself. I don't know what to do. We have people looking for him, everywhere we can think of, but we haven't found him yet. All this and his poor mother has to make funeral arrangements." He couldn't speak any more. He had just run out of words, and he was fighting back tears.

Linda sat there, absolutely stunned. She had seen this before. The whole world changes in an instant. It will never be the same. Never. She found tears trickling down her own cheek. "What can I do?"

"Nothing right now. I will keep you posted. John is here for his session, but he is pretty screwed up. I'll send someone else into you for the second hour. I don't know who it will be yet, but it will be a junior, so your preparation will be the same."

Diane said, "Coach, is there anything I can do? Just tell me. Anything."

"Thanks, Diane. I will let you know. You and Linda should stay in touch about his assignments. I don't know how long it will be until we get him back here, but he is going to need a lot of help when we do." Again, he made a visible effort to pull himself together. "Anyhow, thanks for coming in. Both of you."

Before they left, Linda turned and asked, "Sorry to bother you, in a time like this, but—do you know if the quarterback that was taken off the field during the game is all right? Dan?"

Coach Pearson said, "He is mostly all right. He has a concussion and he won't be playing for a few weeks. He will have to clear the concussion protocol. We are keeping an eye on him, but we will be using someone else at that position for a while."

"Okay," Linda said. "Well, thanks for letting me know. I was worried about him."

Diane and Linda got up and walked out together. Linda walked over to the study room and Diane came with her. "What a nightmare," she said. "That poor mother. My heart goes out to her. What terrible suffering." She and Linda just sat down together in silence, neither one of them knowing what to say or what to do. Fifteen minutes went by and no one showed up to be tutored. Linda wondered if she should go looking for John, or just wait.

Suddenly, John came in. As soon as he came in the room, Diane excused herself and left, promising to stay in touch about assignments. John walked in, his face streaked with tears. All of his youth and strength had been broken. He collapsed in the chair and looked at Linda, shaking his head back and forth. He was wearing his varsity jacket, with a big number 87 on it, and patches for previous championships. But he didn't look like a champion right now. He looked lost. Utterly lost. And broken. He slumped forward, putting his arms on the table, and dropping his head in the middle of his arms. And cried.

Linda sat beside him, crying with him. There were no words that would work right now, so she said nothing. They sat there in silence for almost fifteen minutes. Linda decided that she would wait until John was ready to talk.

Quietly, he began to do just that. "Ms. Miller. I don't know what to do. I don't know how to help Kelly or even what to say. He like my brother. And I loved his brother James. Looked up to him. Thought maybe we be teammates someday. And that he be there when I got there. Now, I just don't know about anything." Linda noticed that John had allowed his speaking style to relax. Ordinarily, he spoke almost textbook English, but right now, his words were coming from a different place. Not from any textbook. He looked down at his hands, and Linda realized that he was in his own world, and for all intents and purposes, she wasn't even there. He was looking at the abyss, and it was there, and he knew it. She was almost afraid to speak.

"Have you seen Kelly?"

"Nope. And he ain't answerin' his phone. No text. No nothin'. Like a black hole. I don't know what to do."

"Neither do I," Linda admitted. "Neither do I." She waited another couple minutes and then said. "We better look at your homework. Show me your assignments for the week. If you fall further behind, you will be in even worse shape than you feel right now."

John looked at her, his eyes almost black pools of pain. Bottomless pools of darkness. He really didn't care about his assignments, but he was too polite to say that. So, he opened his Chromebook and found the assignments for the week. They were supposed to read a poem by Robert Hayden and write a short paragraph about who the speaker was and what conflicting emotions he was trying to describe in the poem.

Linda knew the poem and was almost afraid to explore it with John, with his emotions so fragile. It was a poem about a father and son, and love unspoken. It seemed like almost a dangerous topic to explore right now. She realized that Diane Davidson had made her lesson plans long ago, never expecting that her students would be dealing with this kind of loss at this moment in their young lives. But still.

She knew that Kelly's father had died of cancer, several years back, and that Kelly's mom was raising her sons by herself, but she wasn't sure about John's situation at home. There was nothing to do but plunge on and hope for the best. She opened the lit book to the right page and read to John, who sat quietly beside her. She wasn't even sure if he was really listening:

Those Winter Sundays

Sundays too my father got up early
And put on his clothes in the blueblack cold,
Then with cracked hands that ached
From labor in the weekday weather made
Banked fires blaze. No one ever thanked him.

I'd wake and hear the cold splintering, breaking,
When the rooms were warm, he'd call
And slowly I would rise and dress,
Fearing the chronic angers of that house.

Speaking indifferently to him,
Who had driven out the cold
And polished my good shoes as well.
What did I know, what did I know
Of love's austere and lonely offices?

The poem done, Linda let the words hang in the air, saying nothing, waiting for John to speak. At first, she wasn't sure that he had been listening, that he had any idea what was going on. But she was wrong.

John's voice seemed to come from far away, as though he were almost in a dream state. His eyes were open, but he wasn't looking at anything. He was staring at the wall across the room, but she knew that he wasn't looking at it. His was an interior landscape at this moment. At first, Linda thought that he was not going to answer the question about the poem, that he was not even connected to the assignment. But she was wrong about that, too.

"My father comes to all my games. Always. All my life. Still does. Never misses a game. He was my first coach, too." He spoke without looking at Linda, his eyes down, his hands folded in his lap, in his own mind and memories. "Sometimes, we had trouble payin' for my new cleats. My feet got big fast. He always came up with the money, but he did it by not getting new stuff for himself. I saw him wear the same pair of pants for years. They had little holes in the back pocket, where his wallet pressed against them. He never complained."

He seemed to have run out of steam, and just sat there, still not looking at Linda. It was like she wasn't even in the room. She didn't know if she should speak or be quiet and wait. She waited. John was far away, looking at a memory.

"I'm not sure if I ever said thank you. I think I did when I was younger. Maybe not so much now. Maybe I been too full of myself to see what he still doing for me. And for Mom. And my little brother. Me, the big man on campus, and all that." He looked at Linda now. "I'm gonna go to college. My dad never had that chance. And he the smartest man I know. He can fix anything. Any broken thing." He looked at the poem written on the page, tears gathering in his eyes. "But he can't fix this. No one can." Linda realized that John had made a leap in his thoughts. She sat quietly and looked at him, filled with wonder. And with sadness.

Finally, she spoke. "I think you understand this poem perfectly. You have done a wonderful job, not only with understanding it, but also with linking it to your own life. And learning from what the poet, Robert Hayden, had to say. Here's paper and pen. Could you take the last ten minutes of our hour together and just write down what you've said? Just the way you said it to me right now. It was perfect."

"I don't know if I can write right now."

"You can. You have to. Do it for Kelly. Do it for your father. Do it for James. Don't worry about if it's eloquent, or perfect. Just get the ideas down. Mrs. Davidson will be so proud of you. I already am." She handed him a sheet of notebook paper and a pen. He sat quietly and wrote, and then the hour was up, and he got ready to head out to the practice field.

Linda rose to her feet as he stood up to leave, and he reached out and hugged her. It caught Linda off-guard. She wasn't sure if there were rules about this, but it didn't seem like a time for rules anyhow. She hugged him back, and then he grabbed up his books and his laptop and left. Another young man came in, introduced himself as Mike Nealy and asked for help with a grammar assignment. He had a different teacher than John and Kelly.

Linda got him through the assignment, and suddenly it was 5:00. Quitting time. She sent Mike out to practice and gathered up her stuff. She decided to walk by the football field on her way out and see how the boys were doing. When she got the fence, Coach Pearson saw her and waved her over. He looked terrible—like the weight of the world was on his shoulders. His eyes had dark circles under them.

"I just found out that the funeral Mass for James will be this Friday. I am hoping that you will be there. Visitation will be Thursday night and it would be great if you could drop by. Just to show Kelly that you care. I will give you all the information when you come in for your Thursday sessions."

"I will be there, of course," Linda said. "Thank you for thinking of me. Have you talked to Kelly? Do you know how he is doing?" She didn't know what to say, but she felt she had to say something.

"No. I talked to his mom, and she's a mess. Kelly wouldn't come to the phone. She said he was in his room and she was letting him be. I think I might drive over there tonight and see if I can see him." He shook his head, not meeting her eyes. His eyes were staring out over the field, but Linda felt pretty certain that he wasn't seeing that either. He was staring that 1,000- yard stare of grief. She knew the look.

"Okay. Well, thank you. If you do see him, please tell him that I am keeping him and his mom in my prayers. And I am," she added. He nodded and went back to the middle of the field. She wondered what he had said to the boys. What could you say?

Chapter 20

Linda went to the visitation on Thursday night, but she couldn't get anywhere near Kelly. She could see him in the reception line, standing next to his mother, who was absolutely doubled over in grief. She was a petite woman, her head only coming up to Kelly's shoulder, and she literally seemed to be having trouble even standing. Kelly stood on one side of her, and the Mom's sister stood on the other. Kelly's mom had her arms through theirs, and Linda thought that they were probably holding her up. At one moment, she thought that Kelly saw her across the crowded room, but she couldn't be sure. There were hundreds of people there, milling around, crying, speaking the words we say in grief.

Linda signed the visitors' book and slipped out, making room for others to come and pay their respects. The room was practically drowning in roses and elaborate bouquets of flowers, their aroma hanging in the air like a pall. Linda found her car in the parking lot and backed out. There were several cars looking for a place to park, and her spot was quickly taken. As she drove away, she found that her heart was focusing not so much on

Kelly as on his mom. That poor woman's face was etched into her very soul. The funeral tomorrow would be unbearable. Absolutely not humanly bearable. She resolved to pray for that woman tonight before she fell asleep—pray that God would send her graces to somehow just survive the day.

When she got home, she took a long hot shower, but nothing could wash that sorrow away. As she settled in with her book, her cell phone rang, and she saw that it was Carly. Hoping that nothing was wrong, she quickly picked it up.

"Are you all right?" were the first words out of her mouth.

Carly laughed, "What a thing to say! Yes. I'm fine. I'm better than all right. Are *you* all right?"

"No," Linda replied. "I'm actually terrible. One of my students that I tutor—a young man I really like—his older brother, whom he idolized, just got kicked out of college, lost his scholarship, came home to Miami, got some bad heroin, overdosed, and died. It's just heartbreaking. Such a waste. I am just heartsick, Carly." She caught her breath and realized that she sounded frantic. At the breaking point. She pulled herself together and added, "I'm sorry to dump all of that on you. You said that you were better than all right. What does that mean?"

"Oh, honey," Carly said. "I'm so sorry. I don't even know what to say. And here I am calling you with happy news. I almost feel bad about telling you now."

"Don't be stupid," Linda said. "What news? Honestly, I could use some happy news right now."

"Well," Carly said, drawing it out. "I'm in love. And I'm engaged! I'm going to get married, Linda. I never thought I would, but I am going to get married!" Excitement and joy spilled into her voice. Linda had never heard her sound so happy.

"You are? Oh, Carly. That's just wonderful. I honestly can't believe it. You said that you would never get married, that you were going to stay single all your life. Who is the guy that changed your mind? Is it anyone I know?"

"No," Carly answered. "Honestly, I still can't believe it myself. His name is Tyler Henry. He works for another firm up here. I argued a case against him about two months ago, and all through the trial, I couldn't take my eyes off of him. The way he wears his suit, the way he walks, the way his hair falls in his eyes sometimes, the way he grins—this lopsided grin, his blue eyes. All of it. I am absolutely smitten. Sometimes, I even had trouble keeping my mind on the issues and the arguments. I am pretty sure that I made a fool of myself a couple of times. And I know he caught me grinning at him, and I caught him smiling at me. And—long story short, we started seeing each other. We've been together almost every night for about two months, and I moved in with him last weekend." She was almost breathless.

Linda said cautiously, "Are you sure you're not moving too fast? This all sounds pretty sudden." She felt a little bit bad about saying this, but she sort of felt like she had to.

"I know," Carly admitted. "It seems completely unlike me. But, I'm in love for the first time in my life. I've never felt like this before. And here's where you come in. We're going to the Keys over Thanksgiving, for a little getaway. But, we're going to fly in to Fort Lauderdale and then drive down to Key West. I want you to meet him. It's really important to me. So, is it okay if Tyler and I join you for Thanksgiving dinner? We'll stay at the Marriott right across the street from your condo, have turkey dinner with you, and then be on our way south after dinner. Does that work for you?"

"Yes, of course," Linda said quickly. "That's wonderful. Matt's coming for dinner, so you will be able to see him too. I'm so happy for you, my darling. I honestly never thought I'd see the day that you got married." And that was true. Both parts of it.

"I know. I know. Crazy stuff. Life has a way of surprising us. You know that old saying—Man plans and God laughs. Woman too, apparently. I guess I'm living proof of it."

"So, I'll see you next week?" Linda said.

"Yes. I will keep you posted on our flight plans and everything. And I'm so sorry about your student, Linda. What a terrible thing."

"It is, but that makes your news all the more welcome. I will see you next week then," she added and said her good-nights.

As she crawled into bed, she thought about life. How big it is. How unpredictable. She remembered learning about Nietzsche and Schopenhauer, and their theory that each of us is in his or her own boat. And we are all being swept along on some primordial sea, to some destination we cannot see. And even though we are all on the same sea, the water can be very different for all of us at any given moment. One of us can be in the warm, shallow, sun-dappled waters close to shore, and another one of us can be out in the grasp of violent waves that are threatening to overturn our fragile little craft. And no matter how much we want to help each other, we cannot crawl into someone else's boat. We can, however, reach out to one another, reaching over the dangerous and unpredictable water. We can, at least for a moment, touch each other's hands. And that moment—the moment of shared understanding—is sacred. And so it is.

   She realized that she was living the truth of their allegory right now. She had seen the bottomless sorrow and loss in Kelly's mother's eyes, and she had heard the bubbling-over joy in her sister's voice, describing her new-found love. All within the space of a few minutes, an hour or so. Kelly's mom in the dangerous seas, and Carly in the smiling, sun-dappled waters. She closed her eyes and prayed for both of them. And for Kelly. Poor lost Kelly.

Chapter 21

The next day was the funeral Mass. The priest who was the principal at the school said the Mass, and he did a good job trying to comfort the family and friends of James. But the truth is—nothing helps at moments like this. The loss is just too overwhelming. Linda saw Kelly sitting in the front row with his mom, but she never caught his eye. Coach Pearson gave the eulogy, talking about what a hard worker James was, both on and off the field. How he was such a leader in the locker room, how he was honored to have known him and worked with him. He told the congregation that a scholarship program was being started in James's name and explained that an award would be given in his name every year going forward—an award to the hardest working player on the team. How there was going to be a game this season where they would honor James at halftime and talk about what he meant to the program. How he was going to miss him.

The church was filled with mourners who were sitting quietly, reverently, tears streaming down their faces. Linda had never even known this young man, but she knew Kelly, and she felt that, by extension, she knew James. She felt the loss deep in her soul, in a place beyond the reach of words.

Somehow, they got through the Mass, and then there was going to be the procession to the cemetery. Linda did not think she should go; she thought maybe it would be a time for intimate friends and family. She watched Kelly escort his mom from the church, and once again, it seemed as if he were holding her erect—that she could not even stand on her own. As he walked his mom down the aisle, Linda looked hard at his face. It seemed that he had aged ten years since last Thursday's tutoring session—before the world as they knew it ended for Kelly and his mom. She realized that she was in the presence of something sacred—a sorrow so profound that it was the deepest essence of what it is to be human and to love. She bowed her head as Kelly and his mom walked by, tears streaming down her face as well. The organist played one of her favorite hymn, "On Eagle's Wings." As she listened to the music and the words, Linda prayed that James was already in heaven. That he had been lifted there on eagle's wings.

As Linda pulled out of the church parking lot, she saw Coach Pearson talking with some of the assistant coaches, and she suddenly remembered that they had a game tonight. An away game against a local high school. It was not supposed to be a very good game; most people thought that St. Michael's would crush them. But—could they even focus now? The whole team had been at the funeral Mass, wearing their jerseys in honor of James. Could they somehow get their heads back in the game and play tonight? Linda cared, but at the same time, she realized that she was just too tired, too emotionally spent, to go. She headed home, stopping at the grocery store to get something for dinner. Something she didn't have to cook or even think about.

When she got back to her place, she put her bathing suit on and went down to the pool. It was early Friday afternoon, and most people were still at work, so she had the whole pool to herself. She swam laps until she couldn't lift her arms anymore, and as she swam, she prayed for Kelly and his mom. The sunlight sparkled on the water, making ever-changing light patterns that danced in the blue. By some weird alchemy—the water, the sunlight dancing, the sound of her breathing, the quiet—she felt blessed with a quiet sense of grace. A sense that James was all right. She didn't know why she felt that way, but suddenly, she did. She knew that he was all right, and she knew that she had to let Kelly know. Someday.

But Kelly did not show up for school on Tuesday, and suddenly, it was Thanksgiving week. There was no school on the Wednesday before Thanksgiving, so the kids had five days off. There would be a football game on Friday after Thanksgiving, but Linda thought that she might skip that one, particularly if Matt stayed the night. He had called to tell her that he would be over Thursday morning. Andrea and Tyler were arriving late Wednesday night, and they were going to have dinner with Linda on Thanksgiving.

She suddenly realized that she had better go shopping and get herself ready to cook a Thanksgiving feast. Having eaten most of her meals alone lately, this was a welcome diversion. She got out her cookbook and made a list of all the things she needed and then headed to the grocery store, where every other woman in Fort Lauderdale was doing the very same thing. She felt very lucky to find a turkey that was already thawed since she had been so preoccupied that she had not been thinking about that. She got the fixings for dressing, mashed potatoes, sweet potatoes, and salad. She thought that she should get a nice French baguette, and she realized that she had not been to her favorite French bakery in way too long. So, she stopped there on the way home, finding the last parking spot available. As she entered the bakery, the warm, salty smell of freshly baked bread wafted over her, and it smelled like an embrace. Like a welcome home.

She got in line, with about four other women in front of her. She looked behind the counter to see if there was much bread left. Back in the kitchen, the two handsome young bakers were frantically pulling more loaves out of the oven. They had smears of flour on their faces and in their hair, and they looked like an advertisement for Paris. Dark hair, twinkling eyes, flour on their aprons, big smiles. She grinned at them, and one of them waved, seeming to remember her.

Michel was at the counter, and Marie was frantically working to package up bread and rolls. Both of them smiled at her and seemed genuinely happy to see her, but they were both so busy that there was clearly no time for idle chatter. She paid for her baguettes and went on her way, struck once again by how handsome Michel was. She wondered, in passing, if she saw a kind of sadness in his eyes. However, it was entirely possible that he was just exhausted. The whole family was working very hard in there, the ovens roaring in the background.

She got home and assembled all the ingredients to make a pumpkin pie, and soon the apartment took on that wonderful, spicy smell of the holidays. Her turkey was still thawing in the sink, her pie was in the oven, and there was a moment of calm. She wandered out on the balcony and watched the afternoon settle in. Thinking that maybe she could give Andrea a call before the madness of the big drinking night got started up there in Chicago, she grabbed her phone and called, while standing out on the balcony in the early evening breeze.

Andrea answered at once. Breathlessly. "Mom. How are you? Is everything all right?"

"Yes, darling," Linda reassured her. "I just wanted to catch you, to hear your voice before your big night started."

"Well, Mom, you're a little late for that. I would say that the night has started here already. In fact, it started about noon. The drinking lamp has officially been lit, and I am already scrambling. But it sure is good to hear your voice."

"Wow," Linda said. "It's not even five o'clock yet. You had an early lamp-lighting ceremony, that's for sure. Is it crowded there already?"

Andrea laughed. "I don't think there's an empty chair in the house, not at the bar and not on the floor. Is Matt coming to your place for dinner tomorrow? Is that right?"

"Yes," Linda said. "He is. And so are Carly and her fiancé, Tyler. They get in late tonight and are staying at the Marriott down the street. They're going to have dinner with me tomorrow and then head down to the Keys for a couple of days. So, I will have a full house tomorrow. I only wish you could be here."

"Believe me, Mom. So do I. But I am going to be very busy tonight and tomorrow. However, I can already tell that I am going to make a lot of money tonight. That's for sure. How is the French baker, by the way?"

"I really don't know. I stopped in to buy a couple of baguettes today, but the place was so busy that I didn't even really get a chance to talk to him. But he smiled at me when I checked out. Although—it's funny—I thought I saw a kind of sadness in his smile. But I might have been just imagining it. Anyhow. Happy Thanksgiving, my darling girl. Take care of yourself. Where are you having dinner tomorrow?"

"Oh, a bunch of us are getting together for a "Friendsgiving"—I think that's what they call it. I have been assigned the task of bringing some good wine. I think they were playing to my strengths and avoiding my weaknesses—like cooking. So, don't worry. I will have a turkey dinner. Anyhow, I've got to go. Things are getting away from me here. Love you, Mom."

"Love you, honey. Be careful."

Linda hung up and set her phone down on the chair. She stood at the railing and closed her eyes, letting the wind caress her face and her hair. She let her mind drift back over memories of earlier Thanksgivings—the cooking of the big turkey, her mom and dad coming over, the kids watching the parades, her dad watching the football games. The kids pouring through the sales flyers that had come in the mail, starting their Christmas lists.

And Rick sitting in the living room with her dad, the two of them talking football and drinking bourbon together. A fire in the fireplace. And all the dishes!

The memory filled her heart, and, for a moment, she thought that maybe she missed Rick. She thought about that and realized that maybe what she really missed was being married. And having the kids be little—when their problems were small and their desires were only as complicated as a new video game or a new sweater. But those days were gone. She thought about that famous old saying. Heraclitus, was it? You can't step in the same river twice. Well, it was true. You can't go back in time. Once the river moves on, it will never be the same. You just have to hold those thoughts in a special place in your heart—so that you can access them when you need to. But you have to look forward. You have to keep your eyes on the far horizon, because otherwise, you will have wasted your chance to do something good with the time you have. So, she went into the house, poured a glass of wine, checked on the pie, and then came back out to the balcony. She sat down, sipped her wine, closed her eyes, and let the wind blow on her face. Let the river flow.

Chapter 22

Carly texted her at midnight to let her know that she was safely in town. She said that she would be over by two in the afternoon on Thanksgiving. Matt texted to say that he would arrive at about the same time. Linda got up early in the morning to get her preparations underway. She set the table with her best linens and china, polished her crystal stemware, and set out candles. Then, she started a pot of coffee and got busy with the turkey and the stuffing. Just for old time's sake, she turned on the television to sort of watch the Macy's Thanksgiving parade and the Detroit parade. As she looked at the screen, she realized that she didn't really know the hosts of the parades. Time had passed her by, and she didn't even really know who these people were. That damn river. It never stops flowing.

But the marching bands were essentially the same, and the floats looked very familiar. She smiled at some of the floats that she remembered from when the kids were little. As she busied herself around the kitchen, the place started to smell wonderful. With everything under control in the kitchen, she allowed herself time to take a quick shower and put something nice on.

Before she knew it, it was almost two o'clock, and Matt arrived. Clarence, who is usually the evening attendant on the desk, called up to announce his arrival, and Linda went to the door to greet him.

He came in, looking only slightly disheveled, carrying a big laundry basket, with a bottle of wine balanced on the top. He set the basket down, grinned at her, and gave her a big hug.

Linda laughed. "I see you brought me a present," nodding at the laundry.

"I know, Mom, I'm sorry. But it would be such a big help to me," he smiled sheepishly.

"Take it into the laundry room and get it started," Linda said. "Or better yet, why don't I start it and you open this lovely bottle of wine and pour us both a glass."

"Deal," he said. "But let me carry it back there for you. And thank you so much, Mom. I really appreciate it. By the way, you look great," he added.

"Thank you, my darling. I don't know what makes me look great today, but I am not going to question your pronouncement."

She got his laundry started and joined him back in the kitchen, where he was pouring both of them a glass of wine. "The turkey smells great, Mom. I haven't eaten real food in a long time." He was prowling around the kitchen, looking for something to eat.

"You look thin," Linda said. She realized, even as she said it, that moms always say stuff like that. He laughed, probably realizing the same thing.

"Well, not super thin," he added. "But I have been almost too busy to eat sometimes. Semester exams are right around the corner, and I got a job clerking for a judge down in Miami. Only about ten hours a week, but it's some spending money and even better connections. It will look good on my resume, when it's time to start looking for a real job." He sat down at the kitchen table, ready to nibble on something.

"Does this mean that you got over the jitters?" Linda asked, putting out a platter of crackers and cheese. "Last time you were here you were telling me about some doubts you were having."

"I think it was just a fleeting panic. I guess everyone my age has that moment when they suddenly realize that they are not going to see the whole world, go backpacking in Europe, join the Peace Corps, and write the great American novel. But I'm okay with that now."

"What changed your mind?"

"Well, Mom, I'm so excited to tell you. I met someone." There was a happy twinkle in his eye. He had purposely understated it, wanting to surprise her.

Linda gasped. "What? You met someone? Who? Where? When? Why didn't you tell me? Does Andrea know?" She felt like she could hardly stand up. Matt laughed and led her over to the couch, bringing her the glass of wine.

"Here, sit down before you fall down, and I will answer all your questions." He joined her on the couch. "Her name is Lucia Fernandez, but everyone calls her Lucy. She goes to school with me. We met in a tax law class. I told Andrea yesterday, but I made her swear that she wouldn't tell you because I wanted to tell you myself today." His eyes twinkled merrily. "I think she might be the one, Mom. She's smart and pretty. She's hard-working and kind. In fact, she's a lot like you."

"Well, where is she? Why didn't you invite her to come with you today?"

"She went to her mom and dad's. She has a big, extended family, all of whom live in Miami. I met them a couple weeks ago, and they are actually a little overwhelming. I think I passed muster, but Lucy has three brothers, and they were none too certain about me at first."

"Nonsense," Linda said. "You're quite a catch for any woman." She felt a little miffed that she was, apparently, the last one to know that any of this was going on. Andrea knew, and they had talked last night, and she hadn't hinted at anything at all. And Lucy's family knew. "Well, when can I meet her?"

"It's a crazy time for us right now. Finals are in two weeks. I'm even taking a leave of absence from my clerking job for the next couple weeks until I make it through exams. But as soon as they're over, Lucy and I will get up here and spend an evening with you. It won't be long." He gave her a big hug. "You're going to love her, Mom. I just know it."

He was kneeling on the floor in front of her. She stood up and he rose with her. He was so much taller than she was. He took her in his arms and wrapped his long arms all around her. She buried her face in his chest and wondered how he had grown so tall. In her heart, she still thought of him as about five years old. But that was long ago. "I'm so happy for you, my darling.

What a wonderful bit of news. I can't wait to meet her. What did Andrea have to say?"

"Well, I think that she and Patrick might be getting kind of serious up in Chicago. He is a lawyer there, and I gather, a rather frequent visitor to the bar, especially when Andrea is running the place. I haven't met him yet, but she seems to really like him."

"Wow. That is very interesting. I didn't really think that they were serious at all. I will have to ask her about that. She's been pretty cagey in her conversations with me lately. I had the feeling that she wasn't telling me something, but I couldn't imagine what it could be. And I knew that I would have to wait until she was ready to say something."

"I think she's getting ready to tell you, Mom, but I think she didn't want to spoil my little announcement."

"Announcement? Is there something you want to tell me, Matt?"

"No. Not yet. I want you to meet Lucy first. But, just between you and me, I think I'm going to ask this girl to marry me. Someday soon."

"Oh, honey, that's wonderful. But don't move too fast."

"Don't worry, Mom. I won't. But I just wanted you to know that I'm moving in that direction. So, when you meet her, you can realize where I'm coming from."

The phone rang, and Clarence said that Carly and Tyler were here. Linda thanked him and asked him to send them up. She asked Clarence if he might like a little plate of turkey dinner when she had it ready, and he said that that would be wonderful.

She promised that she would send Matt down with a plate when dinner was ready.

Then, she gave Matt a big hug and told him again how happy she was for him. She told him that Carly and her fiancé were on their way up. As she said that, she realized that three very important people in her life had all fallen in love: Carly and Tyler, Andrea and Patrick, Matt and Lucy. Love. Serious love. The "getting married" kind of love. A tiny little twinge of jealousy floated through the river—she couldn't help but wonder if that river held anything for her. After all, you can't step in the same river twice. Damn you, Heraclitus.

Soon, the front door exploded and in came Carly and Tyler. Carly practically jumped into Linda's arms, covering her with kisses and squealing with delight. Then, she noticed Matt standing quietly over by the window wall, immediately abandoned Linda, and ran into his arms.

"Matt," she cried. "You are about four inches taller than when I saw you a couple months ago! What are they feeding you down there?"

"Laws. Constitutional, tax, criminal, and intellectual properties," Matt growled. He held Carly tight in his long arms and she squealed with delight.

"I'm so proud of you," she said, disengaging. "This is my fiancé Tyler." With all the commotion, Linda hadn't properly greeted Tyler. Now, she turned her attention to him. He was not quite six feet tall, and he had a muscular build. He looked like he might have played a little football in high school, but was certainly not big enough to play at the university level. He had thick, dark hair that was a little bit curly, and dark brown eyes that spoke of laughter, and a warm, easy smile.

Linda walked over to him and put out her hand. Instead, he took her in his arms and hugged her. It all seemed so natural to him, and Linda found herself instantly warming to his easy manner. "I'm so happy to finally meet you," he said, still hugging her. "Carly has told me so much about you that I feel like we've been friends for years. She says you are the bravest and smartest woman in the world. But she didn't quite prepare me for the fact that you are also very beautiful."

She smiled at him and looked at Carly, "You told me he was full of life and mischief. You didn't let me know that he was such a smooth talker."

Carly laughed and said, "Oh, I knew you'd figure that out pretty quickly. Man, it's so good to see you, sis. The place looks great. You've really settled in here and made it so much more comfortable. I love it. Come here, Tyler. Let me show you the best part."

She led Tyler out to the balcony, and they all followed. The sun was already on its downward arc in the sky, sparkling millions of diamonds on the ocean. The breeze was steady and warm, but with a little edge of coolness to it. A flock of seagulls flew overhead, yawping in the sky. Below, on A1A, a stream of cars headed south. People were out walking, laughing in the afternoon. Tyler was flabbergasted.

"Wow," he said. "I can't believe how spectacular this is. Carly, I think we should move down here. We're both lawyers. We could find work down here. I bet they need lawyers here too." He grinned at her playfully. She put her arm around his waist and smiled back at him.

"Man, that would be great. And when Matt gets his degree, we could open a law practice together."

"Sounds good to me," Matt chimed in. "The idea of interviewing and looking for a job sort of intimidates me. This sounds like a very good plan."

They headed into the apartment, which now smelled absolutely heavenly. The turkey was nearly done, the potatoes were about to boil, and the pie sat on the counter waiting for their attention. Carly had on jeans and a simple white shirt, but they fit her so well that Linda could tell that they were probably an expensive version of the old favorites. She told Carly that she looked good, and Carly laughed, saying that love had improved her. She opened a bottle of very nice Chardonnay and poured them both a glass. The men got beers out of the refrigerator and turned on the football game. The Detroit Lions were winning, miracle of miracles. Could it last? It turned out that they both knew quite a bit about football and about the Lions' chances, so their conversation bubbled easily in the background.

Carly turned her attention to Linda. "How are you doing? You told me about the young man whose brother died. I am so sorry. How are you handling it? How is he doing?" She took a sip of her wine and held Linda's eyes with her own. Linda found herself struggling to find the right words—the words that would convey the depth of the loss that Kelly had suffered.

"Actually, I'm just heartsick. I went to the funeral last Friday, and I can't get his mother's face out of my mind. I looked in her eyes and saw bottomless sorrow. She's been so brave, raising those two boys by herself, and James was on his way. At the University of Florida, maybe even with a chance of being drafted to play in the NFL, and now, everything has changed. I didn't know James, but I have come to know Kelly, and he just idolized his brother. I haven't seen Kelly since the funeral, and there, I only saw him from a distance. I don't know what's going to happen, but I'm scared for him."

Carly took a long, deep drink of the wine and looked hard at her sister. "You have really become involved in this program. You know, they're not paying you that much money. If it's taking too big a toll on you emotionally, you don't have to do it, you know. If money is tight, I would gladly send you some every—"

"Stop right there. I was doing it for the money in the beginning. I'll admit that," Linda said, while chopping lettuce for the salad. Carly leaned on the counter, drinking her glass of wine, looking at her meditatively. She said nothing, waiting for Linda to explain.

One of the really good things about Carly is that she was a true active listener. When you were talking about something important, she focused her whole attention on you. This was one of those times. "But, it's not about the money any more. I've met some really nice people through the school. The department head—Diane Davidson—is one of them. And I like Coach Pearson and I respect what he's doing."

"Still," said Carly. "They're not paying you enough for it—"

"Hear me out," said Linda. "I work primarily with these two young men—Kelly Dunn and John White. Both of them are juniors, and they're in the same class. American Lit. And I know all that stuff since I taught it for 30 years. So, there's no preparation. And no papers to grade. But, I know I'm making a difference in the lives of these young men. I care about them, and they are always glad to see me. So, that means that when something bad happens to one of them, it is going to affect me. That's all there is to it. And I'm willing to be that involved with their lives."

Carly stared at her. "This isn't one of those movie scripts in the making. Like that movie Sandra Bullock was in—what was that called? Oh, yeah. *The Blind Side.* You're not having a fantasy that one of these guys is going to make it into the NFL and become a millionaire, are you?"

Linda guffawed. She threw a dish towel at Carly, laughing. "Honestly, that never occurred to me, and I don't think that kind of stuff ever really happens. These kids are just trying to win a scholarship to play at the university level. It would mean a lot to their families financially." She put oven mitts on and pulled the turkey out of the oven. "Now, help me get these dishes to the table and get the men to sit down."

"You got it," said Carly. "Anyhow, just let me know if it gets to be too much for you. I'm always here for you." She turned her attention to the men who were busily shouting at the football game, arguing over a disputed call.

The dining room was open to the living room, so the men asked if they could leave the game on during dinner. Linda and Carly agreed—it was Thanksgiving after all—and the dinner was a huge success. Evening came on, and Carly and Tyler got ready to go. They were going to drive down to the Keys and check in to their hotel so they could wake up on the beach in the morning. Before she left, Carly hugged Linda and reminded her not to get too strung out by what had happened to Kelly. Linda promised to stay in touch and they went over their plans to be together for Christmas.

"We will gladly fly down here," Carly said. "We may have to have Christmas day with Tyler's family, but I will be down here right after that. I will need another dose of Fort Lauderdale sun by then. When I get the arrangements all settled, I will let you know what's going on."

"That would be so great," said Linda, hugging her goodbye.

She reached out to hug Tyler goodbye, and he grabbed her and pulled her tight. "Thank you for an absolutely perfect Thanksgiving dinner," he said. "Wonderful food, charming company, and football. I am a very happy man." He and Carly headed for the door.

"Have fun in the Keys, you crazy kids," Linda called as they got in the elevator.

Matt was gathering up his stuff, getting ready to go too. "I'm heading out, Mom. I've got studying to do, and a brief to write. But first, let me take the garbage out for you."

He took the trash out to the trash chute while Linda found her purse. She pulled out three twenty dollar bills and pressed them into his hand when he came back. "Buy yourself a treat," she said.

"No, Mom," he said. "Not necessary. I thought I overheard you and Aunt Carly talking about money, like it might be tight for you?"

"She's wrong. It's not tight. I'm making an extra couple hundred dollars a week from my tutoring, and my pension and investments cover my monthly expenses. Please. Get yourself a little treat. Or a nice coffee in the morning." He pulled her into his arms and hugged her hard. She hugged him back. Knowing that he had to go.

"I'm really proud of you, Mom. A lesser woman might be whining about her situation, bemoaning her losses. But you just dive in, involve yourself in life, and keep pressing forward. I think it's really cool, and I think those two young men are really lucky to have you in their corner. Thanks for a wonderful day. I love you so much. Happy Thanksgiving." He kissed her on the forehead and headed for the door.

"Happy Thanksgiving, my darling. Please keep in touch. I can't wait to meet Lucy. I know you're coming up on finals, and that will be a pressure-packed time for you. If there's anything I can do, let me know. Or just bring me your laundry. You can sit on the balcony and study while I do it for you."

"You're the best, Mom. Thank you again for a wonderful day." He stuffed the twenties in his jeans pocket, hugged her one more time, grabbed his laundry basket and took off. She went out of the balcony and watched for his car to go by, and then she went back into her apartment. Night had fallen. The TV was still on, and another football game was going on. She collapsed on the couch and let the play-by-play announcer's voice wash over her. Before she knew it, she started to doze off. So, she turned the television off, took one last look around the kitchen to make sure she had cleaned everything up, blew out the candles and climbed into bed. She had survived Thanksgiving. Her first one without Rick. And the funny thing was, she hadn't really thought about him at all. Maybe she was going to be all right. Maybe.

Chapter 23

She woke up to the sun streaming in and the sudden awareness that it was Black Friday, the most important shopping day of the year. She remembered that when she was young, she and her mom used to go out together, starting the shopping day at 6:00 a.m. There were a few stores that opened that early, and they had crazy door-buster specials, usually on toys that the kids wanted. So, she and her mom braved the darkness and the cold mornings up in Michigan to get out there with all the other crazy women who were doing the same thing. Now, she looked back on those morning trips with a bittersweet nostalgia. She missed her mom most powerfully around the holidays, although there was always an emptiness in her life. She remembered talking to her doctor one time, in the midst of her grief. She hadn't been able to eat or sleep normally and felt all screwed up. She remembered asking him when the ache would go away, and he wisely answered, "Never. You are forever changed. There will always be an emptiness in you now. You will learn to carry it better as time goes on, but your world has changed once and for all." She had not expected that answer, and the brutal honesty of it had caught her off guard. However, she had since learned that he was right.

Anyhow, those days were gone. She looked at the morning paper online (even that had changed from the good, old days of paper newspapers!) and scanned the ads for the Black Friday specials. There wasn't really anything she needed. Both Andrea and Matt would have very specific requests—usually one rather expensive thing—and they had not as yet told her what they wanted. Still, she wanted to make the scene, just for old time's sake. On a whim, she called Diane Davidson to see if she wanted to head out to the stores, just for the fun of it. Diane readily agreed, and they met at the Galleria Mall in the food court.

They walked up and down the mall, watching all the young moms dragging their kids around, getting in line to see Santa. They each shared horror stories about trying to get their kids to smile for their Santa pictures long ago, and having walked the whole mall, decided that a nice lunch was in order.

They picked the best restaurant in the place, ordered a glass of wine and some fancy salads and settled in for a talk. Linda found herself enjoying Diane's company, and the easy way she had about her. Like her, she had two children who were all grown up. However, unlike her, she and her husband were still happily married. Soon, the conversation turned to Kelly, one concern they shared.

"Have you seen him since his brother died?" Linda asked.

"Not once. He missed the whole week of school after it happened. And then he missed the next two days too—Monday and Tuesday of this week. Actually, that's not terrible, because

210

nothing much was accomplished on those days. But I have not heard anything from Coach Pearson as to how he is doing or when he's coming back. I heard that he was not at last Friday's game either. I tried to talk to John White about him, but he didn't seem to know anything. What have you heard?"

"Nothing at all," said Linda. "But, of course, you would be much more likely to hear things than I. I only see him twice a week, and only for an hour. I hope someone at the school is reaching out to him. Don't they have a game tonight, too?"

"You're right, they do. It's not against a very good team, but it's getting to that part of the season where every game counts. I think the playoffs start next week."

"You're right. They do," Linda agreed. "I remember hearing that." She took a long drink of her wine. It was funny to be drinking wine at one in the afternoon, but it actually seemed to be a nice treat, and she was grateful to Diane for making the whole thing possible. Having someone to talk to, and somewhere to be.

They finished their salads and split the bill. When they left the restaurant, the mall was busier than ever. They hugged goodbye and each headed for her car. As Linda walked through the mall on the way to the parking garage, she went by the Santa village again. Now, the line was very long, with more than twenty moms and dads trying to corral kids and keep them quiet. A symphony of crying babies added a soprano line to the underscoring Christmas music playing over the mall speakers. Linda couldn't help but smile, as she saw herself in every young mother who was barely holding it together. She thought to herself that it had been a lovely afternoon and morning, and she had almost finished off Black Friday without too many memories high-jacking her heart.

She went out on the balcony with her book and a cup of tea, had a cup of soup for dinner, fielded calls from both Andrea and Matt, who seemed to be checking on her for some reason, and crawled into bed. Feeling almost content.

She had just dropped off to sleep when the phone rang. Clarence, the night attendant on the desk, was calling.

"Ms. Miller?" he said, in his deep, gravelly voice.

"Yes," Linda said. "Clarence, is that you? Is everything all right?"

"Yesssss, Ms. Miller. I'm sorry to disturb you. There's a young man down here to see you. I know it's late. He says he's your student. Name is Kelly Dunn."

"Oh, my goodness. Yes. He is my student. Please have him sit down. I'll be right down," Linda said. She scrambled out of bed and pulled on sweatpants and a St. Michael hoodie. She ran a brush through her hair, found her flip-flops and went down to the lobby.

Kelly stood there, his back to her. He was standing at the front door, looking like he was about to make a run for it. Like he had changed his mind about being here.

"Kelly," she said, walking over to him. "Please come sit down over here, just for a few minutes." The lobby had very comfortable chairs and couches, arranged in two different sitting areas. Linda led him over to one of them and sat down, him on the couch, her on a chair across from him.

She looked at him and saw a young man who was completely broken. He had lost all that swagger, all that confidence, all that sense of who he was and what his plans were. His eyes were deep pools of darkness, staring into the abyss. He scared her.

"Kelly," she said softly. "I'm so sorry about your brother. I don't even know what to say. I've been thinking about you and your mom nonstop ever since I heard."

He said nothing. He just sat there, looking at his hands, trying not to cry.

"How did you find me?" she said. She didn't even know why she said it, adding hastily, "I'm so glad you did. I mean I'm really honored that you did."

"Ms. Davidson," he said. "A while ago she told me where you lived. I don't even know how I got here tonight, or why I'm here. Sorry to bother you." He spoke very softly. Hardly more than a whisper.

"No, no, no," she said quickly. "You're not a bother. Honestly, I'm really glad to see you. I tried to see you at the funeral, but I really couldn't get anywhere near you. Like I said, I'm honored that you're here. Is there anything I can do for you?" She felt completely at a loss.

"You could sit with me here for a while," he said softly.

She nodded. "That I can do." She sat quietly for a minute. "Does your mom know where you are?"

"No."

"Do you mind if we call her, just in case she's worried."

"No. I don't mind. Probably a good idea." But he didn't move. Luckily, she had grabbed her cell phone on the way out of the apartment. She pulled it out of her pocket,

"What's your number?"

He told her and she dialed it. His mom answered on the third ring. There was both panic and sadness in her voice. "Ms. Dunn," she said. "This is Linda Miller. I'm one of Kelly's teachers at St. Michael. Yes. His English tutor." She listened for a minute and then said, "Yes. He just stopped by for a little bit of help. We are sitting together in the lobby of my condo. We're working on one of the assignments that he missed, and then I will drive him home to you if that's all right with you." She chose her words carefully, knowing that the poor woman was probably almost out of her mind with worry and grief.

His mom was mostly just grateful to know that he was all right. She said that she wanted him home in an hour, at the latest, and Linda agreed that it was a good idea, and she would see him safely home. When she hung up the phone, Kelly grinned, kind of a sad little smile at her.

"That was pretty good, Ms. Miller. Thanks for covering for me."

"Well, in a way, it's true. Because what has happened to you is a sacred hurt, and I need to teach you about that since you are going to be reading *The Great Gatsby* next quarter. One of the most important American novels ever written."

"Hmmmm. What's so great about this Gatsby guy, and what's a sacred hurt? And what's it got to do with me?"

"Well, you've just suffered one, and your life will never be the same." She wondered if Kelly had eaten today. She excused herself and walked over to Clarence.

"Clarence, I need your help. This young man has just lost his brother. And I don't think he has eaten anything today. I know you keep a pot of coffee brewing back in the office, and I am going to run upstairs and make a sandwich. Just something to hold him together. Could you make him a cup of coffee? Cream and sugar? He needs nourishment, and quickly."

"Of course, Ms. Linda," Clarence said. "You run upstairs and get that sandwich. I'll put a cup of coffee together for the young man." He went back in his little office to do that and Linda ran over to Kelly.

"Listen, Kelly. Please don't leave. My friend Clarence is making you a cup of coffee. I'm going to run upstairs and make you a sandwich. I will just be a minute. Please promise me that you will stay right there. I will be back before you know it." Kelly looked up at her, and she suddenly realized that he was actually just too tired and too spent to even stand up. She wondered what he had been doing for the past few days. He looked wrung out, and somehow thinner and smaller than he usually looked. He promised not to leave.

She ran back to the elevator, which thankfully was right there, resting, and apparently waiting for her. She flew into her kitchen, threw a peanut butter and jelly sandwich together, grabbed some small candy bars out of her candy dish, a small bag of chips, and a napkin. She ran back to the elevator, which was, once again, just waiting for her. She got back down to the lobby and ran over to Kelly.

She need not have run because it really looked as if he had not even moved. He was sitting there with his hands folded in his lap, his head hanging down. She noticed how thick his hair was, how young his skin was. Dark brown skin, and it was so smooth. No wrinkles yet. Not even laugh lines at the corners of his eyes. But huge, dark circles under his eyes. The past few days had aged him. Sitting on the coffee table in front of him was a big mug of coffee, steaming hot. He hadn't touched it. She smiled at Clarence and thanked him, and then sat down across from Kelly.

"Please eat," she said. "I ran all the way upstairs and all the way back down. I'm not as young as I used to be, and that was a lot of effort for me. You're going to hurt my feelings if you don't eat what I've brought you. A feast fit for a king, you know. Breakfast of champions, and all that." She smiled, trying to make a little joke, knowing full well how lame it probably sounded. She understood completely just how fragile Kelly was at this moment. After all, he had been staring right into the abyss for the past ten days, and it is hard to avert your eyes from that, once you have had a good look at the darkness.

However, he picked up the sandwich and started to eat. He even took a sip of the coffee, which Clarence had sweetened enough for a young man's tastes. Linda could see the strength flow into him, and she smiled over at Clarence, who was watching them quietly from behind his reception desk. He caught her eye and smiled back at her, nodded gently, and then went back to reading his paper. She realized that, in some small way, they felt like co-conspirators in the attempt to save this young man. At least tonight.

Kelly ate quietly, suddenly realizing that he was hungry and finished everything she had brought down. Then he looked at her and said very quietly, "Thank you very much. I really don't even know why I'm here. That was very kind of you." He got up and walked over to Clarence and spoke to him directly, "Thank you, sir. I've never had a cup of coffee before, and I didn't expect to like it. But that was really good."

Clarence smiled at him. "Ms. Linda told me you just lost your brother. I'm very sorry for your loss. What's your name, young man?"

"Kelly. Kelly Dunn. My brother's name was James." He put out his hand and Clarence took it and held in his two big hands.

"I will keep you and your brother in my prayers," Clarence said.

"Thank you, sir," Kelly said and walked back over to Linda. "Well, I guess I better be going." He looked and sounded exhausted. And very quiet.

"Sit for a minute," Linda said. "I promised your mom that I would drive you home, and I will. But I wanted to talk for a minute."

"Pardon me, Ms. Linda, but what is there to say. He's gone. And that's it."

"I understand what you are feeling. Honestly, I understand completely." She led him back over to the couch.

"How could you? Did this ever happen to you?"

"Yes, it did." She sat quietly and let the words sink in. "Not exactly like you, but similar in some ways." The night fell quiet all around them. Outside, the cars streamed by, their lights winking red and white out the window. In the distance, an ambulance wailed. And yet, inside the lobby of her condo, all was quiet. Clarence had disappeared into his back office, and Linda felt like she and Kelly were inside a noiseless bubble. It felt, for a bit, like they were the only two people around. He raised his eyes and looked at her.

"How do you mean?"

"I had an older brother named Tony. He was nine years older than me and I completely and totally adored him. He went to West Point when I was about ten, and he was killed in a training accident there. I don't think we ever got the whole story, but he came home in a box. He was just gone from my life. And I was in despair."

Her words seemed to hang in the air. Kelly looked at her, but he said nothing. She went on, quietly. Slowly. "My poor Mom and Dad were never the same. They had me, so they had to hang in there and raise me. I was just a kid. But they were never the same." She thought about it, trying to gather her thoughts. "We eventually learned to laugh again, and to enjoy times together. We got past the raw, cold, unspeakable abyss of the first few months. And we stayed true to our love for each other. I think we did that to honor Tony, because that's what he would have wanted. And we all knew it. In some ways, we became better protectors of each other than we had ever been before." She was speaking from her heart, and the words were right there, because they were true. Her loss had happened years ago, and she had had time to find the words to describe it. Kelly's loss was too immediate. There were no words for him yet. Just howling.

"I'm sorry for your loss, too," Kelly said.

"Well." She stopped for a minute, as she heard her own voice break a little. "It was a long time ago. But in some ways, it was just yesterday. And it doesn't take much for me to get right back to tears if I'm not careful." She pulled herself into the moment, with an effort. "But. And here's what I want to tell you. What you have just suffered is a sacred hurt. The plain fact of the matter is that your life will never be the same. Never. Your brother's death has changed everything for you and for your mom. Irrevocably. You have to allow yourself to feel this pain. This loss. And grieve. Go right down to the bottom of your pain and howl."

Kelly was listening hard, paying attention to every word. "That sounds pretty dangerous, Ms. Miller. Because I do believe I can do that right now. I can howl. I can scream. And I'm a little bit afraid that it might tear me apart. So bad that I can't come back from it." He looked her right in the eyes. This was an important moment, and she prayed to God that she could get it right. Say the right words. The true words.

"I get it. But it doesn't do any good to try to hold it in. To bury it and not acknowledge it. To try to be all brave." She waited a minute, feeling for the right words. "But after some time, you will come back to life. Like a tree after winter. Slowly and irregularly, life will return. And, although the pain never

219

goes away, you learn to carry it. And you try to be the best you can be, in his honor. Because he existed, because he was a good brother, you try to be the very best you can be, in his honor. Every day I live, I commit myself to be kind. And I do it in Tony's honor."

"Do you miss him still?"

"Every day. Every day. With every breath I take. With every beat of my heart." Linda reached out and took Kelly's hand in hers. "And I know this sounds crazy, but I talk to him all day long. He's my spirit guide. In fact, he's right here with us now."

Kelly almost jumped, looking around the lobby.

She laughed softly. "No, I don't mean like that. Although he might very well be here. He was always kind of a prankster. But what I do mean is, I open my soul to him and it sometimes feels like he is helping me find the right words to say. He was the coolest guy I ever knew—so full of life. It made you happy just to be around him. He had this incredible 'cool factor'—I don't know what to call it. But, what I'm trying to say is that he lived his life with so much gusto. Just enjoyed everything." She worried that maybe she was talking too much.

"Go on," Kelly said.

"Well. Anyhow. In some crazy way, he is more present with me now than ever before. Like I said, I talk to him on and off all day long. And right now—sitting here with you—I really didn't know what I was going to say, and it sort of feels like Tony is helping me find the right words. Or, at least, I hope they're the right words."

Kelly looked down at his feet, gathering the courage to say what he had to say. Then he spoke very quietly. "I worry about James. I mean. I believe in God, and I think I believe in heaven. I dunno about hell. Maybe." Linda didn't even move. She knew he had more to say. "But I worry about James. I mean, is there a chance that he's in hell 'cuz he took H and killed himself? I can't even hardly say it, but I'm worrying about it." He looked at Linda. There were tears in the corners of his eyes, but he was trying very hard not to blink so they could not fall.

Linda said, "If you ask me, and I'm no expert, but I say there's absolutely no chance of that. I'm pretty sure he's in heaven, looking down on us right now. First of all, he was a good big brother to you and a good son to your mom. He made one mistake that night, and his death was an accident. And I feel very sure that his heavenly Father welcomed him home. I think there's half a chance that my brother Tony was there to help him. Tony would know that you're important to me, and that James was your brother. He'd be there, showing him the ropes."

Kelly stared at her. "But how do you know this stuff, Ms. Miller? How do you know?"

"I don't really know, the way you know some things. I mean—no one can really know. Unless you are on the other side. Like my brother and your brother. But, on the other hand, I sort of just know. With a different kind of 'knowing.' I guess it's faith. And right now—that's the best we can do," she said. "When you think about the parables in the Bible, one of the most famous ones is the story of the Prodigal Son. A man has two sons, and one is loyal and hard-working and stays with his dad. The other one goes off and wastes his whole inheritance on wine and wild women. He loses all his money and he's starving. And he limps back home with nothing but the shirt on his back, and his father welcomes him home and declares a feast. That's what it's like for James right now. He's at the feast. At least, that's what I think."

Then Kelly blinked.

And the tears slid down his cheeks. Clarence quietly noticed and came over with a box of Kleenex. Linda came and sat beside him on the couch and held him in her arms. And he cried, his sobs shaking his shoulders. Linda didn't move, afraid to even breathe. She thought to herself, Tony—tell me what to do. And she somehow knew that she should do nothing, say nothing. Just wait. Just hold him and let him cry. Clarence went back to his seat behind the reception desk, moving slowly, not making a sound.

Then, the front doors slid open, and a couple came in, fresh from the bars and dinner. They were laughing and talking, and didn't even notice Kelly and Linda sitting over to the side on the couch. They went back to the elevators and up to their unit, lost in their own little world. Once again, Linda thought about Nietzsche and Schopenhauer. How some people can be in the warm, sun-dappled, shallow waters and some can be in the dangerous seas—staring at the abyss. And all of this happens at the same moment in time, and in close physical proximity. The reality of your individual situation depends on your waters. Can you keep your frail craft afloat?

Linda handed Kelly the box of Kleenex and said, "I should get you home. I promised your mom that after I went over your assignment, I would get you home. Do you think that's okay?"

He nodded. "Yes," he said. "I should get home. I could tell mom about what you've told me tonight." He smiled a very small smile. "Maybe she and I can howl for a while together tonight. I think I might still be in the howling phase."

Linda smiled at him. "You definitely are. If you like, we can howl all the way to your house so you can practice a little. Show your mom how it's done. I'll go get my car."

She got up to go to the elevators. "I'll bring the car around front and pick you up," she said. "Three minutes."

He nodded. She went back to the elevator and went up to her unit, grabbed her keys, and went down to her car. When she pulled around front, she saw that Kelly was standing over at the reception desk, talking to Clarence. She quietly thanked him in her heart for his help tonight, promising herself that she would bake him a batch of cookies. Or something.

Kelly shook hands with Clarence and came out and got in her car. It was almost midnight, and his mom was probably worried sick and alone. He got in the front seat on the passenger side and she looked for her son's playlist, silently thanking Matt for making it for her. The playlist started with Post Malone singing "Sunflower," and he followed that one up with "Circles." Then, Juice WRLD roared in with "Lucid Dreams" and "Bandit." Then Post started in on "Goodbyes."

Kelly looked at her, surprise in his eyes. "I never expected to hear this music in your car?" His words were more of a challenge than a question.

Linda kept her eyes on the road. There was a lot of traffic tonight. "My son Matt makes me playlists. This is the start of his newest one. He keeps me up to date on music."

"This the son that doesn't like poetry?"

Linda laughed. "He's the only one I've got. But yes, that's the one." She carefully negotiated her way through a busy intersection and headed south down US1, letting her navigation system guide her. Kelly had plugged his address in for her. "But you know. I listen to the lyrics," she added. "And whether he realizes it or not, that's poetry." She looked over at Kelly.

He sat quietly for a minute, listening to the words that Post was singing. "I guess you're right," he said. "Poetry you can sing." He grinned, just a little, looking sideways at her. "Or howl."

Linda smiled, realizing what he was referring to. Pleased with him. Proud of him. Even in his pain, he could make a little joke. It was a very good sign. A sign of a brave heart. She smiled over at him. "You're right," she said. "It's poetry you can sing. Or howl. And—as for me, I feel like howling right now." She didn't know where she got the guts to do it, but she just started singing right along with Post, loudly and out of key. But singing. Or howling. Kelly laughed, and then surprised her by joining in, loudly and almost angrily. Linda put the windows down, letting the wind roar in and their howling run out into the night. And they howled their pain, their loss, their brokenness. Kelly knew every word, and Linda knew most of them. They sang at the top of their lungs, not trusting themselves to find any more of the 'right words' that night. Leaving it all in the hands of Post and Juice, who knew exactly how to howl. Before they knew it, they reached Kelly's house.

"Thanks a lot for tonight," he said, his hand ready to open the door. "You taught me a lot. Or, at least, you gave me a lot to think about."

"I'll see you Tuesday at our regular session, right?" she asked hopefully.

"I'll be there. A few nights ago, I was thinking about quitting. But I didn't really want to. But I also didn't know what I wanted to do. I'm still pretty mixed up, but I'm figuring things out a little bit now. Anyhow. Good night, and thank you. And your friend Clarence—he's cool."

"Oh, yes, he is," she said. "Good night. See you Tuesday." She watched him walk into his house. As soon as he opened the door, his mother was standing there, waiting for him. He took her into his arms and shut the front door.

She drove home with Post Malone and Juice WRLD still roaring away, interested that there was so much traffic this late at night. The bars and restaurants were still crowded, and hundreds of people were strolling down A1A, hand-n-hand, laughing and talking. She felt a weird sense of peace in her own heart. She felt happy that there were so many people out, enjoying the night. Happy that there were people whose world was still innocent of the kind of pain that Kelly was trying to process. Grateful that she had felt her brother's presence and that he had kind of guided her—or so it seemed—in what to say. Grateful for Clarence. She parked the car and went down to the lobby. Clarence was still at his desk. He had one more hour before his shift was over.

"Clarence," she said. "I just wanted to say thank you. You were just amazing tonight." He bowed his head, acknowledging the compliment.

"Well, Ms. Linda, I think we were a good team tonight. And that young man needed a good team behind him at this moment in his life." He shook his head sadly. "I'm afraid he has many long nights ahead of him as he tries to get through this loss. I feel kind of worn out from just watching him suffer, but he's lucky to have a teacher like you."

"And I'm lucky to have a friend like you. Thank you again," she said, getting ready to go upstairs and get in the shower.

"Good night, Ms. Linda. You sure wore me out tonight. But also, thank you." He nodded gravely at her, as if to dismiss her. She was very ready to be dismissed.

She went upstairs and took a long, hot shower, climbed in bed, said her prayers, thanking Tony for being there for her tonight. And her mom, who had also been there, guiding her behavior. Her mom had always taught her that most sadness can at least be somewhat ameliorated by food. Even grief. Even sacred hurts. She fell asleep thinking about Tony, wondering if he could arrange to find James and show him around. She hoped so.

Chapter 24

That next Tuesday, she showed up for her regular tutoring sessions a few minutes early, and Coach Pearson called her into his office. There were several assistant coaches and players buzzing around the room, as usual, but Coach asked them if he and Linda could have the space for a minute. They all seemed a little surprised, glanced quickly at Linda as if to see who she was, but they made their way out of the room quickly.

Linda wondered if she might be in trouble, but she sat there quietly, waiting for Coach to speak.

He looked long and hard at her. "I'm very grateful that you came into our lives." He paused for a minute and then went on. He was very solemn, speaking slowly. "Kelly showed up for school yesterday. I was so glad that he was back here. I called him on Sunday and talked to him, and he said that he had dropped by to see you on Saturday night, and that you were a big help to him." He looked puzzled, as if trying to understand how this could be.

Linda found herself breathing again. "I hope it's okay that I met with him and drove him home. We just sat in the lobby of my condo building for about an hour and talked. I don't know exactly how he found me, but he did. And I fed him a sandwich and we talked. And then I drove him home. That's all that happened." She found herself worrying that maybe Coach Pearson was worried that she had behaved inappropriately. She was about to reassure him, but he waved her words away.

"I'm just very grateful. Kelly is a very good, young man, and this has been a devastating blow to him. It would be tempting—even easy—for him to make a series of bad choices at this moment in his life. Choices that would jeopardize his future in so many ways that I shudder to think about them. But, for some reason, he sought you out at a crucial moment, and whatever you said, it helped him to get through that night and to get back here to school." He sat quietly for a minute, collecting his thoughts. Linda thought, once again, that he was very young, but that it seemed like this tragedy was rapidly aging him. His dark brown eyes held hers for a minute. "You know—I have two sons myself. Ages eight and nine. I hope they never go through anything like this, but I would be very grateful if someone like you were in their lives if they did."

Linda didn't even know what to say. She just sat there, waiting for what would come next.

Coach Pearson was ready to move on to his next topic. "Okay. This is what I wanted to talk to you about today. First to thank you. And then to ask you to do me a favor."

"Of course. I will if I can," she said.

He cleared his throat and adjusted the way he was sitting in his chair. He leaned back contemplatively, as if he were thinking even as he was speaking. "You know we have a big game this Friday. It's the second round of the playoffs. Running up to the state championship. We won last Friday, but it wasn't pretty. And it was a team we should have beaten easily."

Linda said quietly, "Kelly wasn't there."

"True," he said. "He wasn't. But there's more to it. The whole team felt flat. So did the coaching staff. Me too, if I'm going to be honest. James's death has taken a lot out of us. All of us."

"I understand completely."

Now, he looked right at her. "That's where you come in."

"Excuse me?" she said, flabbergasted, having absolutely no idea where this was going.

"I've got someone coming in every day this week to give an inspirational speech. There are several players who are alumni and are active in the NFL. I've got one coming in today, Wednesday, and Friday right before the game." He looked hard at her, as if wondering if he should say what he was thinking of next. "But I need someone for Thursday. Instead of doing your regular tutoring sessions that day, I'd like you to address the team. Say something inspirational to them. Read something. I don't know. A poem, a famous speech. Whatever you think might work. I'm putting this in your hands, and believing that you'll come up with something that will work."

Linda could hardly move. She was completely flabbergasted. "You want me to address the whole team? They don't even know me!"

"You're right. They don't. But Kelly and John do, and they think very highly of you. I don't know where I came up with this idea, but I like to try different things to motivate the team. And you would sure be different!"

Now that he had said it out loud, he actually seemed to be warming to the idea. "So. Prepare something. You don't have to tell me what it is. I trust you. Be here at the regular time, 3:00— and be prepared to speak for about fifteen minutes to the boys. And all the coaches." He grinned at her. "We'll pay you for the whole two hours you usually work. Your usual fee." He smiled at her again and then kind of motioned that their conversation was over. "That's all. Now, I believe Kelly is waiting for his regular tutoring session, in the film room." Linda suddenly realized that she was being dismissed and tried to stand up.

She looked at him, halfway afraid that her jaw was hanging open. A most unbecoming look. She quickly checked that her mouth was, in fact, shut. Then said, "But do you have any suggestions as to what you would like me to read or say to them?" She felt a deep sense of panic setting in.

"Nope," he said, clearly ready to move on now. "You'll think of something. Both Kelly and John say that you know what you're doing." He grinned at her, kind of enjoying her bewilderment. He nodded toward the door, "I believe Kelly is waiting." She grabbed her briefcase and headed for the door, unable to speak. When she got to the film room, Kelly was waiting.

"Hey, Ms. Miller," he said. "You've got a funny look on your face."

She sat down in the chair next to him and looked at him. "You are never going to believe what Coach just asked me to do."

"What?"

"He wants me to talk to the whole team on Thursday. We won't have our regular tutoring session, and instead I'm supposed to talk to the whole team. Say something inspirational to help them get pumped up for the big game on Friday."

"But that's great," he said. "That's really a cool honor. What are you going to talk about?"

She looked at him. Speechless. "I have absolutely no idea."

Kelly started laughing at her. She couldn't help it, and she started laughing too. It made her happy to see him laugh. Then, she pulled herself together. "I'm not doing my job, am I? You probably have a lot to catch up on. How can I help?"

"Ms. Davidson is being very cool. I missed a lot, but she is giving me as much time as I need to get caught up." Linda heard this gratefully, reminding herself to thank Diane when she saw her, and see if she could get some sense of what Kelly needed to do to get caught up. "Well," she said. "What's for today?"

"Do you think I should do the stuff I missed or the stuff that the class is working on right now?"

"Personally, and I know this seems sort of backwards, I think we should concentrate on the stuff that the class is working on right now. So, you feel current with them. I'm going to talk to Ms. Davidson and see if I can get the list of assignments that you missed. And also see if I can arrange to get it pared down a little, given your extenuating circumstances."

"That would be awesome," Kelly said. He opened his computer and took a look at the day's assignment. He ran his finger down the screen until he found the listing. "We're supposed to write a short paragraph about a poem by some guy named Robert Frost."

"Oh, that's wonderful," Linda said. "He's one of my favorites. Which poem?"

"Something called *The Road Not Taken*," Kelly said. "Page 442." The poem was available to Kelly through an online program that the school subscribed to, but Linda had a paper copy of the textbook, and she opened that instead. She had always believed in the power of the printed page.

"It's an awesome poem," Linda said. "Here it is. You read it out loud for me."

"Really," said Kelly. "I like it best when you read to me. Please? I promise I will listen hard." He didn't look at her. He kept his eyes on the book.

"Okay," said Linda. "Actually, I'd love to. It's one of my favorites. Here goes.

The Road Not Taken

Two roads diverged in a yellow wood,
And sorry I could not travel both
And be one traveler, long I stood
And looked down one as far as I could
To see where it bent in the undergrowth.

Then took the other, as just as fair,

And having perhaps the better claim,

Because it was grassy and wanted wear;

Though as for that the passing there

Had worn them really about the same.

And both that morning equally lay

In leaves no step had trodden black.

Oh, I kept the first for another day!

Yet, knowing how way leads on to way,

I doubted if I should ever come back.

I shall be telling this with a sigh,

Somewhere ages and ages hence:

Two roads diverged in a wood, and I—

I took the one less traveled by,

And that has made all the difference."

She let the words hang there in the air. Magical words, so simple and so eloquent.

"Wow," Kelly said. "What does that mean?"

"What do you think it means?" Linda said. "Let's just talk about that, and then we will look at the writing assignment Ms. Davidson has given you. But first, what does it mean to you?" Kelly sat there, thinking, unsure how to proceed, or even where to start. "Start with this idea. Who seems to be speaking?"

"Some guy standing in a forest, looking at two different paths and trying to decide which one to take. That much I got. But that's about it," Kelly said.

"Well, that's a very good start. Always start with those questions. Who is speaking and what does the setting seem to be. And you did that very well." He was staring at the words. "Can you picture this setting—this man standing at this crossroads, trying to decide which way to go?"

"Yes," said Kelly, very quietly. Linda could feel him thinking, his eyes boring a hole in the paper, his finger tracing the lines as he thought.

"How are the roads the same?" said Linda.

Kelly ran his finger down to the fourth stanza. "I think that no one is on either road this morning. He says that no step had trodden on them, and they were laying there equally."

"Right," said Linda. "Now. How are they different?"

"One is more worn out."

"Which means?"

"I guess maybe more people go down that one."

"And what does he decide to do?" Linda asked.

"He takes the other one, the one that hasn't been taken as much," Kelly said.

Linda could hardly breathe. She could feel Kelly thinking, ready to leap ahead. Like a wide receiver about to leap for a pass.

"How does he feel about the road he has decided not to take?" she said.

Kelly stopped to think about that, and didn't quite know what to say. The ball was just slightly out of reach, but it hung there in midair, waiting for his hands to reach it. She pointed to line two—And sorry I could not travel both. He nodded. And then she read him lines 13-15, once again: "Oh, I kept the first for another day! Yet knowing how way leads on to way, I doubted if I should ever come back."

"I think there's a part of him that feels sad that he can't take the other road. And he kind of tells himself that he will come back and take that road some other day, but he knows that he really won't. That once he takes this one road, he won't get a chance to take the other one. Ever." He looked at her, asking with his eyes if he was right.

She smiled at him. "That's really good, Kelly. Now, here's the big question. Is he satisfied with his choice, or does he wish now that he would have chosen differently?"

He said nothing, staring at the page.

She read the last three lines again: "Two roads diverged in a wood, and I—I took the one less traveled by, and that has made all the difference." She sat quietly, waiting for him to speak.

He looked at her and said, "I'm not sure."

She smiled. "Perfect answer. Tell me why you say that."

"Well, because I think I could read it either way. He says that his choice made all the difference, but he doesn't really tell us if that ended up being a good thing or a bad thing."

"You are so smart," Linda said. "Most people miss that completely. They read it and they're absolutely sure it's one thing or the other, depending upon their mindset at the moment, I guess. But you saw through that. So, now, let's look at what Ms. Davidson wants you to write about." She found the assignment back on his computer screen. "She says—write a short paragraph in which you explain who is speaking and what decision he is facing. Tell what he decides, and how he feels about his decision."

"That's pretty much what we just talked about," Kelly said.

"That's right," said Linda. "And we still have twenty minutes left, so I think you can get that done right now. But, before you do. Let me ask you one more thing." She paused for a minute, trying to get this right. "Do you think it's possible that this whole thing is about more than two roads in a forest."

Kelly nodded. "I've been thinking that all along, ever since you read it to me the first time."

"What's it about?"

"Choices in life. You go down one road, and it leads to other roads. You make a decision at one moment in your life, and it has consequences."

"Wow," said Linda. "I think you're ready to write. You write the paragraph and I'll look it over before you leave. You did a great job with that. Are you supposed to write it on paper or online?"

Kelly looked at the assignment, and said, "Online." He created a new document and started typing. His fingers flew on the keyboard as the words came pouring out of him. When he was done, Linda proofread it quickly for errors. It was really good. She told him so and sent him off to practice. He gave her a high five and headed out to the football stadium. And John White came in and sat down.

Chapter 25

Later that evening, she called Matt. She told him about what happened with Kelly and how she had driven him home. And how Matt's playlist had been such a big help. He was pleased.

"You know, Mom," he said. "Just one small thought. You shouldn't make a practice of driving students home, having any one of them alone in the car with you. Just saying. In this litigious world we live in, it's just not a good idea."

"You know, I was actually aware of that," Linda said, "and I was even thinking about it even while I was doing it, but the circumstances seemed to call for me to take a chance on doing what I thought was the right thing and getting the kid home safely to his mother. But I know you're right. Anyhow, I need your help on something else."

"How so?" Matt said.

She explained what the coach had asked her to do, and how she really didn't know any of the team very well. Only the couple of kids she was tutoring. And how they were in the playoffs, where it was a single-game elimination platform, and how the coach felt like the team was somewhat unfocused or even traumatized by the death of Kelly's brother. And how he had asked her to come up with something inspirational to talk to them about. And she had less than 48 hours to get this right.

Matt laughed. "Wow. What an honor, and what a crazy assignment. All at the same time. I'm not sure these are your people, Mom. I mean that in the kindest way. You are used to teaching poetry and Shakespeare. What could you possibly have to say to a football team, many of whose members are definitely not into poetry?"

"My point exactly," Linda agreed. "I don't know what Coach Pearson was thinking or what he sees in me, but I also don't want to let him down. And even more important, I don't want to let Kelly and John down. So, what do you think? Your music helped me to connect with Kelly at a very important moment, so I'm sort of hoping you can come up with something."

"Mom, I'm at a loss. I hate to disappoint you, but I think you're on your own here. However, I guess if I were you, I would try to find something that recognizes their status as warriors. Thinking back to my own time on the football field, and admittedly I was never in the same class as these kids, I honestly felt like I was going into battle every time I took the field. I would know that I was going to get hit, and there would be pain. But I would also know that I was going to hit someone right back. I would never want to really hurt someone, but I would hit someone, if you know what I mean. And I learned to play with pain. After every game, I had cuts and bruises. You know that. If you think of it, football is war. One man is trying to get another man to bend to his will. And that other man is fighting with all his might not to give ground."

"Hmmmmm. You're right."

Matt continued, "In some weird way, I've started to feel that practicing law is a little bit like football. The field of battle is the courtroom, and one person is still trying to get another person to bend to his will. Not physically, of course, but through the use of facts and logic. Does any of that help?"

"You know," Linda said. "In a way it does. You've given me something to think about. Thank you so much, my darling. I'll let you get back to your studies. I love you."

"Good night, Mom. Let me know how it goes. One other thought. I don't know if it's useful. But—there is a weird and sacred kind of brotherhood on a football team. Doesn't matter what color you are. You are brothers. A band of brothers." He was quiet for a minute, as if remembering his days on the football field. Linda waited for him to finish his thought. But, apparently, he was done. He just added one thing. "And remember—don't talk too long. Brevity is the soul of wit."

Linda laughed. "I love it when you quote Shakespeare to me. Good night, son. And thanks."

She hung up and went out on the balcony to look out at the night sky. She felt the cool breeze and went in to get a light blanket. Then she lay back on a chaise and let the night work on her. Thought about what Matt had said, and about her brother. Who died on the field of battle, even though it wasn't active combat. She realized that what Matt had said was true, and that every warrior is trying to obtain and maintain power. And that usually involves exerting your will to power.

And then it came to her.

Machiavelli.

In the year 1513, he had written a little book called *The Prince*.

Linda thought of the chalkboard in Coach Pearson's office with all the diagrams of x's and o's. And suddenly, she had it. She went into her study to find her copy of *The Prince*. She would be up late tonight, listening to a voice from the 1500's.

Chapter 26

She was still collecting her thoughts in the morning, but a daring scheme had started to emerge. Machiavelli says that a prince is, first and foremost, a warrior. That he must never forget the importance of war, and that he must train both his body and his mind for battle. Linda started thinking about these ideas and she let them overlap with images of St. Michael, the archangel warrior—the patron saint of the school. She did some quick research on the stories about St. Michael, recalling her grade school lessons.

On and off all day, she let ideas run through her brain, remembering her son's advice. Don't talk too long. That night, she struggled with a way to fit it all together. Make it mean something to the team. In the morning, she went to her computer and wrote her speech. She practiced it ten times, drilling herself on the main ideas. She called Andrea to run the ideas by her. Andrea was cautiously optimistic—at best.

"This is kind of brainy, Mom. I mean—you have a lot of really good ideas here, but these are high school kids. A football team. Not honor students or AP students. And some of this might be over their heads. Honestly, they might not even know what you're talking about."

"Andrea, you're not helping."

"I don't mean to be a stumbling block, but I'm just worried that you're going to get in there and speak to them, and you're going to be met with a sea of absolutely blank faces. They're there to play football, not go to war."

"But, Andrea," Linda disagreed, "football is war. Of a sort. I was talking to your brother and he said that every time he went out on that field, he felt like he was going into combat. In fact, he indirectly gave me the idea for the whole thing."

"Oh, sure," Andrea laughed. "Blame Matt! He'll love that." She took a deep breath. "Well, anyhow, I guess when all is said and done, you've got to trust your own instincts, and you've worked really hard on this. So—I guess I would say...Go for it! If it doesn't work, just smile and say 'Go Warriors' and get off the stage as fast as you can."

"Well, I'll practice it a couple more times and see if I think it will work. Anyhow, thanks for listening. Tell me about you and Patrick."

Andrea babbled on about work and Patrick and the holidays coming up and their plans for a getaway vacation after Christmas. Linda listened patiently, not saying anything at all, but her mind was racing over her thoughts about what she was going to say to the team. As soon as she could politely disengage from the conversation and hang up, she did so, and went back to her notes. She read them over several more times, and she became even more convinced that the ideas would work. But apparently, she was the only one who thought so.

Thursday afternoon came, and she felt jumpy. She decided to pull on blue jeans and a St. Michael sweatshirt. Dark navy blue with a graphic of St. Michael slaying the dragon. Ordinarily, she dressed up for her tutoring job, but this was different. She was going to address the whole team, and she thought she should have St. Michael garb on. Go team, and all that. The navy blue would be good because it was dark enough that they couldn't see her sweat. Never let them see you sweat. If they smell weakness, they will eat you alive. Every teacher knows that rule.

She parked her car in the faculty lot and reported to Coach Pearson's office. For some reason, he wasn't in there, but three of the assistant coaches were. She didn't really know any of them by name. One of them, a big guy with a bald head and a big smile spoke to her right away. "Are you the guest speaker for today? Coach Pearson told me to make sure you were comfortable and let you know that we will be ready for you soon. He's in the locker room with the team. My name is Rob. Rob DeLuca. I'm the strength and conditioning coach for the team." He put out his hand to shake her hand. His hands were huge and his grip was like iron. "Coach told me to see if there was anything you need," he added.

"Thank you," said Linda. "I'm wondering if you could make copies of this one page document for me. I think you said that there are 100 boys on the team, so I need 100 copies. Plus one for all the coaches, however many that is."

"Sure," said Rob, taking the paper from her hands. He glanced down at the title on the page. Machiavelli and the

Warrior Prince. He looked askance at her. "Machiavelli? Are you kidding me? You're going to talk to them about Machiavelli?" His face registered complete disbelief, his ready smile having been replaced by a worried frown. The other two coaches laughed out loud, muttering things to themselves—things like 'this'll be good,' and 'what the hell is Coach thinking'. They got up and left the room, still laughing to themselves.

Linda felt a blush start at the deep part of her neck and start to work its way up her whole face. She felt herself actually kind of shaking in her shoes. Rob shrugged and took the document and started running off 100 copies. The copy machine was right behind Coach Pearson's desk. When he finished, he handed them to her and wished her luck. She wasn't at all sure that he meant it.

She sat down in her chair across from Coach Pearson's chair and whispered a quick prayer—to her brother, to St. Michael, to the Holy Spirit, to her mom and dad, to anybody that might be listening up there. She felt herself still shaking a little and hugged the papers, still warm from the printer.

Suddenly Coach Pearson was there. "Hey, Ms. Miller. Glad to see you could make it. You ready? I've got the team all mostly dressed and they're waiting for you." She looked at him, with something like terror on her face, suddenly unsure of what she was doing or if this had any hope of success. He seemed to read her feelings perfectly and reached out and put his hand on her shoulder. "Come on," he said. "You'll be great."

Linda suddenly pulled herself together, finding that kind of mentality where you just march into battle because there is really nothing else you can do at the moment. All the preparation is behind you, and your battle plan will either work or it won't. The hell with it. Time to meet the enemy on the field of battle and see what happens. She looked at Coach and said, "Could you have your guys give one of these to each of the players and the coaches." She handed him the papers, keeping one for herself to speak from. The rest was in her head. Or at least she hoped it was. They walked down the hall together and he opened the door to the boys' locker room for her, ushering her in ahead of him.

Linda was struck with a wave of the raw smell of man. It almost knocked her over. She'd been in plenty of women's locker rooms before, but she had never smelled anything like this. She almost choked, completely unprepared for the wall of smelly sweat and testosterone that hit her in the face. Luckily, she did not choke, stifling that urge. That, too, would have been a sign of weakness.

Coach Pearson seemed completely oblivious to her momentary panic. He said loudly, "All right, men. Everybody sit down. Either on the floor or on a bench. And eyes right here. And quiet. And I do mean quiet." A couple of the boys were still talking, but when he roared at them, they shut up and sat down. Coach Pearson handed the sheets of paper to one of his assistants and told him to pass them out.

When the boys were quiet, he went on. "This is Ms. Miller. Some of you may know that she has been tutoring a couple of our players in English. She taught English up in Michigan for 30 years, and she has been with our program since September. I want you to welcome her and listen to what she has to say to you.

245

Ms. Miller, the floor is yours." He kind of bowed slightly and gave her the room. She swallowed hard and started to speak.

"Thank you very much for letting me speak to you today at this very important moment in your lives. I've been watching you play football for this whole season, and I've come to realize something. You young men are part of something much bigger than yourselves. You take the whole school on your shoulders, the whole city of Fort Lauderdale, every Friday night when you take the field. You are warriors. And I was thinking about that, and I thought you might like to know a little bit about what it means to be a warrior—from one of the most famous warriors of all."

She moved her eyes around the room to make sure that she had the boys' attention. They seemed to be listening. She went on. "There was a man named Niccolo Machiavelli who lived from 1469 to 1527. He wrote a book called *The Prince* which has been studied ever since. Now, I know you're probably sitting there thinking that a guy who lived that long ago could not possibly have anything in common with you. But, you have to realize that some things about the human condition never change." She suddenly felt that she might be losing them, and she realized that she had better get to specifics and try to involve them.

"Look at the sheet of paper you have in your hands, if you would. Let's read it together and think about what he is saying to us." All of a sudden, all 100 boys started to read the paper, in that sing-song voice that kids use when told to do a choral reading. Suddenly, she laughed, and the ice was broken. "No, no, no. I'll read it to you. You can save your strength for the upcoming battle, but I would appreciate it if you would read silently along with me." She heard a quiet sigh of relief pass through the room. They didn't want to read out loud. Not at all.

She read the first idea: "A prince is always, first and foremost, a warrior. And a warrior is always either fighting a war or preparing for the next one. He must train his body and he must train his mind for battle." She looked up to see if this idea was working, and it was. They were quiet, and they were thinking.

She went on, "When a warrior has a time of peace, he must train himself for the next battle. He can do that by learning about his own country and how best to defend it if it comes under attack. Secondly, he must study his enemy and how he behaves under certain conditions. He must acquire knowledge and experience of the terrain." She paused for a minute and then said, "Does this sound like something you do?"

A young man in the front row, sitting almost right at her feet, raised his hand. He was dark-skinned, with a lot of curly, black hair, and a sprinkling of acne across the top of his forehead. He had a big smile, but it was a tentative smile right now. He was trying to get the answer right, trying not to make a fool of himself. "Is that like what we do when we study the other team's offense and defense, and when we watch film to get ready for the game?"

"Yes!" said Linda. "That's exactly what you do. You see, you are behaving like a prince, like a warrior. You are doing exactly what Machiavelli says you should."

She waited for a minute. They *were* listening. She went on. He further says, "It is important for a warrior to exercise his mind. He should read the histories and study the deeds of great men. Never in peaceful times should he be idle. He must use the times of peace to prepare for the next battle. He must nurture his body and train it for hardship. When Fortune changes, and she will, she will find him prepared to withstand the challenges of war. Remember that Fortune is a whore, who loves no man. She cannot be depended upon. She will reach over and spin her wheel, whenever the whim strikes her. So, a prince must be prepared for the unexpected. He must be ready to adjust his plans, and he must know his options beforehand. This kind of readiness comes only from study and preparation."

She paused, as much to catch her breath as anything.

A hand went up in the back of the room. A big kid. She nodded to him. "Excuse me, Miss, but did you just say the word whore?" Apparently, he was saying what a lot of the kids were thinking, because a nervous sort of laughter rippled through the room. Even the coaches joined in. The laughter continued for a minute, and several of the players were whispering to each other. Linda wondered for a minute if she had screwed up by using the word whore.

Rob DeLuca—the strength and conditioning coach she had met a little while ago, also speaking from the back of the room, said, "Could you explain that thing about Fortune and the wheel? Are you referencing the Wheel of Fortune, like the game show? I'm confused. And why is she a whore?"

Linda realized that he was helping her out, and she smiled gratefully. "Yes, of course. I mean, the ideas are related, but, let me back up. The ancient Greeks and Romans believed in a whole pantheon of gods, who lived on Mount Olympus. One of them was the Goddess Fortune. It was said that she loved no man, was true to no man."

One of the boys in the front row chuckled and said, "I think I know that girl."

Everyone laughed, including Linda. She smiled. She could feel herself relax a little. "Well, the story goes that there was a great big wheel on Mount Olympus, and when you were born, you were assigned a spot on the circumference of the wheel. And the thing is—sometimes everything is going great for you, that means you're up at the top of the wheel—and then sometimes, for no reason at all, things change and start going very badly for you." She let this idea sink in.

The same boy who had spoken a minute ago said, "You mean—sometimes bad things happen to good people. Who don't deserve it, and nothing they did made it happen. But it happened anyhow. Shit happens." Linda smiled and nodded.

"Yes. Bad stuff happens." She was sort of gently correcting the use of the word shit. But she knew exactly what he meant. "On the other hand, of course. You could be at the bottom of the wheel—things are going very badly for you—and she could spin the wheel, and things could suddenly improve, again not necessarily a result of anything you did. The ancient Greeks and Romans used this image to explain that sometimes life is completely unpredictable. They blame it on that whore Fortune, spinning her wheel for no reason."

"Makes sense," said the kid in the front row. Several of the other players were nodding in agreement.

"Anyhow, the big thing is, that life is going to throw you curve balls. Bad things. Unexpected things. Have you guys ever had to battle back from a bad call by an official at a crucial moment in the game? Have you ever lost a teammate to injury?"

Almost everybody had something to say about that. They were all talking to each other, remembering a time they were victims of this kind of call. Remembering the loss of their quarterback in the California game. Linda raised her voice to bring them back. "Well, blame it on Fortune, if you like. But the big thing is—when it happens, you have to be ready to shrug it off and keep fighting. Adjust your plans and stay in the fight."

She felt the boys were with her now. She had finished working her way through Machiavelli's main ideas, and now it was time to bring it home. Raising her voice above their talking, she said, "So anyhow, you are warriors. You are princes. In fact, you are the St. Michael Warriors. And look at the picture of St. Michael we are all familiar with. What do you see him doing? Slaying a dragon! So, get out there and slay the dragon."

Suddenly, all the boys were cheering. She wanted to share one more idea. "One more thing I want to say. Right now, you can't even understand how important this game of football is to you. It is something you will carry with you for the rest of your life. Something you will tell your children and your grandchildren about. Right now, you are brothers. You are a band of brothers. There is something very special about that. Something sacred. So, go out there and make yourselves proud. Make your coaches proud. Make your families proud. Make your school proud! What you do matters, in more ways than you can ever know right now. So, be princes. Be Warriors! And thank you for letting me speak to you today!" She realized that she was shouting, and had raised her hand in a fist. She didn't know what had gotten into her, but the boys were on their feet, clapping and cheering. Hitting each other on the back.

Suddenly, Coach Pearson was right beside her. He looked a little sweaty. He put his right arm around her shoulders and started yelling. "Do you men hear me!! This woman gets it!! She understands what it's all about. And she has given you something to think about. Show her your appreciation. She gets it! She gets it! Now, let's get out there and do it! Be on the field. Five minutes." All the players started clapping and hooting their approval.

As he was shouting to the team, he kept his arm around her shoulders, but he was also jumping up and down at the same time. Linda was sort of forced to jump with him, knocked off balance and not even sure what was going on. It occurred to her that he might have been thrilled that it had gone well, even relieved. Because how could he know that it would? He hadn't even asked to review what she was about to say. She didn't know who was more relieved, the more she thought about it—him or her. Then the boys started to head out to the football field, picking up gear as they left the locker room. They were all talking at once. She could hear the words whore and Fortune being whispered as they left the room. Some of them were laughing.

Coach Pearson turned and thanked her again, and gave her a big hug. Then, suddenly, he was gone. Linda felt her knees shaking. Some of the boys thanked her as they filed out of the room, and several of the kids mentioned that they liked the part about Fortune the whore best of all. She smiled at them, and they grinned right back at her, saying that they would see her around, and to make sure she was at Friday's game. She assured them that she would be on the 50-yard line, like always. Top row. The last ones out of the room were Rob DeLuca and a couple of the other coaches. They stopped to talk to her. One of them introduced himself as Dave Eddings. He said he was the defensive coordinator.

"Do you happen to have a couple extra copies of the Machiavelli paper," he asked. "My brother coaches over at a small school up in Boca, and I think he might get a kick out of this. I could give him mine, but I don't really want to give it up."

Linda laughed. "Well, I've got about five left over. Please. Take them all. I'm really glad you liked it. Really glad, and really relieved. I honestly had no idea if this was going to work or not."

Dave was a short, tough-looking young black man. When Linda looked at him, she was reminded of Barry Sanders, one of the gods on Mount Olympus if you grew up in Detroit. He was about to leave, and then he changed his mind. "Could I ask you something?"

"Sure," she said. Only Rob and Dave and she were left in the room now, but the smell and the noise and the cheers seemed to linger in the air. Linda was half drunk on the euphoria of not having made a fool of herself.

"So," said Dave, "I understand now who this Machiavelli dude was. And what I was wondering is—why did Tupac call himself Machiavelli? Although, he actually called himself Makavelli. He said it a little differently. Do you know anything about that?" He was standing right in front of her, and his face was very earnest.

Linda was caught completely off-guard. Luckily, thanks to Matt and his ongoing education of her musical interests through his playlists, she knew who Tupac was. She thought about it, but she wasn't sure about the answer, so she just waited. Rob was clearly thinking about the question, and suddenly, he got an idea about the answer—without any help from her. He said, "I think maybe Tupac thought of himself as a warrior prince. He was at war with the world. Fighting for a black man's rights and identity."

"That seems right to me," said Linda. "You know—I didn't really get the chance to tell the boys all of his ideas, but let me tell you this, and you see if you think it fits. Machiavelli advocated using deception to outsmart his enemies. He also said that for a leader, it is better to be feared than loved. And always, he advocated studying the smart men who had gone before himself, to see if he could avoid their failures and reach even higher heights. Does that work for you, and for Tupac as a fan of Machiavelli?"

Dave and Rob looked at her and nodded slowly. "It really does," said Dave. "Tupac was a highly skilled rapper, but he always talked about maintaining power and getting even better. And he lived a violent life. He definitely thought it was better to be feared than loved. One of his songs—he says—grab your Glocks when you see Tupac. Somethin' like that. I think it works." He put his hand out to shake Linda's hand. "Thanks a lot for today. You gave me something to think about. I can't wait to tell my brother about it. Have a good night. See you at the game tomorrow. Go, Warriors." He smiled and left, leaving only Rob DeLuca behind.

He ushered her out of the room, saying, "When I saw you before the speech, I thought to myself—this ain't ever gonna work. I was even a little worried about you. I see I got that wrong."

"You and me both," she said. "Honestly, I was more than a little worried about it all. But it seemed to work out okay."

"No. It was great," he said.

She took one last look at the locker room, knowing full well that she might never be back there. You can only do a show like that once. Or, as Robert Frost had said in his famous poem: "yet knowing how way leads on to way, I doubted if I should ever come back." The words of that poem really resonated with her at that moment. She smiled and thanked Rob for his kind words and walked out to the parking lot as he locked the room behind her.

As she walked to her car in the autumnal air, she remembered that Frost concludes his poem with the words: "Two roads diverged in a wood, and I—I took the one less traveled by, and that has made all the difference." Kelly had been right when he said that he wasn't sure if the speaker was happy or sad about having made the choice he did. But tonight, Linda was pretty sure that he was happy. Or she was. Or at least content. And sometimes, that is good enough. In fact, right now, it felt pretty damn good.

She breathed a silent prayer of thanks to all the "guardian angels" who had helped her through this presentation—including her brother and St. Michael. And, of course, Machiavelli. Overhead, a flock of seagulls flew into the gathering darkness, yawping merrily.

Chapter 27

Friday night. The game. The semi-finals in the state championship. By luck of the draw, St. Michael's got to host the games all the way up until the final, if they got that far. This year, the team from Tampa had to drive across the state to play here, in Fort Lauderdale, on St. Michael's field. Next year, if St. Michael managed to get to the playoffs, they would be the team that traveled.

But this year, they had home field advantage. Not that it seemed to matter all that much. The team from Tampa Central had brought twenty buses full of fans and players. Dressed in white, they were the White Knights, and their fans all had white t-shirts on, trying for that infamous "white out" look that Penn State had made so famous. And they looked very intimidating. The fans completely filled the bleachers on the visitors' side, and auxiliary bleachers had been brought in to accommodate the vast numbers who had come to see the game. Their marching band was big and loud, and they were already in their place in the bleachers when Linda got to the game and made her way to her seat on the 50-yard line.

It was the first Friday of December, and the weather had cooperated by bringing in a chill, with a wind coming straight out of the north. At one end of the football field, the gigantic American flag snapped in the wind. The scoreboard was lit up and ready to go. So were the fans. They were laughing, talking, and shouting encouragement. They jumped to their feet when the team ran out of the locker room and onto the field, the marching band roaring their way through the school's fight song. Linda was on her feet with 5,000 other people, shouting encouragement and clapping her hands. She shivered slightly, although she wasn't exactly sure if it was from nervousness or cold. She ran her eyes up and down the sidelines, looking for Kelly and John. She knew their numbers, so that was how she found them. They already had their helmets on. She said a silent prayer that they would both do well, and then she added a quick prayer that no one would get hurt.

A prayer was said by one of the students, and then the National Anthem was sung by a senior girl with a beautiful voice. Her soprano voice rang out in the night, echoing around the stadium. A light breeze blew her hair around her head, almost like a halo. Linda felt some kind of magic in the air. Then, suddenly, that moment passed and it was all business. The captains for both teams met at the 50-yard line for the coin toss. Both Kelly and John were out there representing their team.

St. Michael's won the toss and elected to defer. The referee blew his whistle, and the game started with the St. Michael's kicker driving the ball into the end zone with no return. The ball was spotted at the Tampa 20-yard line, and their offense took the field. There had been a lot of noise about this team from Tampa because they had finished their regular season undefeated and had moved rather easily through the playoffs so far. They had two wide receivers and two running backs who were supposed to be unstoppable. They called themselves the "four horsemen of the apocalypse"—with a play on the idea of the white knights. They were all Division I recruits, all seniors, and all fiercely competitive. The first drive resulted in a touchdown for Tampa. In fact, they had scored rather easily, mixing up running plays and passing plays. The touchdown was scored by one of the famous wide receivers, who leapt up in the air, snagging the ball mid-flight, tucking it into his chest, and finishing with a spectacular run down the sidelines, right into the end zone.

Too easy. Linda thought that the team's season might be about to come to a screeching halt. All the men sitting around her were talking to each other, complaining about the defense being too soft. You got to hit somebody, you can't let them do that. Linda felt her guts tightening up. The team was not just some amorphous and anonymous blob of boys to her anymore. They were young men with dreams and hopes. Guts and glory. They had broken bread together. If you could consider Machiavelli bread. And she did. The White Knights converted on the point after, and the St. Michael's Warriors were down 7-0.

Linda felt sympathy for the young quarterback. She had met him once—she remembered that his name was Dan, and that he was only a sophomore. Just a kid. Well, he was growing up tonight, as he put the whole team on his back and took the field. Kelly and John were both in the game. Linda watched Kelly most of all, but she tried to keep her eyes on John too. Dan dropped back, staying in the pocket and threw a long pass to Kelly, down the right sideline. Linda felt herself holding her breath as Kelly went up for the ball. He got hit hard, while he was in mid-air, and she winced at the blow. But he landed, safely inbounds, and the reception was good for a gain of forty yards. The crowd roared its approval, and Kelly ran back to the huddle.

Now, Dan handed off to the star running back, who ground out another hard nine yards, his legs pumping like pistons. Then, Dan tucked the ball into his stomach and successfully executed a quarterback sneak to get the new set of downs. The Tampa team had not expected that—they had their defense set for another run from the running back, and were caught off-guard when Dan tucked the ball and basically blasted forward, his offensive line pushing forward to open a gap for him.

First down, and goal to go. They were on the five-yard line of Tampa. The St. Michael's crowd was on its feet, a wave of sound rolling through the air above the stadium. The Tampa team's marching band was playing as loudly as they could, trying to make it difficult for the young quarterback to call out the plays. Everyone expected a handoff to the running back. Everyone.

Instead, Dan dropped back in the pocket, checked his receivers, and lofted a ball to the deep part of the end zone, where Kelly was waiting to leap. He timed his jump perfectly, snatched the ball out of mid-air, and landed in bounds. The crowd went wild. Everyone on the St. Michael's side knew Kelly's story, knew that he was fighting through unimaginable sorrow, knew that he was playing for his brother, his teammates, his school, and himself. People were shouting, laughing, crying, clapping, roaring their approval into the night.

Kelly quietly knelt down in the end zone, just for a second, and then he looked up at the sky, pointing up to the heavens. Linda knew exactly what that meant. So did everyone else. Then, suddenly his teammates were on him, slapping him on the back, hugging him, screaming joyfully at him, dragging him back to the sidelines, where several members of the coaching staff were waiting for him. Coach Pearson, in a rare moment of in-game emotion, opened his arms and hugged him to his chest. Then, he slapped his helmet and let him go. Time to direct his attention to the point-after attempt.

Kelly made his way to the bench that they had set out for the players who were not on the field at the time, and one of the water-boys ran over to him with a Gatorade squirt bottle, which Kelly accepted gratefully. The point-after attempt was good, and the defense ran on the field. The crown continued to roar joyfully, and a lot of chatter was going on all around Linda, but she never took her eyes off Kelly. It was almost as if he felt her eyes on the back of his head, because, all of a sudden, he turned around and faced her. He knew where she would be—top row, right on the 50-yard line. So, their eyes met instantly. Probably no one else in the whole stadium noticed what happened next, but Linda did, and she would never forget it.

He smiled at her and nodded his head, ever so slightly. She smiled back. She was so proud of him in that moment. Her heart ached, but in a good way.

The rest of the game was a happy blur for her. The truth is, an aficionado of football might have objected to the game, saying that there was a lot of offense, but nobody was playing defense very effectively. The four horsemen of the apocalypse put on quite a show, leaping and running for five touchdowns during the course of the game.

However, the St. Michael's team scored six, and when all was said and done, the Warriors had won the game 42-35. They had not only won the game; they had also won the right to represent the southern half of the state in the State Championship game, to be played the next Friday in the UCF stadium up in Orlando. As Linda drove home from the game, she found herself looking forward to her tutoring session on Tuesday, where she would get a chance to tell Kelly and John how proud she was of them. She also knew that she had to go to the state championship game. She had to see this thing through to the end.

Chapter 28

Tuesday came, and she arrived a little bit early for her sessions with the boys. Coach Pearson was there in his office, and he waved her in. "What a game," he said. "I hear you were there." He nodded at the chair across from his desk, wordlessly inviting her to take a seat.

She laughed. "I wouldn't have missed it for the world. What a great game." She wasn't sure if she should ask him about the next one, or if that was inappropriate somehow. "I don't know if I should ask this, but—I'm curious. What do you know about your next opponent? Your last opponent for the season."

Coach Pearson smiled. "Oh no. It's the right question to ask. In fact, I've been concentrating on them since last Friday night. After the game, and after all the boys left for the night, the whole coaching staff met in the film room and we started watching film on the team from Tallahassee. We are going to have our hands full. They're big and they're tough, and they are very well coached."

"Wow," Linda said. "You mean you started working that very night? Right after the big win? You must have been exhausted."

"Not really. We were all too pumped up to go home. So, it's best if we stay together for a couple hours and put our heads together. Start thinking about the next game. Keep the focus tight." He grinned at her. "You've got to study your enemy during times of peace. Study the way he behaves so you're ready for him. Study the terrain. That way, you can be a little bit better prepared for the unexpected. You never know when that whore Fortune is going to spin her wheel."

Linda felt herself blushing slightly. "Oh boy. Are you annoyed that I ended up using that word with the team? I never ran things by you. Was that really inappropriate? Did you take some blowback on that?"

Coach Pearson laughed. "Are you kidding? That was their favorite part—most of them. Including the coaching staff. Listen—you play this game long enough, you learn all about unexpected and unfair bad things that can happen. At least we now have a vocabulary to work with to explain some of them. Fortune and her Wheel." He looked at his watch. "You better go. Kelly will be waiting for you in the film room. Have a good session." He stood up, and Linda said goodbye and went into the film room, where Kelly was indeed waiting, his computer opened up on the desk in front of him.

"Hey," she said, as she walked in the room.

"Hey yourself," he said. Then, he surprised her by standing as she walked in to take her seat. He gave her a quick hug.

"Saw you at the game on Friday."

"I know. I saw you too," Linda said, smiling. "I don't know if I've ever been so proud of someone in my whole life." She wanted to be careful not to overstep. "But, I know what you've been going through, and what you're trying to deal with, and you went out there—on the field of battle—and you brought great honor to yourself, your brother, your family, and your team. With a quiet kind of elegance that is actually quite refreshing in the world today. The way you just knelt for a minute and then pointed to the heavens." She swallowed hard, feeling herself getting a little bit emotional. "Anyhow, I was really proud of you." She then turned her attention to the computer screen. "So, what do we have today?"

"Thanks, Ms. Miller. Thanks for saying that, and for noticing." He was very quiet, and she realized, not for the first time, that he was a very proud young man. Trying to do the right thing in a complicated world. Having grown up way too fast and trying to deal with that sacred hurt. That loss.

He said, "I'm supposed to read a short story called "The Open Boat." I started reading it last night, but I couldn't get into it at all. It just seemed like nonsense to me. The people in the story don't even have names," Kelly said. It was pretty clear to Linda that he was genuinely puzzled and a little bit frustrated by the story. He couldn't see how it could be relevant to anything he was going through, and he was going through a lot.

"Did Ms. Davidson give you any background on the story?" Linda asked. "Tell you about the author, or the setting, or the philosophy behind the story?"

"She said it was based on something that really happened in 1897. And that it took place here in Florida. Off the coast of Daytona Beach."

"That's right. And the guy who wrote it was an athlete, and a good one. He went to Syracuse University on a baseball scholarship. Then, he got a job covering foreign wars for the newspaper. So, he is actually one of the characters in the story. He's the correspondent. Or the journalist—like a reporter." Linda could tell that none of this was making any difference or any impression on Kelly. She switched tactics. "Have you ever been swimming in the ocean in January or February off the coast of Daytona Beach?"

Kelly looked at her strangely, uncertain of where she was going with this. "No," he said.

"Do you have any idea what the surf temperature is that time of year up there?"

"Not a clue."

"Well," said Linda, "it's about 55 degrees. Do you know how long you can stay alive in water that cold if you are completely submerged? Swimming? Before hypothermia sets in?"

Now, he was interested. Something had changed. "No idea," he said. But he was listening. He was a South Florida boy, and she could almost see him mentally shiver at the thought of the cold ocean.

"You would have maybe fifteen to twenty minutes, and then you would start to lose consciousness. The cold would get inside you, and you would slip under water, sinking to your death." She felt a little bad to be talking about death to him. But it was at the core of what the story was about, so there didn't seem to be any way around it if she was going to teach him about the story. He had a faraway look in his eyes.

"So, the story is about these guys who are shipwrecked off the coast of Florida, in January of 1897. The ship sinks, and the four survivors have to get in a little rowboat—referred to as the "open boat" and try to row themselves for several miles across the open ocean to get to shore. The boat is very little. They can hardly fit four of them in it, and they have no food and no water. Which is ironic, of course, because they're surrounded by water. But as you know, you can't drink salt water. Anyhow, the waves are absolutely huge, and they threaten to overwhelm their little boat at any moment. The water is icy cold. One of the men has a broken arm and won't be much help with the rowing. They will have to take turns at the oars, and there is a very good chance that none of them will survive." Telling the story, even she shivered a little, feeling the cold and desperation creep into her bones. At least in her imagination.

Now, Kelly was really listening. Linda looked at him and could tell that his imagination was engaged. She let him think about what she had just said, and then she asked him, "When do you have to be done with the reading of the story?"

Kelly consulted his assignment board on the computer. "I have to read it by next week. I won't be able to meet with you this Thursday because the team is going up to Orlando Thursday afternoon." Suddenly, he remembered to ask her about the game. "Hey. That reminds me. Are you going to come to the championship game this Friday night? Up in Orlando?"

"Wouldn't miss it for the world," she answered quickly, although she still wasn't sure how she was going to get there. She really didn't want to drive that far alone at night. "Okay. Then, let me start to read the story to you with the time we have left today, and you finish it when you get the time, but make sure you have it done by next Tuesday, when we have our next session." She quickly consulted her calendar of school events. "That will be our last session until after Christmas vacation, because your last day of school is Wednesday of that week. Can you believe it's almost Christmas?" She caught a note of sadness in her own voice, and saw that sadness reflected in his eyes.

"I can't. But the truth is, I really can't see past the game on Friday," Kelly admitted. "And Christmas—I don't even want to think about it. It's going to be so hard with James gone. My poor Mom is gonna be a mess. I can't even think about it." Linda had absolutely nothing to say to that, nothing that could take away the pain. She sat silently and waited a minute. What to say? Sensing the importance, the sacredness of the moment, she chose her words carefully. The room was very quiet, the only sound a faint hum from the overhead light.

Then she said quietly, "Look, Kelly, I'm not going to lie or give you false hope. You're right. It's going to be very hard. But you're also right about the game on Friday. That's what you have to focus on right now. I saw you play your heart out in last

Friday's game. And something good comes from that. I'm not sure exactly what it is, but I know that it is right and good. I'll be there this Friday, somewhere up in those stands. And I'll be cheering for you. Watching every play."

She had run out of words, and she was halfway afraid that she was babbling. So, she said, "Now, go out there on that field and have a good practice. Your last one before the championship game. And I'll see you Friday night at the game. And then next Tuesday." It was 4:00, and the session was over. Kelly seemed to understand that. He glanced up at the clock, nodded at her, took a minute to visibly gather himself, grabbed his things and left.

Linda sat there for a minute, feeling completely drained, and not at all sure that she had said anything meaningful. A minute later, John White came in, flung his back pack on the floor, opened his computer and brought up the text to "The Open Boat."

"Ms. Miller," he said, "I do not understand this story at all." He was clearly frustrated. Linda began the lesson again.

That night, she went home mentally and spiritually exhausted. However, she was certain about one thing. She had to get up to Orlando to the big game this Friday. On a whim, she called her son Matt. She knew that this was the last week of his finals, and she hesitated to interrupt him in his studies. But still.

He answered right away, and he sounded good. Strong. "Hey, Mom. I've got one final to go. I'm almost half way through law school. Imagine that."

"Oh, my darling," she said. "I'm so glad to hear your voice. You sound good. I can't even imagine how stressful this past week or two has been for you. One final left. Which one?"

"Contracts," he said. "And it's bound to be terrible. But, I have it first thing tomorrow morning, and then I'm done for a month. How are you doing?"

"Well, I've called to ask a favor," she said and explained everything about the boys and the team, and the big game up in Orlando. She told him that she really didn't want to drive that far alone, and that she could buy a ride on the fan bus, but she didn't really want to do that either. She didn't know that many people there. And could he go with her?

"This Friday night?" He hesitated, and she imagined that he probably had other plans. She almost told him to forget about it, but he surprised her and said, "I'd love to come. Is it all right if I bring Lucy? I'd like you to meet her, and she's certainly ready to meet you. She has her last final tomorrow afternoon, so we will both be ready to party."

Linda felt a thrill of relief pass through her and said, "Oh, thank you so much, Matt. I don't know why exactly, but this game means a lot to me. After what Kelly's been through, and is still going through, I just want to be there for him. I know it's a huge imposition."

"Not at all," said Matt. "But, I want to have the right gear. Could you buy me a St. Michael's sweatshirt before the game, and I think you should probably pick one up for Lucy too. Please get me a large and her a small."

"Done," said Linda, planning to run by the school bookstore tomorrow. She should get herself a sweatshirt too. It was bound to be chillier in Orlando than it was down here in Fort Lauderdale. She said good night to Matt, thanked him again, and wished him well on the Contracts exam. She watched some mindless television and fell into bed gratefully, where, for some reason, her mind went back to "The Open Boat." The water so cold and so endless, the universe indifferent to the plight of the men in the little boat, the waves looming gray and cold overhead, the seagulls yawping in the air, landing on masses of seaweed with the black, glittering eyes on the men in the boat. The feeling of quiet desperation, of rowing and rowing endlessly, feeling like they were getting nowhere. The cold, indifferent stars twinkling above.

Chapter 29

Matt and Lucy came and picked her up Friday afternoon. They were glowing, in part because they had just finished their final exams and were half way through law school. However, the most important part of the glow was that sort of crazy, light-footed look that young lovers have, as though they do not quite touch the ground when they walk. They were giggling about something as they came into her condo, clearly very happy together and very much in their own world.

Then, Matt turned his attention to Linda and proudly introduced Lucy.

"Mom, this is Lucia Fernandez." He presented her almost formally to Linda, and Linda knew that this was a special moment, and this was a special young woman to her son.

"I'm so pleased to meet you. I've already heard so many wonderful things about you. Also, I have to say, I can't tell you how grateful I am that you and Matt would give up your Friday night to do this for me." She reached out her arms and Lucy stepped right into them for a hug. She was petite and dark, with hair almost black in color. It was shoulder length and very full, and it swung when she walked. She had dark brown eyes, very white teeth, and a big smile. Her eyes seemed to twinkle joyfully.

"I'm so pleased to meet you, Ms. Miller. I've heard so many things about you too. Matt is very proud of you and the way you've been working with these kids on the football team. I think it's amazing." She looked Linda right in the eyes as she spoke, a quality that Linda found completely endearing.

"Well, to tell you the truth," Linda said. "I think these kids are teaching me as much as I'm teaching them."

"You see," said Matt. "What did I tell you? That's why she's the best teacher in the world." He gave Linda a big hug, wrapping his long arms all the way around her. Linda loved the feeling of being held in his arms. She let him hold her for a minute and then stepped back.

"I almost forgot," she said. "Here are your sweatshirts, so you can be properly dressed for the big game."

Lucy and Matt pulled their new hoodies on, and they all went down to Matt's car. Linda climbed in the back seat and Matt started up a new playlist. She asked about it.

"Matt, this is a different playlist, isn't it? Could you please send it to me when you get a minute? I can't even begin to tell you how important it is that I know something about today's music scene. The music you've taught me has come up several times in the past couple months, and, in some weird way, it makes me more approachable since I know some of it." She listened to a new song by The Killers, a band she knew she liked. Then, she turned her attention to Lucy.

"So, Lucy, tell me about you? And how it is you have my son so completely happy and so completely smitten?" Lucy giggled and reached over for Matt's hand. She smiled at Linda, with delight in her eyes.

"Well, Matthew, I guess our secret's out," Lucy said.

"No surprise. Mom could always read me like a book." He merged on to the Florida Turnpike and headed north. Many of the cars that were on the highway were painted up for St. Michael's. Go Warriors, and all that. The kids had the day off school in honor of the game, and there were twenty fan busses and hundreds of cars making the pilgrimage to Orlando. Somewhere, in a hotel conference room, the team was having their last chalk talk before the game.

Lucy told Linda how she and Matt had met in Contracts, and how they also had Constitutional Law together. How she had a family that lived in Miami, and she had a younger sister named Michelle. Her mom and dad had met Matt a couple weekends ago, and loved him. Linda could tell that Matt and Lucy were very happy together. They babbled merrily all the way up to Orlando, and before she knew it, they were there. Matt found a place to park the car, paid the parking guy, and they got out. The gigantic University of Central Florida stadium loomed in front of them, ablaze with lights on this December night. Thousands of people were streaming into the stadium. There were people hawking programs and sweatshirts for both teams. It was a battle of the northern powerhouse—Tallahassee vs. the southern powerhouse—the Warriors of St. Michael School in Fort

Lauderdale. The night was chilly and a light breeze was blowing. A perfect night for football.

They filed in to the stadium, and Linda realized what a thrill this must be for the boys. There was a gigantic Jumbotron at one end of the field and an immense scoreboard at the other, all lit up. St. Michael's had been assigned the designation of the visiting team. The stadium was huge, with room for 65,000 fans. The announcers were talking away about the two teams, and they mentioned that they were expecting a crowd of 13,000 tonight—a very big crowd for a high school football game. Matt and Lucy led the way over to the 50-yard line area, and then started climbing up to a place where there were still open seats.

Linda settled into her seat, shivered a little—whether from excitement or cold, she wasn't sure—and looked down at the field to see if she could see Kelly or John. The coaching staff was milling around, grabbing players and talking to them individually. The offensive line coach had his men sitting together and he was giving them last minute instructions. All around Linda, students from St. Michael's were joyfully taking pictures of themselves, hamming it up for the camera. It was a festive atmosphere, with the St. Michael's team in their green jerseys and white pants. The team from Tallahassee had red and white as their school colors, but they had opted for an all-white uniform tonight. In some way, maybe an optical illusion, Linda thought it made their players look huge. The captains went out to the middle of the field, the coin was tossed, the National Anthem was sung, and the teams took the field.

The Tallahassee Dreadnaughts went on offense first. Their offensive line was huge, and stood in there stoutly to protect their quarterback. The quarterback was a dual threat—he could pass the ball, as he had a very good arm, but he could also run. Matt knew all about him and told Linda that the kid was going to the University of Georgia next year, a Division I powerhouse. He put together a nice, long drive, converting third downs three times in the course of the drive. Then, he ran a quarterback sneak into the end zone, and the Tallahassee Dreadnaughts had drawn first blood.

Now, it was time to see what the team from St. Michael's could do. With their young quarterback at the helm, the team lined up. Somebody jumped. Illegal procedure. Five-yard penalty against St. Mike's. Linda hoped they could shake off the jitters. From up here in the stands, the young quarterback looked small. Linda could see Kelly lined up on the far right. Dan handed the ball off to their star running back and he gained five yards, right up the middle. Got the penalty yards back, thought Linda. But still. A long way to go. Then, the ball was snapped and Dan dropped back, hanging in the pocket, his offensive line protecting him. He let a deep ball fly and John ran under it, tucking it away and heading downfield hard. A great, hard run, gaining 45 yards. Touchdown. The crowd went wild. Linda felt herself starting to breathe again. At least, they wouldn't be blown out. They were going to be fine. Win or lose—they were going to compete well. And, in the final analysis, that is really what matters.

Matt and Lucy jabbered away happily as the game went on, Matt explaining some of the fine points of the game to her. But it was clear to Linda that Lucy could hold her own in the discussion, and she found herself feeling glad that Lucy understood the game so well. Ever since Matt had played, he had been a big fan of football. The science of it. Understandably. If you've ever been on that particular field of battle, you are always—at some level—a student of the game. Or so it seemed to Linda. She enjoyed hearing her son talk about it to Lucy.

She actually had started watching football with Rick long ago, and although she had started to watch because he was so interested in it, she now was a big fan of the game on her own. And maybe even more so since she knew some of the players and the coaches out there on the field. Dan was engineering a brilliant drive, converting two third downs. Then, from the 20-yard line, he fired a ball down the right-hand side of the field. It was the first time that Kelly had been targeted. Linda felt herself running with him, timing the leap, snatching the ball out of the sky, landing in-bounds, and tearing into the end zone. Then, just like before, he knelt briefly, pointed a finger into the heavens, and then leapt up, into the center's arms.

The team was jumping around in the end zone, celebrating with each other. Then, all of a sudden, Kelly looked up at the stands. Right up at the 50-yard line. She was pretty sure that he could not see her—she was way too far up in the stands. But, she felt his eyes looking toward her, for just a moment. The kicker made the extra point, and the game was tied. Both teams were very talented, and both quarterbacks were connecting on their passes. Linda started to feel like it might come down to who made a big mistake first. Halftime came, and the game was tied 21-21.

They all ran down to the restrooms and the concession stands to grab popcorn and a soft drink. She and Lucy told Matt that they would meet him back at the seats. Linda was very pleased at how comfortable she felt with Lucy. She didn't feel like she had to try to make conversation, and Lucy was clearly absolutely crazy about Matt. She told Linda just that, not playing hard to get. Linda told her in return how happy she seemed to make Matt—how he seemed more confident, more peaceful.

Lucy grinned. "I know exactly what you mean. I feel the same way myself." Then, they were back at their seats, and the second half began. So far, the announcers were saying, the game had lived up to everyone's expectations. It was a clash of two heavyweights, and both teams were firing on all cylinders. St. Michael's would go on offense to start the second half. The temperature was dropping, and Linda was glad to have her sweatshirt on. She scanned the sidelines to see if she could spot Kelly and John as the team got ready for the second half. She noticed, out of the corner of her eye, that Matt had his arm around Lucy, and that she was snuggled up tight against his chest. She felt so happy for Matt.

After the kickoff return, St. Michael's began on their own 40-yard line, so they had a nice short field to work with. A promising beginning. Dan dropped back to throw a pass, coming right for Kelly along the right side of the field, but a tackle for Tallahassee jumped up and hit the ball in mid-air. The ball wobbled weakly in the air, and a Tallahassee linebacker was there to grab it. He cut to the outside and tore down the field for the end zone. Touchdown. Pick six. A big mistake. The Tallahassee players went crazy and so did their fans. Linda marveled, once again, at how quickly things can change. One minute you're riding high, and the next minute, that whore Fortune spins her wheel and you're down six points.

This would be a real test for the boys. How would they handle this change in fortune? The Tallahassee team converted the extra point, and the St. Michael's offense had to go right back on the field, still jittery from that bad mistake. Linda looked out at the field and saw the boys lining up, with Kelly flanked out on the left instead of the right. Dan looked kind of small for some reason. Maybe it was just her imagination. She shivered—it was getting colder. Nothing worked. Three attempts resulted in nothing. In fact, they lost a couple yards. Too far for a field goal attempt, so they had to punt.

A nice run back for the kick returner, and the Tallahassee team took over at midfield. The crowd was really pumped now, and the Tallahassee team was feeling invincible. You could tell that the momentum had changed, and they believed in themselves, could even smell victory and a championship ring. They drove down the field, almost professionally—every pass connecting, every run producing good yardage. Touchdown—a pass to the corner of the end zone. And St. Michael was down 35-21. End of the third quarter.

Matt leaned over Lucy and said, "Doesn't look good, Mom. Sorry." He waited a minute and said, "You look kind of cold. Are you sure you want to stay to the end of the game? This might be getting out of control?"

Suddenly, Linda was afraid that she had imposed too much on Matt and Lucy. They probably had a hundred other places they would rather be. She turned to Lucy and said, "I'm sorry to drag you two way up here for a game you really don't even care about. Would you like to leave early? It's all right with me if we go."

"Heck, no!" said Lucy. "No way. We are going to stay to the end and see this thing through. You have way too much invested in this team. Matt has told me all about you giving them a speech about Machiavelli. That is one of the craziest and bravest things I've heard about for a while. So, no way. We see this through. Right?" Linda was so flabbergasted, and so genuinely pleased, that she started grinning, from ear to ear. She reached out to Lucy and hugged her, and then together they turned to Matt and said, "We're staying to the end!"

"Whoa! Well, all right. You two look pretty fierce together. I'm not going to try to mess with that woman-power! We stay. So, let's go, Warriors!"

"Yeah," said Lucy. "Let's go, Warriors! And Fortune, honey, spin the damn wheel!" Linda looked at Lucy with delight and laughed. She really did know her Machiavelli!

"Damn right," said Linda. "Fortune, you whore! Spin the wheel!" She looked out at the field, scanning the players on the sidelines, looking again for Kelly and John. She could see one of the assistant coaches had Kelly cornered and was talking hard to him, his arm around his shoulder. The night temperature continued to drop, well into the low 50's, and the wind was coming straight out of the north, according to the flags blowing overhead. One quarter to go. One twelve-minute period to decide the championship.

The crowd from Tallahassee was on their feet, cheering and yelling. Not wanting to be outdone, the crowd from Fort Lauderdale took to their feet, screaming encouragement. Linda wondered how many little silver flasks had been "utilized" (as Hemingway would say) during the break. The boys on the sidelines raised four fingers in the air—their time-honored sign for acknowledging the beginning of the fourth quarter.

The Warriors successfully shut down the Dreadnaughts on their first drive, and they had to punt. The punter dropped back to send the ball downfield, but the ball came off his foot a little funny, and the punt returner had to run forward to catch it. Not only did he catch the ball, he then also ripped off another thirty yards before he was tackled. St. Michael's had the ball on the Dreadnaughts' 35-yard line. Could they reach deeper and find just the right play? Even though they were exhausted? Did they have one more miracle in their pocket? Had Fortune spun her wheel?

Sometimes, there is a moment in a football game when you can feel things change. Linda didn't know exactly what she meant, but she started to think about a line from Shakespeare's play Julius Caesar: "There is a tide in the affairs of men, which, taken at the flood, leads on to fortune; Omitted, all the voyage of their life is bound in shallows and in miseries." She thought back to what she had said to the boys. She told them that this was an important moment in their lives. They didn't even really understand its significance right now, but in time, they would. And she was glad she had said that, and that some of the boys seemed to understand what she was saying. She felt that way right now. This was the moment. Do it—somehow—or forever after regret it.

And they did it. Dan tried two passes, but neither one connected. Then, he dropped back as if to pass again, but he had really already handed the ball to the star running back—Matt checked the program and said that his name was Jacob Bailey—a senior and an Alabama commit. He pounded through the line with a fierceness that could not be denied and ended up standing in the end zone. The drive had only taken about three minutes and there was still plenty of time. The Warriors had closed the gap, now down only by seven points. The St. Michael's crowd was roaring, everyone in the stands on their feet. Linda felt the pendulum swing, felt the wheel turn.

Tallahassee seemed somehow to be doubting themselves all of a sudden. Afraid to throw the ball, afraid to make a mistake, or maybe just trying to run some time off the clock. They tried two runs up the middle and a run to the right. Nothing. They had to punt, and St. Michael's had the ball back, down seven points, with four minutes left on the clock. It might have been true that Matt and Lucy didn't care all that much about the game at the beginning of the night, but they were fully invested in it now. They looked like St. Michael's veterans, jumping and screaming, wearing their Warrior sweatshirts. Lucy gave Linda a quick hug and said, "I think that Fortune might have spun the wheel!"

Linda laughed and said, "I sure hope so. I think you might be right." She looked out at the field and saw the team in formation, Dan tucked under center. They tried two runs up the middle, putting the ball in Jacob Bailey's hands, hoping he could grind out another miracle, but it was not to be. The Tallahassee defense was stout, and they were keying on him. Third down. Kelly wide right, with single coverage. Dan dropped back and stood in the pocket, his feet always moving, looking left, center, and right. Running through his progressions, while Kelly raced down the right side and suddenly had a step on the defender. Dan let the ball fly, and Kelly went up, up, up. Like Jerry Rice. Like an angel. Like a Warrior, and caught the ball, all the while the defender's arms wrapped around his middle. He somehow came down in-bounds and hung on to the ball. First down, goal to go.

The crowds on both sides of the field were screaming, the marching bands were roaring, the announcer was babbling over the speakers, unable to control or conceal his own excitement. It was that moment when absolutely anything could happen, and everybody in the stadium knew it. The flags stood out straight in the night sky, the stars wheeling overhead, completely indifferent to the beautiful cacophony below. And absolutely anything was possible. Anything.

Linda felt a magical shiver. For a moment, she felt time stop. She closed her eyes and listened to the roar. Smelled the night and imagined the stars overhead, shining in the dark sky.

She felt the cool wind on her face, and she felt her son put his arm around her shoulders. She could taste the night, the moment, the possibility. Then, she opened her eyes to see the center hike the ball and Dan drop back. The Tallahassee team expected a run up the middle by Jacob Bailey. A good guess. Or maybe a quarterback sneak by Dan. They only had two yards to go to get into the end zone. Another good guess. But instead, John White drifted into the corner of the end zone, with a step or two on his man, and Dan lofted the ball to him. It landed perfectly in his arms, he brought both feet down. Touchdown. And the game was tied. Two minutes to go. Still that wonderful feeling—anything, anything could happen.

The Warriors converted the extra point. Some of the people in the stands were calling for the coaches to try for a two-point conversion, but cooler heads had prevailed. Now, it was all in the hands of the defense. Linda looked down at the field and saw the defensive coordinator and Coach Pearson talking to the defense before they took the field. Their heads together, saying something to them. Very intense. Was it a prayer? A plan of action? Linda realized that sometimes, those were one and the same. The score was tied 35-35, with two minutes to go. Overtime loomed as a real possibility.

The Tallahassee offense took the field. They tried two runs and a pass to the left, but St. Michael's shut everything down. Tallahassee punted, and the punt returner ran the ball back to midfield. The offense took the field on the 50-yard line with just under a minute to go. They had to make a first down, and they had to use the sidelines because they only had one time-out left. In a weird change of dynamic, the St. Michael's crowd grew quiet, although the people on the Tallahassee side were still screaming their heads off. Their marching band was roaring away, playing as loudly as they could in a desperate attempt to make sure the St. Michael's players would not be able to hear themselves think, let alone hear the play call.

Dan dropped back and passed the ball to the wide receiver on the right side. Matt checked the program for the kid's name—Steve Campbell. A senior. Gain of six yards. Jacob Bailey ran the ball up the middle for a first down before going out of bounds to stop the clock. All of a sudden, time was the enemy.

Dan dropped back and passed the ball to Kelly, who flew up in the air, caught the ball, and made it out of bounds at the 30-yard line, stopping the clock. There were only ten seconds left. Dan tried a deep pass into the end zone, but the ball sailed on him, too high for anyone to catch.

Time running out. Only five seconds left. Coach Pearson called a timeout to settle his kicker, who had been kicking on the sidelines into a practice net for the past twenty minutes. Matt checked the program for the boy's name. Nick Diaz. A senior. Going to go to Miami next year, the program said. Linda saw Coach Pearson talking to him, his arm around his shoulders. She wondered what he was saying. What do you say to a young man who has the whole team, the whole season, on his shoulders in a championship game?

She wondered what she would say, if it were up to her. She decided that she would say—just do your job. You know what to do. You've been preparing for this moment all of your life. You know what to do. Trust in your teammates. And go out there and do it. There is a time in the affairs of men. Fortune has brought you to this moment. Now, take advantage of it.

Nick walked out to the center of the field, his teammates surrounding him. As Linda watched, she saw Kelly go over to him and pat him quickly on the butt before he ran to his spot. She was so proud of him.

And then. The stars continued their flight across the night sky. The marching band roared, the fans screamed, the players on the sidelines held their breath, the flags floated against the darkness. The center snapped the ball, the holder placed the ball on the ground, Nick took two steps forward and kicked the ball— straight through the middle of the uprights! All zeroes on the clock! St. Michael's wins, 38-35.

Suddenly, a wave of sound swept over the stadium— shouts, laughter, screams, the marching band blaring the fight song, the announcer hollering over it all, and everyone jumping, clapping, hugging, high-fiving, even crying. Making a joyful noise. At least on the St. Michael's side of the stadium. On the Tallahassee side, players just fell to the ground in anguish. Linda was struck by the difference. The agony and the ecstasy.

The announcer was asking everyone to remain to see the medals awarded to the two teams—the runner-up to receive theirs first.

Matt turned to Linda, "Do you want to stay for the medal ceremony?"

Linda looked at her watch. It was almost 11:00 already, and they had a three-hour drive ahead of them. She shook her head. "No, but thank you, Matt. I saw what I came to see. Let's get home. It's really late, and you two have done enough." She could tell that he was relieved, and the three of them started to wind their way down to the lower levels and out to the parking lot. Just as she came level with the field, Linda looked out at the team. Kelly happened to be standing near the fence, only about twenty feet away. She was about to call out to him when suddenly, he turned his head and saw her. He slowly smiled, and nodded his head. That was all, but that was enough. She was so proud of him. She smiled back, called out "Well done!" and then followed Matt and Lucy out and down the tunnel and out into the parking lot.

The drive home was actually quite pleasant. Matt played his new playlist for her, narrating something about each song and the artist. Linda, always an avid student, listened carefully, drinking it all in, remembering how important the music had been to her on that dangerous night when Kelly had come by her house, needing a friend.

Matt pulled up to her condo at about 1:30, and Clarence unlocked the front door to let her in. She hugged Matt good-night, and she hugged Lucy too, telling her how much she had enjoyed being with her that night.

Lucy smiled and said, "Thank you for bringing us to that game. I have always loved football, and that was a game to remember. It's so cool that you are working with the team. That made it really special." She looped her arm through Matt's and added, "And thank you for this guy. He's pretty special too."

Linda said, "He certainly is. Thank you so much for taking me tonight. Love you." Then, she went in, said good-night to Clarence and went up to her little window on the world. She walked out on the balcony and drew in a deep breath, smelling the ocean air, seeing the stars faintly through the haze of the city lights, thinking of conquering heroes, lost loved ones, and saying good-night to them too.

Chapter 30

The next morning, she slept later than she meant too, probably worn out from the night before. The sun was fully up in the sky when she got outside for her morning walk/run. She put her earbuds in and brought up Matt's new playlist and set a good pace for herself. As she walked past the French café, she could see that it was bustling. Michel and Maria had actually bought an old-style Florida house, built around 1940, and converted it into their café. There was an outside part, with little café tables under colorful umbrellas advertising Dom Perignon champagne and Peroni beer. A light breeze was in the air this morning, just enough to flutter the umbrellas merrily in the morning sunlight. The tables were all full—the place was doing a very nice business this morning. Linda knew that inside, the ovens would be roaring away, and the sons would be back there baking, covered in flour. Marie would be working the cash register while Michel waited on tables. As she walked by, she saw him come out carrying breakfast to two of his patrons. She smiled and waved, and he smiled back, but his hands were full.

The morning was absolutely beautiful—the kind of morning you get in south Florida in December—the kind her mom used to call a "Chamber of Commerce" morning. The sky was bright blue, with white wispy clouds moving gracefully across the heavens in the morning breeze. The ocean was dark this morning, with white caps dancing into shore in their endless parade, crashing on the beach where children played with boogie boards and noodles. A flock of pelicans soared overhead, keeping their formation in a perfect V, and Linda thought of her dad. Yes, she thought, there goes the Fort Lauderdale air force. She walked two miles on the beach sidewalk, carried along by the beautiful morning and Matt's music. Then, she turned around and headed for home.

She was approaching the French café when suddenly a flock of seagulls flew right over her head, yawping and calling to each other. She looked up to see what they were doing when all of a sudden, one of the seagulls let go of his breakfast—right on Linda's head. The warm seagull shit caught the upper corner of her face and ran right into her eyes, steaming hot! It stung! And, for a minute, she was blinded by it. It caught her so off-guard that she clipped the toe of her sneaker on a raised brick paver, tripped, lost her balance, and splattered herself right in front of the café.

The guests at the outside tables jumped to their feet, horrified at the sight of this poor middle-aged woman now plastered to the bricks right outside the little fence that separated their café from the sidewalk. Two male lifeguards just happened to be walking toward her when she fell, and they rushed over to see if she was all right.

Linda couldn't exactly see them—the bird shit had temporarily blinded one of her eyes, but she felt their hands and heard their voices. One of them was trying really hard not to laugh.

"Are you all right," he said. "Do you want us to call an ambulance? Did you hit your head?" As he spoke, they gently helped her to sit up, leaning against the railing that outlined the edge of the café. They got her sitting upright, knees bent, and feet flat on the sidewalk. The good old recovery position.

"No, no, no," said Linda, absolutely mortified. The lifeguards knelt beside her, and through her one good eye, she could see that she had bloodied both of her knees. She had huge abrasions on both legs, having donated a couple inches of her skin to the Fort Lauderdale sidewalk. She was sweaty and hurt, and there was still bird shit on her face and in her eye.

"What would you like?" one of the lifeguards said. "What can we do for you?"

"I would like a hot shower, that's for sure," Linda said. Not really thinking about what she was saying. Just answering the question.

"Well," said one of the lifeguards, chuckling gently, "I'm not really sure we can give you that, but—"

Suddenly, Michel was there, kneeling in front of her. He had a small white towel, dipped in hot water, and another one that was warm and dry. He said to the lifeguards, "Good morning, Carl. Good morning, Mike. This lady is my friend. I will take care of her." The lifeguards and Michel helped her stand up. Linda realized that she kind of hurt all over—she must have really jacked her body when she fell. She also suddenly realized that she had never looked worse in her entire life, and there were three handsome men standing right next to her.

One of the lifeguards—either Carl or Mike apparently— said, "You got her, Michel? Because we can easily call an ambulance. They will be here in a matter of minutes." Michel looked at Linda, who shook her head no.

He said, "I do not think it will be necessary. If we change our mind, I will run across to your lifeguard stand and let you know." The lifeguards wished her well and went on their way, and Michel said, "Come with me, Miss Linda."

He led her into the bakery, into a far corner near the kitchen and away from prying eyes. Maria had seen the whole thing, and she called to him that she was fine and that he should take care of Linda. He brought her to a small chair and knelt before her, gently cleaning her face with the warm, wet towel, wiping the bird shit off her forehead and away from her eyes. Then he got another towel and started to clean her knees. "Would you like me to call your husband so he can come and get you?" he said, so gently.

Now, for some reason, she started to cry. It was the last thing she wanted to do. But the tears started to flow freely down her cheeks. She tried to stop herself, and instead, it got worse.

"I don't have a husband," she managed to say. "Not anymore. I'm divorced." She still felt uncomfortable with that particular word in describing herself to another person. Actually, it felt horrible. Lonely and forlorn. She looked at his handsome face and felt more miserable than ever.

"But, you have children. Grown children. I always thought you were married." He was standing a little bit apart from her, respecting her space.

"I was," she said. "For a long time. But I'm not married any more. He left me for a younger version." She felt herself getting control, such as it was. The tears stopping.

"Hmmm. Then, I think he is a fool. Here," he said. "You look much better now. Come and have a cup of coffee and a croissant. I will sit with you. We are not too busy right now, and my sister is very capable." He added this last part as if trying to make sure she would stay. She looked at him, still with tears in her eyes. But a cup of coffee sounded really good. And a warm croissant sounded like heaven.

Suddenly, her brain caught on one word. Sister? His sister? Maria was his sister? She looked at him, her eyes wide with disbelief, "Wait a minute. I have so many questions! What did you just say? Did you say that Marie is your sister? I thought she was your wife! And, are those your sons? The ones in the back smiling and waving at us? And how do the lifeguards know your name? Do you regularly rescue damsels in distress?"

"Whoa! That is a lot of questions, and I am not sure I remember them all, and certainly not in the correct order." He laughed, genuinely enjoying her confusion, but in the kindest way. No malice. In fact, if there was anything—it looked like joy. "Let me see what I can do to answer at least some of them." One of the boys brought coffee and Marie brought a basket of two croissants, butter, jam, and two small plates. She reassured Michel that she had everything under control, and she did. The rain had moved in, and many of the patrons had dashed for their cars, leaving the café almost empty.

"Okay. The lifeguards know my name because I give them free coffee and croissants—good way to make friends. I always try to rescue a damsel in distress, whenever I get the opportunity—although, I must say, it doesn't happen very often. And never so charmingly as this." His smile was so gentle that she felt her defenses dropping—just a little.

He went on, softly. "Yes. Those are my sons, and I love them very much. Gabriel and Raphael. We named them for archangels." He smiled back at the boys who were busy in the kitchen, but clearly keeping one eye on their dad. "My lovely wife, Victoria, passed away four years ago. After losing a battle with cancer. I've been raising the boys by myself since then. We are doing okay, but Marie is a very big help to me, and the boys love their auntie very much. Both of them are at the university, and work here part-time to help me run the place." He paused for a minute, ticking off questions on his fingers. "How did I do?"

Linda was flabbergasted. She could hardly speak. How could she have been so wrong? "First of all, I am so sorry about your wife. That must have been terrible for you and the boys. I feel very stupid that I never even considered a possibility like that. Please forgive me." In her heart, she was scolding herself for assuming so much about what she thought she was seeing. Lesson learned, she thought.

"Nothing to forgive. Truth is, I miss her every day. I miss her more than ever, and I am pretty sure it's going to be like that until the end. But," he hesitated, as if testing the waters, "I am very sure that she wants me to live my life. And I think she would like you very much."

Linda finished her coffee and stood up. "I can't thank you enough for all you did for me. I think I'm going to get myself home and get cleaned up. You and your sister have always been so very kind to me, and especially today."

He stood up with her. "May I see you sometime?"

"Really?" she gulped. Could this really be happening?

"Yes, really," Michel smiled. "When you are not covered in bird shit. I know it is the Christmas season, and you are very busy, but maybe you could find an opening in your schedule for me? Evenings are best. We close the café at 5:30, so any time after that. Any night."

"Really? I don't know if I'm ready for a date. I'm still getting my head around what happened. I'm not sure I am very good company. That way." She felt a little bit like a teenager—searching for the right words and not having the experience necessary to find them yet. Fumbling along, hoping for the best.

"I think we will be very good friends and keep each other company. Let's just try that. What do you think?" His dark brown eyes were full of some deep experience, probably loss. She felt her fears slipping away. She felt her heart opening slowly. Just a little. Very cautiously. But opening.

"I think yes," Linda said, shocking herself. Feeling just a little bit surprised and daring. I think yes. Just a little bit, she thought.

"Very good," he said. He reached out and took her hand in both of his. Then, he raised her hand to his lips. A small, light kiss. Light as a butterfly. Light as a breeze. Her heart opened up as the seagulls yawped overhead, white wings against the dark blue sky. Opened up, just a little.

"You had best get home," he said, smiling at her. "The birds are saying that a storm is coming. And the sky looks very threatening out over the ocean." He was right. It did. It was a very dark blue—almost indigo.

She stood up gingerly, still mentally checking on her status with regard to aches and pains. She looked down at her knees. "What a mess I have made of myself. Oh well." She smiled ruefully and gathered herself to limp the last couple of blocks home. The remaining customers in the café were gathering their things, sensing the approaching storm. The wind had picked up, and it had a weird kind of electric feeling to it. Some of the customers were moving to the inside seating area, but most were hurriedly paying their bills to get on their way. She saw Marie and the sons busily helping the customers.

"Do you need me to drive you home?" Michel asked.

"No," Linda said. "I'll be fine. But thank you so much. For everything. Honestly, I think your sister needs your help right now. I can get home. It's only a little way." She smiled at him, gently encouraging him to get back to work.

"Please. Give me your number before you leave. I will call later on tonight to check on you."

"No, please, don't trouble yourself," Linda started to say, but he waved her words away.

"No trouble at all, My pleasure. I just want to make sure you're all right."

Linda smiled and gave him her number. She was going to write it down, but he said that if she just said it out loud, he would remember it. She still couldn't quite believe what had just happened. Then, he walked her to the sidewalk, pointed her in the right direction, and said he would call later this evening. The wind freshened suddenly, picking up small scraps of paper and leaves, running them along the sidewalk. Linda felt the air temperature drop quickly, and she knew he was right. A storm was coming. She waved goodbye and hobbled home, the seagulls still yawping in the sky.

A squadron of pelicans flew overhead, holding their deep V formation, pointing out the way. She thought of her dad, watching over her. Sending her home before the storm broke. She felt pretty scraped up and rattled, but she also felt a curious lightness in her step. That is, if one could be said to hobble *lightly*! But in truth—she felt as light as a kiss. Or a butterfly.

Chapter 31

Michel did call that evening, and they made plans to go to dinner at a local French restaurant the following Friday. Not too fancy, he assured her—run by a friend of his, and with absolutely wonderful food. Linda agreed to the plan and marked the date on her calendar. With some trepidation, but also with that weird and curious lightness in her heart.

Tuesday arrived, and she went to school for her regular tutoring sessions. Kelly first, and then John. They were supposed to have read "The Open Boat" over the weekend—a short story by Stephen Crane, and one of the most famous examples of American Naturalism. Kelly came in first and sat down, looking somehow too thin and very tired.

"Are you all right," Linda asked. The minute she said it, she felt stupid. She quickly corrected herself. "I mean, I know you're not all right. You'll never feel quite all right again. I get that. But, what I mean is, should we look at your lesson, or do you want to talk about something else first?" She felt out of her depth here, but the words just came out.

"Let's do the lesson," Kelly said. "I've got to get caught up. Exams are coming, right after Christmas vacation, and I want to do well."

This seemed like a very good sign to Linda. Gratefully, she turned to the questions that Ms. Davidson had asked them to reflect on about the story. He had them printed up on a sheet of paper. The questions focused on the philosophy of Naturalism, and he had missed that lecture, so Linda decided to cover those ideas before they even started to answer the questions.

"Okay," she said. "First of all, this group of writers called themselves Naturalists, but they really considered themselves a branch of the Realists, who were writing at the same time. They believed that their writing should have a neutral, objective tone. They portrayed their characters as victims of their environment, or circumstances beyond their control."

Kelly listened quietly. "I get that," he said. "Things you can't control. Can't even predict. Terrible things that happen." Linda was pretty sure that he was thinking about his brother and the drugs that had killed him.

"Yes," she said. "These writers believe that people do have free will, but that these outside forces are often way too big for anyone to control. Furthermore, they believe that the universe is absolutely indifferent to our plight. That it will go on regardless of what happens to us. Eventually, you are probably going to study a group of writers who have a very different view. As you work your way through the history of American literature. Some of these writers are much more optimistic about the possibilities for humankind. So, don't rush to judgment. Don't think that this is the only way of looking at things."

She wanted to caution him away from despair, but she also wanted to affirm his understanding of the literature. So, she pulled it back to the piece of literature at hand and said, "However, you're right—the view of the Naturalists is pretty bleak. They see the universe as completely indifferent to us, as I said. They see no plan, no form."

Kelly listened intently. "I get what you're saying, but I also get what they're saying. You try to be a man, but there are forces out there ready to crush your dreams. I understand that." Linda felt like they were getting into dangerous and dark waters philosophically. Again, she wanted to caution him away from the darkness, but she also wanted him to take the journey intellectually. To discover the ideas as he read the literature. She looked at the questions that Kelly was supposed to consider.

The first two questions were about the setting and characters, and Kelly got those easily. The third question asked the students to examine a quote about the seagulls, floating on a mass of seaweed, looking at the men who were in this little boat, fighting for their lives. Stephen Crane writes that the seagulls "stared at the men with black bead-like eyes. At these times, they were uncanny and sinister in their unblinking scrutiny." The question asked what the seagulls felt about the men who were fighting to survive, teetering in their open boat among these dangerous waves that were ready to crush them at any moment. Linda asked Kelly what he thought.

"The birds were sinister. That's what it says. That means that the birds wanted the men to die, doesn't it?" Kelly asked.

"Yes, you have read that passage correctly. That's what it says. But—what is the author really trying to say? Do the birds want the men to die? Do they wish them ill?" Kelly looked at her, sensing a trick question, saying nothing. She waited for him to speak.

"It sort of seems that way," he said hesitantly.

"Does it? Think back to what I told you about Naturalism—the philosophy, I mean. What did I tell you?"

"That people have to face forces much greater than themselves. And that the universe is completely indifferent. It doesn't care if we live or die."

"That is exactly right. That's what the philosophy of Naturalism says. So, are the seagulls 'sinister'—are they floating on their bed of seaweed watching the men struggle and sort of enjoying it?" Again, Kelly sensed a trap. He looked at Linda, waiting for help. Suddenly, an inspiration came to her. A way to break the logjam.

"Can we take a time-out and I will tell you a story?" she asked. "It might seem completely unrelated, but I think that you will eventually see that it's not."

His curiosity peaked, Kelly sat back in his chair. "Sure," he said. "We got time."

Linda said, "Saturday morning, I was walking down A1A, listening to one of Matt's playlists. I was walking by this French café, where there is a very handsome man that I kind of have a crush on, and I heard this flock of seagulls yawping overhead, and I looked up to see what was going on, and one of the seagulls squirted a big blob of bird shit, all slimy and gray and hot, right onto my face, right into my eyes."

Kelly started laughing. She could tell that he felt bad about laughing, but he couldn't help it. She actually felt great that she was making him laugh, even a little. Even to see him smile again lightened her heart. She went on. "I started stumbling forward, caught the toe of my sneaker on a raised paver, fell down, bloodied both my knees, and lay there on the sidewalk, blinded by hot bird shit. Right in front of this incredibly handsome man and all the people having breakfast at the café."

She had a long skirt on today, but she demurely raised the hem to show him her knees. They were all scabbed over, but they were still a bloody mess. Red and sore. Ugly.

"Oh, Ms. Miller, I am really sorry. That's terrible. Right in front of the café? Where this hot French guy is?" He was still laughing softly, but trying not to.

"Yes. Absolutely. Right in front of it. And there were about 25 people on the patio having breakfast. They were all horrified." She paused for a moment, remembering the scene.

Kelly dropped his face into his hands, still quietly laughing.

"Now, here's my question," said Linda. "And I want you to think about it. Did that seagull fly over my head and say to itself—oh, there's Linda Miller. I am going to shit on her head?" She couldn't keep herself from laughing a little. It actually did sound pretty funny.

Kelly looked at her. He was still laughing, but he shook his head. "Oh, man. I doubt it. I think that he just had to go."

Linda nodded, enjoying the lightness of the moment with Kelly. "So, that seagull *seemed* sinister and mean-spirited to me, but was it really? If I told you that it was, I would perhaps be imposing an interpretation on the event that was not very realistic. Objectively? Right? I would be what they call an 'unreliable narrator' at that particular moment. You see?"

Kelly went back to the book and examined the passage about the seagulls. He was putting all the ideas together in his head. "So, when the narrator says that the seagulls are sinister, he is putting his own interpretation on the event. The way *he* thinks and feels at the time. But it might not be an accurate description. It might just be *his* idea about what is going on at that moment. Is that right?" He worked his way through the complicated idea carefully and then looked up at her, smiling.

"Exactly!" she said, grinning. "You have just leapt up to a much higher level of understanding of the story. Well done," she added. "And one more thing. You remember that there are four men in the boat, trying to survive? Who are they?"

"Ummmm, let's see. The oiler, the cook, the correspondent, and the captain," Kelly said, running his finger over the text of the story.

"Right," said Linda. "Who is the strongest, and therefore most likely to survive this battle with the elements?"

"The oiler, for sure," said Kelly. "He did most of the rowing. He took over for almost anyone who asked for help. The captain can't even row, 'cuz he has a busted arm. And the cook is sort of fat, not much of an athlete. The correspondent helps a little, but the oiler does most of the work."

"Right. Who survives the battle with the ocean? Who doesn't?"

"I'm not sure," Kelly said. "There were some parts at the end of the story that were unclear to me."

"Let's look at the ending," said Linda. She pointed to a passage and asked Kelly to read it to her.

He did so: "In the shallows, face downward, lay the oiler. His forehead touched sand that was periodically, between each wave, clear of the sea."

He read it slowly, letting the words sink in. Then, he looked up at Linda. "Oh, man. I missed that the first time. So, he didn't make it?"

"Right," she said. "The man who was the strongest does not survive. He wore himself out helping the others by rowing all night, and he was too weak to swim to shore. So. It's a new take on the old 'survival of the fittest' thing. In other words, we kind of come back to our old friend Machiavelli. Sometimes, bad things happen to good people. Things they don't deserve. Things they never could have expected." She spoke very quietly. It seemed like they were the only people in the building at that moment. She could hear herself breathing.

He smiled the smallest smile. A sad smile. "That whore Fortune again."

"Yep," she said. "What a bitch." She couldn't even believe she had said that herself. It just slipped out, but she laughed at herself, and Kelly laughed right along with her.

"Anyhow, sorry about that. I shouldn't have said that. Still, do you think you've got it now?" she asked.

"I do, and I better get out of here. I see John standing out there, waiting for his turn. Anyhow, I have a quiz on this story tomorrow in class, and I know I got it. Then, it's Christmas vacation. No school for two weeks." He stood up to leave. Linda stood up too. Suddenly, Kelly had a thought and turned back to her.

"Just one more thing," he said.

"Yes?" Linda wondered what had caught his attention.

"This idea about the universe being completely indifferent to what happens to us? No one watching over us? No one caring?"

"Yes," she said. "I know. Not a very comforting thought." She wanted him to think it out for himself, so she just waited.

"What do you think of that?" he asked softly.

"Are you asking me what I believe? Me, personally?"

"Yes."

She looked him straight in the eyes, speaking carefully and slowly. "I know that some people might make fun of me for saying this, but when it comes to that theory—well, I just don't buy it. The whole absolutely indifferent universe thing." She paused a minute, trying to gather and organize her thoughts. "On the one hand, I know that there are forces of nature that are just huge. More powerful than us. And the wind doesn't care where it blows, and seagulls don't plan to poop in your eye."

She found it curious that she was somehow censoring herself now, having said the word "shit" enough for one afternoon. "But," she went on slowly, trying to explain, "I have a hard time surrendering to the idea that the whole thing is absolutely random and accidental. That chaos theory sort of thing. I'm not doing a very good job of explaining this, but—I think that there is a plan. Maybe not in all the little things. But in the larger scheme of things. There is a Providence, and there is a God in heaven, waiting for us." She felt herself getting a little emotional, and tried to back down from it. "I don't know. Is that what you mean?" She was struggling to find the right words for this moment.

"I think that's what I mean," he said and gave her a quick hug. "Thanks for everything," he said. "Merry Christmas."

Linda tried not to sound all choked up. "No," she said. "Thank you. And Merry Christmas. I will keep you and your Mom in my prayers. And just one other thing." She wasn't sure if she should say this, but she decided to plunge ahead.

She grinned at him, a little sheepishly. "Just one more thing I should tell you. After the seagull pooped in my eye and I fell down in front of the café, French café, the handsome Frenchman I mentioned came out and rescued me with a warm, wet towel and a cup of coffee."

He was standing in the doorway, about to leave. He stopped moving entirely and looked at her hard, almost laughing. Almost. "Wait a minute?! What did you just say, Ms. Miller! The handsome Frenchman came out and rescued you! You never really explained that part! What's the story!!" He came back in the room and sat down in his chair, obviously not going anywhere right now.

305

Linda felt herself blushing, and she wasn't at all sure that she should be confessing anything at all about this whole scene. But—in for a penny, in for a pound—as her grandma used to say. She took a deep breath and decided to go on with the story.

"This little French café where I fell down. I told you about the handsome Frenchman who works there. I thought he was married, but it turns out he's not. And neither am I, anymore." She grinned at Kelly, who was sitting there with his mouth hanging open and laughing.

"So, let me see," he said. "What you're saying is that the universe is not completely indifferent to us, and the seagull shitting in your eye led you to the handsome Frenchman. Have I got this right?" He grinned at her.

"Well, it sounds pretty stupid when you say it like that, but, anyhow. I'm not sure that the universe is completely indifferent. I know it sounds silly."

"I want to hear more about this handsome Frenchman. Are you sure he's good enough for you?"

Linda smiled at him, thinking—what a lovely thing to say. "I don't know him very well yet, but I think I would like to know him better."

"I would like to hear more of this story."

"Okay. Maybe. But our hour's up and John is waiting. I see him right outside the door."

"All right, but I want to hear more about this guy. You're not getting off the hook that easy." Then, he opened the door, and John came bursting in. As they passed, they kind of shoulder-bumped each other. Like young men do.

John said, "You went five minutes over, man. My turn. Ms. Miller, you better help me. I do *not* understand this story at all." He tossed his book bag down on the table.

Kelly smiled at her over his shoulder and said to John, "Ask her about the seagull. Ask her about the seagull." John looked puzzled.

He laughed as he went out. She would not see him for almost three weeks. She hoped that he and his mom survived the Christmas holiday. Then, she turned her attention to John White and began the lesson again.

Chapter 32

Over the Christmas holiday, she went out on two dates with Michel. They talked for hours about their past, sharing their stories. She heard about his wife's battle with cancer and learned about his sons and what they were studying in school. She told him about her job in Michigan, how she had taught in a public school for 30 years, had retired, and got a job tutoring for a couple hours a week at St. Michael's. She told him about coming home and finding her husband chasing Tiffany around the bedroom, her Hemingway sash tied around her waist.

As she told the story, she sort of warmed up to the telling of it, in some crazy way. For the first time ever, since it had happened, it felt like she could see the scene almost like an outsider. Hearing herself describe what had happened, she couldn't believe how ridiculous it all was. And before she knew it, she was laughing with him, although she was also embarrassed by the whole thing. She found herself in that weird place where the line between laughing and crying seems to disappear.

Michel was a good listener, and he held her hands as they sat on her couch after coming back from dinner. He was trying hard not to laugh, and he knew that he shouldn't, but the whole thing was so ridiculous, he gave in.

"Oh Linda! Bella Linda!" he was laughing with her, but also feeling her pain.

"No. Just Linda," she misunderstood, thinking that he was unclear as to her name. "Just Linda. Linda Miller."

"No. Not just Linda, not to me," he smiled. "Bella Linda to me. Beautiful Linda—that's what that means." He smiled at her. "It will be my nickname for you, if you like it." He shook his head. "I think that your ex-husband might be a fool. Anyhow, as the famous Frenchman Michel Montaigne once said: 'One man's loss is another man's gain.' I think this time I might be the lucky man."

Linda told herself to be careful. She did not want to rush into anything. "Um, Michel. I think I should let you know that, really and truly, I'm still pretty fragile over the whole breakup. I don't know if you understand what I mean, but the truth is that I have no desire to rush into anything right now. I'm just starting to get used to living by myself and I'm still figuring things out." She didn't want to give him the wrong impression—she definitely wasn't ready to enter any kind of a long-term commitment.

"I understand completely," he said. "And I agree. My Victoria died eight years ago, so I have had time to figure things out. Believe me when I tell you that she is always with me. She loves me still, and I will always love her. But to honor her, I am trying to live my life. You are just beginning your journey. But, if you give me permission, I would like to be your friend. After that, time will tell." He was so gracious and so understanding, such a gentleman, that Linda felt a little bit like St. Paul, when the scales fell from his eyes and he could finally see the light. A little bit. Still scared, but hopeful. And just a little bit dazzled by the light pouring into her heart.

She showed him to the door. "You know," she said, thinking back on her story, her confession. "I always wanted to go to Spain and see the bullfights, and I kept that stupid Hemingway sash to remind myself to do that someday. Now—I don't know."

He held both of her hands in his as they stood at her door. "Plenty of time to decide all of that," he said. "No need to rush. And, if you would like to go to the bullfights, I would be honored to take you there. Someday. When you are ready. But I will tell you a secret." His dark eyes searched her eyes. She leaned closer to him, almost unconsciously, ready for the secret.

He smiled gently and whispered, "The bullfights in Hemingway—particularly in *The Sun Also Rises*—are much better, and I mean much better, than they are in real life. The scene with the bullfights in that novel—well, I have been to many bullfights, and I have never seen its equal. Never." His dark eyes were twinkling with something like merriment.

She leaned back, awestruck. "Really?" She realized that he must be very well-read to speak so confidently of Hemingway's works. She had not had time to discover that yet. There was definitely more to this man than what met the eye. Still—what met the eye was also very, very nice.

"Really," he nodded and said sadly. "But I will tell you something that I have seen in real life that no writer has ever been able to do justice to. Do you know what that is?"

"No. What?" Linda realized that this man was not only very well read, but was also very well-spoken. Once again, she felt just a little bit dazzled.

He took a deep breath, closing his eyes, as if remembering his own scene. "Paris at night. No matter how good the writer is—they just don't seem to be able to get that whole feeling in words. Or, at least I have not yet read the passage that makes me feel it completely."

"Hmmm," said Linda. "Now, that's a challenge. I will have to think about that. I bet I could find one that would make you say—That's it exactly!"

Michel bent down and kissed her hand, and then he kissed her lightly on both cheeks. Again, she felt that weird lightness, like scales falling from her eyes, falling from her heart.

"Perhaps you can. We shall see. Good night, Bella Linda," he said, and he was gone.

Linda walked out on her balcony and saw the full moon over the ocean, sprinkling gold and diamonds across the surface of the water. She remembered how Walt Whitman had brilliantly once said that the earth is a Prodigal with her beauty, that she lavished her charms on a world that often left her beauty unregarded, unappreciated. And yet, she continued to spill her beauty on us, ungrateful though we are.

She felt the moonlight enter her that night, coming like a gentle touch, like a whisper, like a kiss on the cheek. She felt a little bit like laughing, or yawping at the moon. It was a very lovely feeling to have a handsome man think that you are beautiful. Bella. She stayed a little longer, drunk on moonlight and imagination, and then went inside to bed.

Chapter 33

She saw both of her children over the break. Both of them seemed to be happy, falling in love, making plans for the future, busy. Andrea and Patrick were thinking about setting a date for their wedding in the fall. Matt and Lucy wanted to get through law school before they got married, but they felt pretty sure about each other. Matt said that he wanted to take Linda to meet Lucy's family—a wild, sprawling bunch of people down in Miami. He made it sound like they were a lot of fun. Linda looked forward to meeting them.

Carly and Tyler were thinking about getting married in Florida, so that Linda could be there. Sometime in the summer. Neither one of them wanted a big wedding. They were madly in love, but in a kind of private way. They had a refreshingly quiet confidence in their love. It had all happened pretty fast, but then, sometimes that happens. They didn't feel the need to put on a big show—they were going to be married, and Linda would be her maid of honor. Matt and Andrea were already making plans to be there. Linda wondered, almost a related thought just passing by, if Carly was too old to have a baby, or if they were thinking of adopting. While Linda was very close to her sister, and treasured her friendship, she also realized that—at least in some ways, Carly was a very private person. But she would be such a wonderful mother, and Linda hoped that she and Tyler would have a child. Carly would tell her about it when she was ready. Linda realized that these were very personal questions, important decisions that Carly and Tyler would face together. However, she was very glad that she had Matt and Andrea in her life. In fact, she couldn't even begin to describe how much their lives had enriched her own.

She had several wonderful conversations with Michel—at his little café where they sometimes shared a morning coffee and a baguette, and on the phone. His sister Marie always welcomed her whenever she stopped by. She told Michel to sit for a few minutes, and she would handle the customers. Linda often saw Gabriel and Raphael smiling and winking at her mischievously from the kitchen. Michel scolded them that they were not to scare Linda with their naughtiness, but Linda could tell how proud he was of them and how much he loved them.

He wanted to hear about her tutoring job; in fact, he was fascinated by it. She told him about Kelly and John, and about how Kelly's brother had died. And how she was worried about him, and admired his courage. He loved hearing about the literature she was teaching, and once again she realized that he must be very well read. He seemed to know all the pieces of literature that she was teaching, and when she talked about teaching the boys about "The Open Boat," and the theory of Naturalism, he reminded her of Albert Camus—the famous

French existentialist. In some of his writings, like *The Stranger*, he took the theory of existentialism even further—to a much darker place. She agreed with him, telling him that she did not like that book at all—that it even scared her a little. He said that he agreed with her—it was a little frightening.

She made him laugh when she told him about her conversation with Kelly. And about the seagull shitting in her eye, leading her to get to know him better, and that maybe the universe was not indifferent at all. He laughed when he heard her theory.

"Well, I have never imagined that Providence includes seagulls shitting in lovely women's eyes. If so, then Providence has a funny sense of humor. But I am awfully glad it happened, and that I am getting to know you better." He was always an attentive listener, and she felt herself opening up whenever they were together. The holidays, which she had been dreading, passed quickly by.

Suddenly, the Christmas vacation was over, and Linda's tutoring responsibilities started up again. She helped both Kelly and John prepare for their first semester final exams, and they both did well. She kept a careful eye on Kelly, watching for signs of him losing focus or getting into dangerous behaviors. However, he had three friends who were like brothers to him. John was one of them, but there were two other young men— both football players—who also stuck pretty close to him. Kelly had brought them in to meet her before his tutoring session one day.

He had introduced them as his teammates and friends—he called them his 'bros.' Their names were Justin Cavanaugh and Ian Clark. They were both taller than Kelly, but slender. And very fit. It was pretty clear to Linda that they were keeping an eye on him too. When the three of them stood shoulder to shoulder in her little work space, they were an impressive presentation of youth and strength. There was an unspoken energy that almost zapped between the three of them. They were like kinetic energy, only barely held in check. She felt honored that Kelly had brought them in to meet her. As they stood there in their school uniforms, they looked almost indestructible, but Linda knew very well that that was an illusion. She had learned the hard way about how fragile life is, how precious. So had Kelly.

The weeks slipped quietly by, and Kelly seemed like he was doing okay, but not great. Since his brother's death, he had lost his easy smile and some of his cockiness. Or his strut. Linda knew that he missed his brother terribly, and he missed football. She was pretty sure that he got something important—something he needed—from the contact, from the hitting. Luckily, the assistant coach that she had met during the Machiavelli presentation with the team—Rob DeLuca—was a strength and conditioning guy, and he was starting up regular and required sessions with all of the football players. They were starting this week. Linda thought that it was not a moment too soon.

That meant that, even though it was only February, the boys would be thinking about football again, and they would be together, working out in the gym and out on the football field. They had had about four or five weeks off, after their championship run, and most of them were ready for some kind of football, even if it was only training for the next year. Linda learned that many of the seniors, most of whom would not be playing at the college level, still attended the workouts, even though they absolutely did not have to. She had learned that football gave these young men something important. A code. A brotherhood. A sense of purpose and focus. A feeling of belonging to something bigger than yourself.

So, on this Tuesday, Kelly came in for his regular session, to be followed by John White. As usual. Apparently, Ms. Davidson was a very brave soul because she was determined to teach Walt Whitman's famous poem, "The Song of Myself." She believed that it was the great American poem, that it absolutely captured the rich complexity of the American scene, and that every student of American literature should know it.

Although Linda privately agreed with her, she thought that Diane was incredibly brave to try to teach it to high school students, because it was a wild, enormous, highly complex, almost unmanageable thing. It didn't even look like poetry. Lots of the passages just looked like prose, and Walt Whitman used this famous—or infamous—technique of cataloguing images. That means that he just runs image after image at you, letting them accumulate before he even gives the slightest hint as to what he's doing. Usually, most people are completely overwhelmed by it. And bewildered. Kelly came in for his session, tossed his book bag down, opened his computer, and got out his poetry book.

Clearly, he was not impressed with this American classic. He was not having it, at all.

"Ms. Miller," he said. "What is this thing? I cannot even tell who the speaker is. You tell me to always start with that. Well, I don't get it. And who writes a poem with 52 sections to it? It's more like a book, told by some crazy person." He looked at her with thinly disguised frustration. "I'm really glad we don't have to read all 52 sections."

Linda laughed. "Well, you have described it perfectly. I wonder if the number 52 means anything to you?"

Kelly frowned lightly, puzzled. "I don't know. The only thing I can think of is 52 weeks in a year."

"You're right. That's it exactly. It's almost like he was saying—this is the poem brought to completion. He meant it to be the great American poem. To celebrate the American spirit— in all its diversity, all its complexity, all its richness. The beauty and the ugliness. The pleasure and the pain. That's what he's trying to capture." She paused for a minute. She knew that she was caught up in the rhetoric, the rapture that sometimes came over her when she spoke about great literature. Kelly was looking at her skeptically, almost shaking his head 'no.' He sighed heavily, unconvinced.

"Well," said Kelly. "All right. I'll give it a chance. That's a cool idea. But man. This poem is 62 pages long! Who writes a poem that long? That is completely out of control!" He saw her start to caution him, and he added, "But okay. I will give it a chance."

"Good. That's all I ask. Remember how we always say that you cannot rush to judgment. You've got to wait until you've read the whole thing, whatever it is, and then you have to think about it. Now, tell me what you have to do with it."

Kelly sighed, surrendering, "Ms. Davidson is setting the whole thing up, and she is going to do the opening sections. Sort of get us going. And then every person in the class gets one section, and we have to explain it to the class when it's our turn. Some of the sections in the middle we get to skip over." He added "thank God," under his breath. He grinned at her.

Linda thought that sounded like a pretty smart way to approach the beast. She admired Diane Davidson's courage and her clever approach. "Okay," she said. "That sounds pretty good to me. You and your fellow students will actually build off of each other. And you'll help each other figure things out as you go along. Which section did you get?"

"You'll never believe it. Section 52. The last one. I get to be the guy that wraps it all up." He did *not* sound thrilled.

"Wow," said Linda. "You got the best section in the whole poem. She must really think a lot of you to entrust you with that one."

"Hmph, I don't know about that."

"Well, I do. I think there is a very special reason that she gave that section to you, and I know you are smart enough to figure it out. When you know a little more about the poem and what Whitman is trying to do." She looked at his assignment sheet. "I don't see that you really have any homework, nothing to write or anything else."

He checked the homework page on his computer and agreed with her.

"So," she said. "Let me just read the opening sections to you. And you just listen, letting the words wash over you. Okay? No judgment. Not yet."

"Okay," he said. "First of all. Who's the speaker? That's what you always say to start with, right?"

"That's right. That's the first question when you look at a poem. And it's a really hard question with this one. The speaker is Walt Whitman, 37 years old—a strong, hard-working, confident, American man." She let that sink in. "But the speaker is also sometimes God, or the Creator, or the poet/artist who perceives the world in all its beauty and pain. The speaker believes that we can transcend space and time through poetic, and sometimes prophetic, visions."

Kelly looked at her and rolled his eyes. "Was this guy on drugs?"

"No," she said. "He was a Romantic. Or a Transcendentalist. Nature was his drug."

He looked at her with bewilderment. "Talk sense, Ms. Miller. Explain."

"Well," she said. "You remember before Christmas when I taught you about the Naturalists, or the Realists. And their philosophy? When we read that story called 'The Open Boat?'"

"I remember," Kelly said. "The universe is completely indifferent to us. It doesn't care if we live or die. There are huge forces out there and we can't control them." He spoke confidently about the story. Clearly, he remembered it well.

She beamed at him. "You are so smart. I'm so proud of you. Well, anyhow. Whitman has a completely different philosophy, and as your class starts to study this poem, you will come face to face with it. He believes that Nature nurtures us and heals us. He believes that if you're out of touch with Nature, you're out of touch with your own divinity. He says that you have to get outside every day, and that you have to get your eyes up to the sky, out to the ocean, up to the mountaintops, or you'll go crazy."

"Hmmmmm," said Kelly. "Pretty hard to see any mountaintops around here."

"True," said Linda. "We don't have mountains in South Florida, but we sure do have the ocean. And everywhere we have the sky."

"Which your brain is wider than," Kelly grinned at her. She was startled for a minute, and then she remembered that he was actually alluding to the Emily Dickinson poem they had studied together, what seemed like ages ago.

"Kelly!" she said. "You amaze me! Your mind makes these leaps sometimes. You're an amazing young man." She pulled herself together, smiling at him. She was so proud of him. "But anyhow, Whitman believes that we have a body and a soul, and that the soul is immortal. He doesn't really subscribe to any given religion. He kind of has his own. In this crazy, long poem, he celebrates life. He invites us to come on a journey with him. He's going to try to capture the American spirit—he loves his country, even with all its flaws—and discover, with him, how precious life is. That we should live every minute to the fullest."

"He sounds really different than those Naturalists."

"Oh, he is. You're absolutely right. Fire and ice." She smiled at him, with a secret nod of the head to Robert Frost. "Well, our hour is almost up, and John will be here for his session. But we have a couple minutes left. So, let's do what I said earlier. Let me just read the opening section to you and we're going to just let the words wash over us. No judgment yet. No attempt at interpretation. Just listening. Unless I can talk you into reading it to me?" she added hopefully.

"No chance," he said. "You read. I'll listen." He settled back in his chair.

"Okay," she said. "Here goes.....

Song of Myself

I celebrate myself, and sing myself,
And what I assume you shall assume,
For every atom belonging to me as good belongs to you.

I loafe and invite my soul,
I lean and loafe at my ease observing a spear of summer grass.

My tongue, every atom of my blood, formed from this soil, this air,

Born here of parents born here from parents the same, and their parents the same,

    I, now thirty-seven years old in perfect health begin,

    Hoping to cease not till death.

    Creeds and schools in abeyance,

    Retiring back a while sufficed at what they are, but never forgotten,

    I harbor for good or bad, I permit to speak at every hazard,

    Nature without check with original energy."

She finished the opening section of the poem, tasting the words like some delicious, heavenly wine, eager for the next drink, her heart beating faster.

She looked over at Kelly, to see if he, too, felt the approaching rapture.

He looked back at her, his face absolutely empty of any emotion. Flat.

"Well," she said, having a hard time hiding her excitement.

"Nothing. I got absolutely nothing."

Apparently, he did not, as yet, feel the approach of rapture. "Well," she said. "It's an introduction. He's saying—here I am. My name is Walt Whitman. I'm 37 years old, and I'm going on a journey, and I would love it if you would come along. Let's go discover the mystery of life together. Are you ready to come? That's what he's saying."

John knocked on the door, ready for his hour.

"Well," said Kelly. "It would have made a hell of a lot more sense if he had just said that!" He grinned at her sheepishly. "Sorry about the hell."

John White came in. "My turn. I need some help with this thing. I got section 6, so I need a lot more help than Kelly here. So, help me, Ms. Miller. Save me." He sort of pushed Kelly out the door, laughing.

Kelly called over his shoulder, "Good luck, bro. This is some really crazy shit. Oops. Sorry about the shit, Ms. Miller." Then he grinned at her before leaving. "Oh, I forgot. We can say shit. Even you say bird shit."

"Get out, you!" she laughed. "Haven't you got something important to do?"

John said, "Wait. What's this about bird shit?"

"Argh! Never mind," Linda said. She was still laughing, in spite of herself. "Okay. Let's talk about Walt Whitman. You say you have section 6, so we better get going. You're one of the early performers." And she began the lesson with John.

Chapter 34

The first thing they did is read his section together. Section 6. "Song of Myself." Like Kelly, he wondered how in the world a poem could need 52 sections, and, again like Kelly, he asked her to read it out loud to him. John explained that each student was supposed to read their section out loud to the class and then tell their classmates what it meant, picking out two or three lines that they felt were the most important ones in the passage. It was supposed to be an experiment in 'student-centered collaborative education.' John thought it was an experiment in Ms. Davidson seeing if she could drive them all crazy and make them do all the work.

"Well," said Linda. "You have probably the most important section in the first half of the poem. The one that gets it all going, so you have got to do a good job for your fellow students. You see that Whitman is working with the image of grass. What do you think it means when he says that the grass is like the handkerchief of the Lord, purposefully dropped in every corner of the world?"

John looked at her, his eyes wide. And blank. "I have absolutely no idea."

She smiled at him. "Not your fault. Understanding the image depends on you understanding something women used to do." She stood up and walked away from him, across the room, dropping an imaginary handkerchief on the floor behind her, and then looking back over her shoulder. "What would you do if I dropped my handkerchief as I walked away from you?"

"Errrr. Tell you that you dropped it?" He said, not getting it.

She laughed. "Given our preoccupation with germs these days, that might be the smart thing to do. But in days of old, ladies used to drop a handkerchief near a man that they kind of wanted to talk to. Ladies weren't supposed to start the conversation, so that was a subtle way of saying—hi. I'd like to talk to you."

"Well, that is the silliest thing I have ever heard," John laughed.

When Linda thought about it, she realized that he was absolutely right. What a way to begin a relationship! She nodded, smiling, "All right. I agree. But—just for argument's sake. Let's say that's what it means. If so, then what is Walt Whitman saying about the fact that God has dropped grass of some kind in almost every corner of the planet?"

He sat there, thinking for a minute, following her logic and the image they were working with. "I guess it means that God is interested in having a talk with us. Or a relationship?

Maybe? Am I way off base here?" He was uncertain, but he was actually absolutely right.

"Well done," Linda said. "Now, let's take it a bit further. "He tells us in the middle of your section that the grass is very dark, rich with color, not pale and ghostly. He tells us that in cemeteries all around the world, the earthly remains of men, women, and children lie under the grass. But not their spirits. He says that the grass is trying to tell us something."

John looked askance at her, clearly puzzled, clearly thinking she had gone too far. "Ms. Miller, are you saying that the grass is speaking to us? Telling us something important?"

She smiled. "I know it sounds crazy, but that is exactly what Whitman is saying. The grass is trying to reassure us that there really is no death. That life goes on. Listen to your closing lines...

"I wish I could translate the hints about the dead young men and women,
And the hints about old men and mothers, and the offspring taken soon
Out of their laps.
What do you think has become of the young and old men?
And what do you think has become of the women and children?
They are alive and well somewhere.
The smallest sprout shows there is really is no death.
And if ever there was it led forward life...
All goes onward and outward, nothing collapses,

327

And to die is different from what any one supposed, and luckier."

She waited a minute and let the lines sink in. It was absolutely radical stuff, and it was written about 150 years ago. Walt Whitman was so far ahead of his time, it still astonished her every time she read the poem. His crazy, wide open style—the world had never seen anything like it. He was writing free verse before they even had a name for it. And his style of cataloguing images—just running image after image at you, letting them accumulate significance. It still baffled readers, to this day.

"Do you see?" she asked. "He has now made this radical declaration, and he is going to spend the rest of the poem trying to prove what he has just said. But you have the very important responsibility of making this opening declaration for him."

John looked at her. "I have to read this whole section to the class, and it's pretty long. And then I have to explain it. This is a big thing." He was processing the assignment in his head, figuring out how to approach this, how to attack it. She was very pleased with him. He had made so much progress as a student, now comfortably thinking about and analyzing complex tasks.

"That's right. And you *can* read it. And do that very well. You have a good strong voice. You'll do a good job with the reading. But then, you also have to tell them the three main points, and have them underline the important lines. So, let's try to figure out together what the three main points are. What do you think is the first thing you should explain, looking back at the whole section?"

He studied the lines. "I think I better explain about the handkerchief thing, because I don't think anybody will get that unless I tell them about it."

She agreed with him. "Perfect. You're right. You had better explain that. And then what?"

He moved his finger down the lines. "I think the part about the men, women, and children—their bodies lying under the grass, but not their spirits. Then, the idea that the grass is everywhere. All over the world."

"Perfect," she said. "So, what does that mean?"

He sat there thinking for a minute, and then he surprised her by going even further than she had hoped. "I guess it means that death is everywhere. That it is universal. Everybody dies, eventually."

Linda sat quietly, letting him follow his own train of thought. Then, she nudged him further. "You're right. Now, what's the last idea? Last, and most important. Look at the closing lines."

John thought deeply for a few minutes. "That death is not the end. That death leads to life. That's what the grass is trying to tell us. And our loved ones who have died—in some ways, they're luckier than us." He paused a minute. "I don't know exactly how that is, but that's what he says." He looked up at her, asking with his eyes if he had it right.

He had it right. "John," she said. "That is absolutely brilliant. No—we don't know exactly what he means, and he's going to spend the rest of the poem trying to help us. But you have explained his position perfectly. I'm so proud of you."

They sat there for a minute together. It was five o'clock. Time for his football training. He looked up at the clock, grinned at her, and said, "Okay. That's enough thinking. I think my head's gonna blow up." He still sat in his chair, unmoving.

She stood up. "Off you go, then. Have fun out there."

"I will," he said. Finally, he stood up. He looked at her and smiled. "And man, thanks a lot. I never could've done that without you."

"Thank you, sir," she grinned. "Not yet, anyhow. Someday."

"Unlikely," he said. "Have a good evening."

She gathered up her stuff and headed out to the car. It was February, and the sky was staying light a little bit later, but not much. There was a South Florida kind of wintry coolness in the air, and as she started up her car, her old buddy Bob Seger came on, singing, "Someday, Lady, I'll accompany you." She sang along with him. And howled, just a little.

Chapter 35

Thursday came, and it was time for Kelly's tutoring section. He came in and looked at her with something close to terror in his eyes.

"Ms. Miller, I've read my section, and I don't know what the hell this man is talking about. And I have to present next Monday or Tuesday, so you gotta help me figure this out today. No kidding. I'm running out of time here."

"Hello to you too!" Linda laughed. "You and John are in the same class, right? So, that means you got to see his presentation on section 6. How did he do?"

"Man, he did great. He got an A on it, and Ms. Davidson was really happy with what he said. He even acted out the dropping the handkerchief thing, and she thought that was great. But his section was a lot easier than mine."

Linda waited until he got settled down, opened his computer, and found his book. "Have you been listening to all the things your classmates have said about the intervening sections?"

"Of course," he said. "And I've been taking good notes. But I still don't know what mine's about, and I want to do well. I've got the last section, and Ms. Davidson told me as I was leaving today that it is the most important section of the whole poem. The really famous one. Just like you told me." He seemed to really feel the weight of the responsibility. Linda was so impressed with him, over and over again. She knew that he was hurting, deep inside, but he was going on. Like a warrior must.

"Well," she said. "First thing. Let's read the section out loud and listen to what he says. Then, we'll find the three big ideas. Okay? You read to me."

"Noooooooo, Ms. Miller. Please? This first time—you read it to me. I think I hear it better when you read it to me."

She acquiesced. "Okay. Here goes. Section 52. The conclusion of 'Song of Myself'—at this point, Whitman is pulling it all together. He is getting ready to say his farewell to the reader. He has laid out everything he knows. Or, at least that's what it feels like at this moment. I think he actually has more to say, and he goes on to write a lot more poetry. But this one—this incredibly complex, wild, sprawling, poem is done. And here's the bottom line. Even the speaker of the poem knows that he must die. But remember—death is not an ending.

The spotted hawk swoops by and accuses me, he complains of my gab and my loitering,

I too am not a bit tamed, I too am untranslatable,
I sound my barbaric yawp over the roofs of the world.

The last scud of day holds back for me,
It flings my likeness after the rest and true as any on the
shadowed wilds,
It coaxes me to the vapor and the dusk.

I depart as air, I shake my white locks at the runaway sun,
I effuse my flesh in eddies, and drift it in lacy jags.

I bequeath myself to the dirt to grow from the grass I love,
If you want me again look for me under your bootsoles.

You will hardly know who I am or what I mean,
But I shall be good health to you nevertheless,
And filter and fiber your blood.

Failing to fetch me at first keep encouraged,
Missing me one place search another,
I stop somewhere waiting for you."

As she finished the reading, Linda found that she could hardly breathe. There were tears in her eyes. She was thinking of her Mom. And her Dad. And her brother. And James. A litany of her everyday saints, her family and friends that had gone before, floated in front of her eyes. Even the air seemed to hold its breath, and she looked at Kelly, with tears in her eyes. She couldn't hide them, and she didn't even try. He looked at her, hard, saying nothing. Then, he looked at the words on the page.

"What does it mean?" His voice was almost a whisper.

"I don't know," she whispered back.

For a minute, he said nothing.

Then, she looked at him and laughed. So did he.

"Not the answer I was looking for," he said. "You're gonna have to do better than that, Ms. Miller." There was a tear in the corner of his eye, which he quickly wiped away.

"Well," she said. "Let's unpack the lines. Like we always do. In the first couple lines, the speaker sounds like he has to leave, like he has stayed long enough. Right? What could that mean?"

"That the poem is almost done?"

"Yes," she agreed. "I think that's it exactly. And maybe, even, on another level, that his life is almost done. It's time for him to fly away, and he is eager and excited to do that. He wants to sound his 'barbaric yawp' over the rooftops."

"Yeah. About that," said Kelly. "What exactly is a yawp anyhow?"

"It's a cry. I don't mean a tearful cry. It's actually more like a warrior's whoop in this case. You see? It's a *barbaric* yawp. I don't mean to say that it can't be a sad cry. I think it sometimes can. I think there is sadness in it, maybe underneath it. But it can also be a triumphant cry. At least, that's what I think."

"Okay," said Kelly. He nodded, understanding the concept. A barbaric yawp. "So, that's something I should explain." He studied the text carefully. "And then, these middle lines—the speaker is departing 'as air'—flying away, I guess. But, he is also allowing his body to be buried."

"You're right," said Linda. "He 'bequeaths himself to the dirt to grow from the grass I love—he is allowing his *body* to be buried. But his spirit is flying away. Is that how you see it?"

"I think that's right," Kelly said, pointing at the middle set of lines. "And then the ending. What do you make of that?"

Linda studied the lines with him. She felt herself getting a little choked up, and she didn't want to screw this up, or to overstate it. She waited for the right words to come to her, and then they did. "He is still with us. He never left us. He is nearby, and if we can't see him or feel him right now, we just have to trust that he is near and keep looking. And sound our barbaric yawp right along with him. We will find him, sooner or later." She was almost whispering now, fighting back tears.

There was a long pause. For a minute, Kelly just sat there.

"Who are we talking about," Kelly said. His voice almost a whisper too.

She looked at him. She swallowed hard and fought for the words. "Our lost loved ones. My brother. Your brother. Your dad. My mom and dad. Walt Whitman. And all the lost loved ones of your classmates that you will take on this journey with you. They are not lost. They have stopped somewhere, and they are waiting for us. In the next room." She felt the idea go all the way through her.

"Well. Okay." He did too.

She couldn't move. She couldn't speak.

He grinned at her, but it was a grin that was touched with sadness. She understood completely. And so did he.

Then, he said, "Yawp."

It was one of the bravest things she had ever heard. She laughed, almost in spite of herself. She grinned right back at him, her own smile touched with sadness too. "Yawp."

He thanked her for the lesson and headed out.

John came in.

Chapter 36

Saturday morning in late February in South Florida. Misty and cool. Well, it was winter after all. Linda put on her running shorts and shoes and a long-sleeved top. It was about 60 degrees out there, and very windy. In South Florida, that felt cool. She got her Iphone and her earbuds and took off, aiming to get four miles in. Listening to Matt's most recent playlist, letting the morning carry her along. Lots of tourists were in town, and the sidewalk was crowded with out-of-towners, determined to get out and enjoy a morning at the ocean, in spite of the gray skies.

Young mothers pushing babies in their fancy jogging strollers, couples keeping fit, all kinds of people joined the parade down the sidewalk that ran along A1A. As she went by the French café, Linda could see that business was booming. The umbrellas fluttered in the morning breeze, and customers huddled together, wearing their sweaters, enjoying the coolness as they drank their coffee. She did not see Michel out on the patio, but that could mean that he was just picking up an order in the kitchen, getting ready to serve it. Maybe she would stop and see him on her way back. Assuming that the seagulls had left her alone.

The wind picked up even more, and the sky darkened as she went along. She turned around when she was two miles out, but she had the feeling that she would be racing the rain, trying to get back before the skies opened up. The tourists who were out on the beach started to gather their towels and beach bags. Everyone could smell the rain approaching. Out on the ocean, you could see a dark wall of rain, moving slowly toward land. Linda quickened her pace and was just across the street from Michel's café when she heard her name being called.

"Ms. Miller! Hey. Ms. Miller!" she turned and looked to see Kelly sitting on the white wall that lined the edge of the beach. She stopped quickly and pulled out her earbuds.

"Kelly! How nice to see you! What are you doing here?"

"Well. I just took a chance. You've told me many times that you walk this route every morning, and I woke up early and thought I would drive over here and see if I ran into you. I thought I might run a couple miles before I head back home. Give the local ladies something to feel good about." He grinned at her.

Linda grinned right back. "I'm sure the local ladies will appreciate your contribution." She climbed over the wall and sat next to him. The wall is low, only about a foot and a half tall. Perfect for sitting on, although children all love to walk on it—as if it were their own little sidewalk.

They sat together companionably, looking at the rain coming across the ocean. Kelly had his St. Michael's sweatshirt on, and Linda was glad she had a long-sleeved shirt on. She was thinking that maybe she could have Kelly join her and go over to Michel's café, trying to get someplace safe and warm before the rain hit.

But Kelly had something on his mind, and she could sense that this was not just a casual visit. She waited for him to speak, to see what he had to say.

He took his time, and then he said, "You know that stuff we were talking about the other day? The part about 'look for me under your bootsoles—I stop somewhere waiting for you'—you remember that part?"

"Of course I do."

"Well. What you said about it. Did you mean it?"

"I did. I do."

He looked at her. "That our loved ones are not lost. That they are waiting for us somewhere, and that we will be together again? Do you believe that? Really?" His dark eyes were boring holes into hers. This was not a time for levity or carelessness. Once again, she searched for the right words.

"I do believe it. I somehow know that my Mom and Dad, and Tony, are all waiting for me. For when I cross over. And they will be there. And I think my brother is going to scoop me up in his big, strong arms and literally carry me across the finish line. I used to think I was going to swim into heaven, but now I think Tony is going to carry me in." She hoped that she did not sound foolish. But, on the other hand, even if she did sound foolish, she was speaking her truth.

Kelly waited for a couple minutes. "So, that means that you believe in heaven and you believe in God, and you believe in an afterlife. You believe that this is not the end."

"I do believe that."

"But how can you believe that when you have absolutely no proof. No one has ever proved it to you." She could hear the pain in his voice, right under the surface. Wanting to know the answer, and knowing that it was impossible to know the answer. At least not yet. Not here. But wanting just the same. She took a deep breath and spoke slowly, feeling her way for the right words.

"Sometimes, you believe in something even though you can't see it. You just know, on some gut-deep level, that it's true. Someone once said that faith is when you believe in something that you can't see. So, I guess it's faith." She was trying to explain, and she felt like her words were falling flat. He didn't say anything.

She tried again. "Sometimes, I swear I get nudges from my loved ones. I hear my Mom's voice. Or my Dad's. Or Tony's. Something they said once washes over me, and I just know they're there."

Out on the horizon, a gigantic cruise ship was chugging along, coming into port. The rain squall was continuing its march across the ocean water, blending ocean and sky, blotting out the horizon. The cruise ship was about to sail right into the wall of rain. The raindrops who were the advance guard were already making their presence felt for Linda and Kelly as they sat on the wall. Suddenly, Linda had an idea. It was one of those moments when you suddenly get an epiphany—you're not even sure if the idea originated with you or was given to you by some kindly spirit. She decided to try it.

"Kelly, do you see that cruise ship out there?"

"Yes," he said. "I think it's about to get clobbered."

"But you see it right now?"

"Yes," he looked at her, puzzled. The rain intensified. She had to raise her voice to be heard. They were both about to get really wet. And it was a surprisingly cold rain.

"Okay," she said. "Wait a minute."

Kelly looked at her like she had lost her mind. The cruise ship sailed on, right into the band of rain, which was huge, deep, and dark gray. In a moment, the ship completely and utterly disappeared from sight.

Linda pointed. "Do you still see the ship?"

"Nope. Can't see it at all." Kelly looked at her, sort of waiting for the lesson to end. He shivered slightly in the cold rain. So did she.

"But you still believe it's there?" she asked.

"Errrrr, yes. Of course."

"But you can't see it?" she persisted, stubbornly.

"No," Kelly was puzzled. He looked at her like she was some kind of broken record, stuck on the same line over and over. She went on.

"But you know it's there? Right? So," she said. "It's kind of like that. But way better. I think that every now and then, we get a glimpse of what lies ahead. We get these little signs that our loved ones are alive and well, waiting for us just beyond the veil.

We hear their voices, or smell them, or they come to us in our dreams, or we suddenly just know what to do or say, and we have the feeling that they just helped us along. Or, they send us signs. Things we would recognize as significant to them. It's personal." She desperately hoped that she was making sense. She waited for him to say something, and the rain poured on.

He didn't look at her. It almost seemed like he was completely in his own head for a minute. He spoke slowly, even as the rain and the wind intensified. He too raised his voice a little since the rain was getting louder. Linda was soaked all the way through, but she dared not move. "So, when I think that I might be hearing James talk to me, or my Dad, it might be true?"

She nodded. "It might." She waited a minute, letting the rain run down her cheeks. "Or, they are so deep inside you that you have become one. Sort of. At least for that moment."

"So, what are we supposed to do in the meantime?" he said. Tears and rain were blending on his face. Hers too.

She looked at him, looked hard at him, unsure of what to say. And then, she knew. "Yawp."

"What!?"

She threw her head back and yelled. Or yawped. It was barbaric. "Yawp! Yawp!"

He laughed and threw his head back too. "Yawp! Yawp!"

She jumped up and started laughing and yawping all at once.

People were driving by in cars, probably wondering what these two crazy people were doing. They ran around on the wet sand, still yawping. Linda flapped her arms ridiculously.

Yawping. Kelly did the same. Soon, they were laughing so hard, they could hardly stand up. Rain and tears commingled on both of their faces.

She looked across the street and saw Michel watching them, and laughing. He was standing under the canopy of the café, holding up two big white towels. He hollered something, but she could not hear him over the rain. She grabbed Kelly and pointed to the café.

"Let's go get dry. I'll buy you a cup of coffee. And one more thing." He was listening hard. She looked him right in the eyes and went on, "We yawp right through the pain. We still miss them. We will always miss them—until the day we die. But we carry them with us—in our hearts. And in our voices. And in our barbaric yawping."

He nodded and grinned at her. "I get it. I think." Then, they ran across the street, jumping over puddles. Which was absolutely silly since they were completely soaked. Shoes and all.

The café was practically empty, as most of the customers had left to avoid the rain. Michel and Marie were both standing there smiling, holding out warm, dry towels.

Michel put one of them around Linda's shoulders, laughing. Marie gave hers to Kelly. Michel said, "Bella Linda! Have you no sense at all! You are completely soaked, and you are shivering! Come in here and let me get you some coffee. And you must be Kelly! I have heard so many wonderful things about you. Come in, come in."

Marie and Michel showed them to a table at the rear of the café, out of the reach of the rain. Gabriel and Raphael came over, bringing hot coffee and croissants, a baguette, butter, and jam. Both of them wanted to meet Kelly.

Gabriel said, "I am so pleased to meet you. I have so many questions. I hear you play football. My brother and I—we play football too. But our kind of football. You call it soccer. We have a lot of questions about the rules to your American football. Which we much admire, but do not understand in the least." Both the boys sat down, dragging up an extra chair. Marie brought Linda another towel, warm from the dryer. It was almost the most heavenly thing she had ever felt.

Soon, they were all talking and laughing, Kelly explaining the rules—Gabriel and Raphael interrupting excitedly, questions and questions. The young men were in their own world, getting to know each other, talking about the sports they loved. Kelly seemed very comfortable with himself, delighted to answer their questions, enjoying the repartee.

Marie drifted back over to the cash register to help a lone remaining customer. Michel smiled at Linda and took her hand in his. Together, they watched the young men talking about passes and catches and touchdowns. All that wonderful stuff.

Chapter 37

The weeks went by, and soon it was May. The school year was almost over. The students were down to their last five weeks. It was time for Spring Football. There were very strict rules regulating football in South Florida, but all the players were looking forward to this very special time. They had a lot of fun during these practices, and there was a lot of emphasis on strength and conditioning. They worked out four days a week, for about an hour and a half a day. Light pads, no heavy tackling. Learning to run the plays and getting to know each other.

However, in spite of these limitations, it really could be seen as the beginning of the football season. The rising seniors stepped up into positions of leadership. Team captains were chosen, and the graduating seniors got a chance to say their farewells. The session concluded with a spring football game against a nearby school who wanted to play a full scrimmage on the field and under the lights. This year, St. Michael would be playing Fort Lauderdale High, and the game was scheduled for the last Friday before Memorial Day. Then, the kids would take the final exams and go off to enjoy their summer. The school year was really coming to a close.

Kelly and John were both named as captains, chosen for this honor by their teammates. They continued their tutoring sessions with Linda, and both of them had told Coach Pearson that they wanted to work with her next year as well. Both Kelly and John had improved their scores on the SAT and the ACT, and they were very pleased with how well they had done. Coach Pearson had passed this information on to Linda, and she had told him that she would be honored to stay on. On the last Thursday before the game against Fort Lauderdale High, there was to be a team meeting, and there would be no tutoring sessions that day.

Coach Pearson asked her to come in a little early on Tuesday so he could talk to her about something, so Linda showed up at his office about a quarter to three—15 minutes before her session with Kelly would begin.

"You know that there will be no tutoring this Thursday, right?" Coach said.

"Yes," said Linda. "I heard that. So, as I understand it, today will be my last session with Kelly and John, until next fall. Is that correct?"

"Yes," he said. "However, I would like you to come in on Thursday and attend our big team meeting. It's the last team meeting we will have until we begin summer practices."

"Really. You want me to attend?" said Linda. She was actually flabbergasted.

"Yes, really," he said. "You see, something pretty important is happening at that meeting. Kelly is addressing the whole team, and he wants you to be there to hear his speech." His eyes were twinkling merrily, and Linda could tell that he was very pleased with himself about something.

She could hardly speak. She thought about Kelly and how brave this was. She remembered how nervous she was the day she spoke to the team about Machiavelli. And what a trip that whole experience was.

"Well," she said. "I am really honored. I mean really honored. Of course, I would love to attend the team meeting. Thank you for thinking of me."

"Well, I would like to take credit for that. I really would. But this is all Kelly. And John agrees. He said that you have to be there. So—that's that!" He smiled at her, but it was clear that he was not going to explain anything more about the meeting.

Then, he grabbed up some papers on his desk, and Linda recognized his traditional signal that the meeting had come to an end. She stood up, thanked him, and went to her little room to wait for Kelly.

When he came in, she tried to pump him for information about what he was going to speak about on Thursday. He elegantly sidestepped all her questions, saying simply, "You'll see. You will be there, won't you?"

"Honestly," she said. "I wouldn't miss it for the world."

Understanding that he was not going to tell her anything about his speech, she turned her attention to the lesson for the day, which was basically a review for the final exam. Ms.

Davidson had given the kids a study sheet, listing the main ideas that would be on the exam, the most important pieces of literature, and the literary terms they had to know.

They went over them together, and Kelly did really well. He spoke confidently about every piece of literature and rattled off good definitions for all the terminology. Linda was both pleased and very proud, and she told him so. He thanked her for the lesson and reminded her to be there on Thursday, grinning mysteriously. She promised that she would be there, and he went on his way. John came in and said hello, and she began the lesson again.

Thursday afternoon rolled around, and Linda drove over to the school. She decided to go check in with Coach Pearson to let him know that she was there. There were lots of football players milling around the office, grabbing protein bars and chatting with the coaches. But, there was no sign of Kelly.

She stepped up to Coach Pearson's door and called a hello, because the door was wide open.

"Oh, good," he said. "I've been watching for you. Come with me. Most of the team is already in the locker room. I'll escort you in and see if Kelly is ready. Come along." He guided her toward the locker room door, paused outside, and opened the door a crack, hollering in, "Is everyone dressed?"

A chorus of ayes and nays came back at him, and a lot of chatter, so he poked his head in the door and found that everyone was indeed dressed, and sitting on the floor. Kelly was standing at the front of the room, with a sheaf of papers in his hands. A couple of the assistant coaches were standing around him, offering encouragement.

Coach Pearson led Linda in to the room, escorting her to a chair at the back. Many of the players nodded and smiled at her as she went by. She took her seat, and Coach Pearson went up to the front of the room. He called everyone to attention.

"Good afternoon, gentleman. We have a big game tomorrow, against Fort Lauderdale High. The coaching staff and I will be looking at you to see if we can find our starting lineup for next year. We may actually try some of you in positions that you are not expecting as we consider various possibilities. After the game tomorrow night, you will drop your equipment off with Coach Sanderson. We will begin summer practices in July. Each of you will receive a schedule in your email and in your mailbox." He waited a minute for that to sink in. Then, he went on. "But our season really begins tomorrow night. And, in order to have you understand how important this is, your newly elected team captain, Kelly Dunn, will speak to you. As the season goes on, each of the other captains will have an opportunity to address you. But we begin our season with Kelly. Please welcome him with a warm round of applause."

The whole team was clapping and whistling, making quite a racket. It kind of broke the tension in the room, and Kelly grinned. Then, he stepped up to the podium and spoke quietly into the microphone. Quietly, but clearly. His voice clean and strong.

"First of all, I want to thank you for naming me as your captain. Along with three of my teammates, my brothers. It is a great honor, and I will try very hard to deserve your trust. You know and I know that it takes a lot of hard work to earn a state championship. You also know that, in spite of our 6:00 a.m. workouts, our weight training, our blood, sweat, and tears, there are things that can happen that will make it very hard for us to do it again. I want you to know that, in addition to leading you on the field, I will also be there for you in a more important way," He looked down at the papers that he held in his hands, and then he set them down on the podium. He must have decided that he didn't really need them. Linda could feel her own heart pounding in her chest.

"I know that a lot of you know my story. My brother James died this year, and my Dad died about four years ago, and it's been really hard. But, I'm standing here today because a lot of you have helped me learn to carry this loss. It still hurts. Every day, and I know it's gonna hurt for the rest of my life. But, I'm gonna try to honor James and my Dad by doing the best I can with the time I got left. Whatever that is." He paused, and looked down at his notes.

"I know that a lot of you remember Ms. Miller," he pointed to her, sitting at the back of the room. "She talked to us about Machiavelli last fall. You remember that, don't you?"

There was a chorus of voices, and a little bit of laughter. One of the players said, "Yeah. And the whore named Fortune who spins the wheel." More laughter, but rather quiet and respectful. Kelly was still very much in command of his audience.

"That's right," said Kelly. "I knew you'd remember. Well, anyhow. Ms. Miller taught me something else. She taught me about a thing she calls a 'sacred hurt.' It's when something really bad happens to you—like you lose someone you love, or they get real sick, or badly hurt. And you know that things are never gonna be the same. Never." He waited for this to sink in. "It happens to everybody eventually. That's just the human condition. Eventually, every single one of you will experience a sacred hurt. Some of you already have." He paused for a moment. The room was completely silent.

"You can't run from it. You can't drink or drug it away. You can't lie to yourself about it. You gotta face it. You gotta look it in the face, admit it, and own it. You gotta allow yourself to hurt. To grieve the loss. And then—you gotta go on." He waited for a minute, almost as if he was collecting himself.

"Now, you know my story. But I know yours too. I know a lot of you here with me today have your own sacred hurts that you're trying to live with. In time, everybody gets hurt. No one escapes. No one. I know I said this before, but it's worth repeating. It's important." The coaches and the players were listening to him very carefully, and every eye in the room was on him. It seemed like no one was even moving.

"And when it happens, no one can take away your hurt. But, you have brothers here, right in this room, that will walk beside you. So, when that time comes, and it will, just know that there are others who will be there for you. I'm going to say this again. And I really mean it. Not that we can take your hurt away. No one can. But, we will walk beside you, shoulder to shoulder, and help you learn to carry it." The players and coaches were starting to whisper in agreement. Their eyes still on Kelly.

"And one last thing. In English class this year, I read this poem by a guy named Walt Whitman. He kind of had his own ideas about a lot of things, but one thing he was sure of is that we have a soul. And it does not die. There is a part of us that is eternal, and it does not die! Some days, you just got to remember that. Your loved ones are alive and well, and waiting for you, and right now, they want you to live." The ground swell of noise was getting larger, but still the team was listening, pulling for Kelly. The coaches were rapt. Linda wasn't even sure that she was breathing.

Kelly went on. "And this guy Whitman said, that when he dies, he would sound his barbaric yawp over the rooftops of the world. And I asked Ms. Miller what a yawp was—and she said it was a cry. But not exactly a sad cry. More like a warrior's whoop. A battle cry. Almost a joyful or a triumphant cry. You have experienced the pain and the loss, and you choose to keep fighting. And when you feel a little overwhelmed, or you think the powers of darkness are getting too close—you gotta stand up and YAWP!! With all your might! Fight against the darkness and YAWP! Like this."

And Kelly threw back his head and yawped.

And all of a sudden, all of the players were on their feet, yawping their heads off. Coaches too. Laughing and yawping and smacking each other on the back. Hugging. A couple of the coaches were almost overwhelmed, or so it seemed. It was the most outrageously beautiful cacophony Linda had ever heard. It had sadness and joy in it. And pain. And something else. Something that felt like determination. Determination to fight and win, or at least go down swinging.

She jumped to her feet, yawping with the team. Laughing so hard that tears were streaming down her face. Coach Pearson came over to the podium and took Kelly in his arms. He just held him there for a minute, and suddenly, everyone was clapping, shouting Kelly's name. Quite a few of them were still yawping. Coach Pearson threw back his head and yawped, with one of his arms still around Kelly. Kelly had tears on his face. Linda thought her heart might burst.

Then Coach Pearson spoke into the microphone once more. "All right, Warriors. Let's get out on the field and have a great practice. Big game tomorrow. The season starts now."

All the players gathered up their equipment and started heading out to the football field. Most of them stopped by to talk to Kelly, telling him how much they enjoyed his speech. Many of them called him "Captain" as they spoke to him. Linda watched the whole thing from the back of the room. Several of the coaches spoke to her before they left, telling her how much they appreciated what she had done for the team. She said the same thing every time, and it was true. These young men had given her as much or more than she had ever given them. She was honored and humbled to be a part of the experience.

Then, only Kelly was left. He was at his locker, gathering his things, and getting ready to head out to the field with the others. She walked over to him, and she could tell that he was still really pumped up.

"I don't know when I have ever been so proud of anyone," she said.

He gave her a quick hug and said, "Never could've done it without you. Thanks for everything, Ms. Miller. You be at the game tomorrow?" He was ready to go.

"Wouldn't miss it for the world," she answered.

He grinned at her and walked out of the locker room, anxious to get out on the football field and hit something. As he left the room, he looked back over his shoulder and grinned as he said the magical word.

"Yawp."

He smiled a great big smile, and then he left.

Linda was alone in the locker room for a minute. She took a deep breath and tried to hold it all in her heart. Every part of the moment. The sights, the smells. Oh, the smells! Then, she gathered her stuff and headed out, whispering as she left the room. "Yawp."

She thought back over the year. It was just about a year ago that she had come home to find Rick and Tiffany in her bedroom. With her Hemingway sash tied around Tiffany! Oddly enough, she felt herself smiling. Almost smiling, anyhow. It didn't really hurt all that much anymore.

She realized that her marriage to Rick had given her Andrea and Matt, whom she loved with all her heart. And, in some weird way, all the amazing things that had happened this year would never have happened had she not found Rick fooling around with Tiffany. So, once again—she was thinking about that profound, bewildering question. Is it Fate? Chance? An indifferent universe? Or Providence? Faith? Hope? Love?

Hard to say.

But a lot of good things had happened to her after her divorce. Her sacred hurt. Her fall from grace. At least, at the time, it had seemed like a fall from grace. Now—she was not so sure. Maybe it was grace disguised.

She felt herself trembling on the edge of one of those unanswerable questions again. She cautioned herself to remember her Hamlet and not be guilty of "thinking too precisely on the event." You can't overthink these things—you could drive yourself crazy.

Sometimes, you just need to put one foot in front of the other and keep walking forward. So, maybe what you need is patience and persistence. And every now and then, maybe you just have to sound your barbaric yawp over the rooftops of the world.

She walked out to her car in the beautiful spring evening. In the distance, she could hear the coaches' whistles as the football players went through their drills.

A flock of seagulls flew overhead, and Linda looked up to see their white wings against the darkening blue of the evening sky. Hoping that none of them would choose to leave a message on her head tonight, she almost ducked reflexively, smiling at herself for even thinking about that. The seagulls yawped noisily in the dusky evening as they headed east, to the ocean.

She could feel some friendly spirits smiling down on her. It had been an amazing year. And, it had been an amazing day. One she would never forget.

She could hardly wait to tell Michel all about it when she got home.

Bonus Materials

When I was finishing up the writing and revising of *Learning to Yawp*, two poems kind of nudged their way into my consciousness, sort of demanding to be written. It was an interesting experience, because I hadn't been writing poetry for a while. I had been concentrating all my efforts on Yawp. But, they kept whispering to me until I finally realized that I had to turn my attention to them and see what they were all about.

After I had written them, I realized that they were both related—thematically—to what I was saying in *Yawp*. Related—but different. So, I decided to include them at the end of the novel. As a teacher and as a writer, I have learned that you never know what is going to be the piece of literature, the image, the set of words that just explodes off the page and lights somebody up. That Eureka moment. That feeling of "Aha! I get it. I knew it!"

So, here they are—two poems that are kind of offshoots of what I am doing with *Yawp*. I hope you enjoy them. Maybe you will even write your own. That would be wonderful. You can do it, you know. Sound your barbaric yawp over the roofs of the world.

The Ocean

The ocean is ever-changing, and
Never changing too.
The tide goes in and the tide goes out.
It has always been this way,
Since the dawn of time.

The moon pulls on the surface of the water,
Calling the ocean to move to her.
She uses her magic every night,
Music that carries across thousands of miles,
And far below,
The water obeys,
Like an eager lover,
And the tide rolls out once again.

I stand tonight at the edge of the ocean,
My toes in the water.
Listening for the music of the spheres,
Hoping that if I listen closely enough,

And keep my heart wide open,
I will feel the pull.

I wait.

I hear the eternal hush of the waves,
Whispering as they kiss the shore.
I imagine that I can hear the music of the moon,
But it eludes me.
Still...

And then, I think maybe I hear it.

She whispers
Not yet.
Not yet.
Not yet.

The Road to Emmaus

(Based on Luke 24:13-35)

Broken-hearted and broken down,
We trudge along the road.
We feel so heavy—we have lost our light.
Even more than that.
We have lost our way, our truth, and our life.
Our direction and our hope.
Gone.

We keep walking, but we don't know why.
And then he comes along.
Just talking, listening.
Listening to our stories.
And we babble on, about everything
We've lost.

And then, he joins us for a while.
And in the breaking of the bread,
Suddenly—we see.

The breaking is the opening.

Are not our hearts burning within us?
Are not our hearts filled with his fire?

Just for a moment, the veil is lifted.
Just for a moment, we see.

O Lord, I believe.
Help my unbelief.

O Lord, I believe.
Help my unbelief.
Walk with me today.

Amen

Acknowledgements

First and foremost, I would like to thank my husband, Christopher, who has been with me every step of the way. He was my first reader and my best critic. He helped me get the football stuff right. Well—he helps me get everything right, when I do. He is my rock.

Then, I need to thank my children and grandchildren. They are constantly teaching me about courage, life, and love. And—in a very special way—my beautiful grandson Brett, who is waiting for me up in heaven. I fell in love with football when he played it with such heart.

I would like to acknowledge my brothers and sisters, my first companions on the journey. I want to thank my Mom and Dad up in heaven—my first and best teachers about the things that really matter.

Thank you to all my friends and students, literally thousands of students over 45 years of teaching. Without you, there would be no Linda Miller.

A special thanks to my son, Nick Stearns, who put the text into a publishable format.

Finally, I would like to thank Debby Priestap. After my husband, the first person to meet Linda and Kelly. Provided all kinds of feedback on characters, style, setting—everything.

Thank you to Sarah and Seamus up in heaven, helping me to think beyond these earthly limits. There are three things that last—faith, hope, and love. And the greatest of these is love.

Love you so much in the whole world, as Bretty says.